by Peter De Vries

NO BUT I SAW THE MOVIE

THE TUNNEL OF LOVE

COMFORT ME WITH APPLES

THE MACKEREL PLAZA

THE TENTS OF WICKEDNESS

THROUGH THE FIELDS OF CLOVER

Through the FIELDS of CLOVER

Through the FIELDS of CLOVER

by Peter De Vries

Boston - Toronto

LITTLE, BROWN AND COMPANY

LIBRARY OF CONGRESS CATALOG CARD NO. 60-12207

FIRST EDITION

The lines on page 53 have been adapted from "Wild Peaches" and taken from the *Collected Poems of Elinor Wylie* with the permission of the publisher, copyright 1921, 1932 by Alfred A. Knopf, Inc.

Published simultaneously in Canada by Little, Brown & Company (Canada) Limited

PRINTED IN THE UNITED STATES OF AMERICA

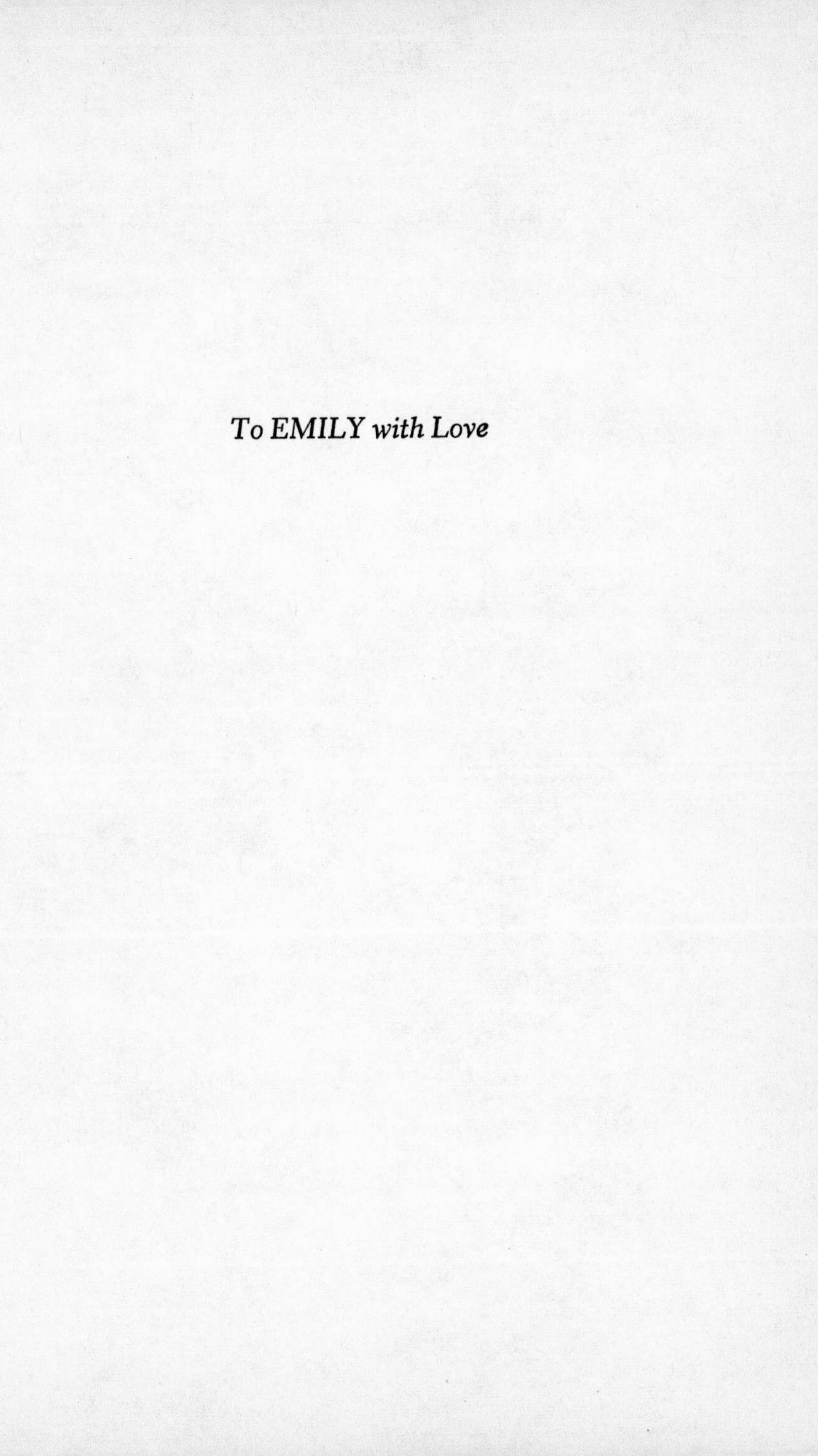

To EMILY with Love

CONTENTS

part one:

BED OF COALS

one

MARVEL was in no mood to talk or even think about a fortieth anniversary. He had gone shopping for his wife that afternoon at a supermarket equipped with one of those electric eye doors that open automatically at the approach of a customer. The mechanism was out of order at the time, unknown to him. He strode into the entranceway with his customary zest, swinging his arms and taking the magic eye on faith, and walked into the door with a force that not only flattened his cigar but broke his nose on the metal crossbar traversing the plate glass at that level.

It was now evening, and he lay in bed on his side, hoping by his appearance to ward off plans for the celebration which he knew his wife, sitting in her window chair with a crossword puzzle on her lap, was impatient to crystallize. He watched her reproachfully with jam-colored eyes above a thick latticework of bandages. Wearing, in the June heat, pajama trousers only, occasionally executing a gnat on his naked chest, he had a demoralized and shipwrecked air.

Mrs. Marvel was a poor speller, which was a great aid in working crossword puzzles. She dashed this one off with more than her usual speed, and after jotting in the last word, "gloming," dropped the paper and set her pencil on the desk. He groaned, though he knew her approach to the subject would be prefaced by a show of sympathy, perhaps an offer to feed him a nutritive goody or fetch him his Poland Water.

"Would you like to go to the hospital?"

"Too sick."

He should have known better than to take the New Age on trust. In sight of the shopping center where the mishap had occurred (and which he would have found allegorically refreshing had it befallen another) were the Massachusetts Knitting Mills where he had first tasted its scientific spirit. It was there, fifteen years ago when he was fifty, that he had worked in the accounting department. The corporation then suddenly underwent modernization, which included the use of aptitude tests for employees. Existing workers as well as new applicants were to be thus screened, to make sure they were soundly placed from a psychological viewpoint and that maximum use was being made of their abilities. Marvel had tested out as executive material. Since they had no openings for executives at the time, and none was anticipated, he was fired.

Marvel asked to see the new personnel head, who received him cordially in his office in the presence of a representative of the firm of New York industrial consultants who had inaugurated the new system and who was staying on long enough to get it rolling on its own.

"I'm sorry," the personnel manager said to Marvel's protests. "But we have no openings of the sort you tested out on."

"But I don't want to be an executive."

"Nevertheless it's what you're suited for. Your qualifications come out Grade-A in the slot." The manager and the expert had been playing with blocks when interrupted, of the kind used in the aptitude test along with ink smears of a mildly salacious sort and a questionnaire answered in the subject's own handwriting. The blocks had more than anything else been Marvel's undoing, in betraying him to be administrative timber. "You're a natural for the category. We hate to see you go."

"Hasn't my work in accounting been satisfactory?"

"Perfectly. But of course now we have no certainty it's been a hundred per cent of what you can give, your potential profiling you out as it did in another direction."

"But I'm happy here."

"I'm sorry to hear that. Of course we'll put your name on . . . and if anything . . . You'll find the customary severance pay in your envelope." They both saw Marvel to the door and the New York expert laid a hand on his shoulder in parting. "I was very interested in your profile. It's a nice study. You could go far."

The last he had heard of the Massachusetts Knitting Mills they were marketing something called thermal underwear. Ben Marvel could remember when those drawers were called long woolens. He could remember when people opened their own doors. He could remember — But what was the use of all that? He could remember when Main Street was a mudhole.

"Be nice to have them all back with us, all the children

from near and far," Alma purred in her window chair. Her stocking feet nuzzled one another like a pair of horrid little beasts. "And I don't mean just a family reunion. I mean the whole town. Open house. Oh, let's!"

Difficult as it was to express pain behind his mask, the registration of apathy was impossible. Marvel feigned sleep. Next, he tried *to* sleep. He lay on his back and willed himself to be a dead leaf, now thoroughly light and dry which a thought would carry away, or, in an act of imagination said to be used in certain acting techniques, he gathered his bones into a fine supposition that they were a bundle of fagots which a flame called slumber would presently consume. But the sodium pentothal was wearing off . . .

"You and I, Ben, stand for something. I see us as doing that. Forty years together in this day and age! Don't you agree with me?"

Marvel affected a light snore, going *Pfff* out of one corner of his mouth as though dislodging a bit of thistledown from his Buffalo Bill mustache. Which betrayed him, for he was normally a light sleeper. "He's no lemon bedwise," Alma had once confided to a friend after a few sherries. This had been in 1950, when they had been married thirty years. Now she saw herself in a grove of grandchildren while the photographers' bulbs exploded in the summer air and the caterers bled him white. Reverend Korn would already have said "Marriage is a sea on which we embark, not a harbor into which we sail," as he had on every such occasion within living memory in Hickory, Mass., speaking with one hand in his pocket in respect of the evening's being jocular and impromptu.

Opening one eye Marvel saw that she had begun her calisthenics, bathrobe pinching and puffing alternately at the flanks as she rose and squatted on her heels with arms outthrust. He remembered her describing herself to statement-thirsty reporters on a previous round-number celebration, their Silver, as "a stout advocate of regular exercise." What would she think if she ever found out they were incompatible? He had never told her. What would he, Ben Marvel, say that wouldn't sound idiotic when quoted next day in the *Blade?* His left eye began to twitch, for he had standards.

"Let's wait ten years," he said, scratching himself with a spurious indolence, being by now a nervous wreck. "That'll be our Golden, what a blowout we'll show them then!" Unaware of the outlay in pain and trouble this exclamation cost his face she merely turned her own and with no intermission in her bobbing gave him a look which intimated their probable whereabouts a decade hence. He crooked his finger lewdly at her and patted the free space on the bed. She rose, catching herself on a corner of the bureau with a report somewhere in her bones like a pistol shot, and lit a cigarette. A marked stockiness was not mitigated by a certain tendency to dishevelment, nor that helped by a taste for frilled blouses and a lifetime's lack of definitive approach to, or coherent viewpoint about, her hair. Sometimes she parted it in the middle, then not at all. Reared in a generation whose mothers prized hair that could be sat on, she sensed that this in itself was a meaningless merit and once out of her mother's clutches had cut it to her shoulders. Since then she had wavered among methods of organizing it with the result that it was now usually loosely baled on top of her head with a few tortoise-shell pins for security. It was at this time the color of woodsmoke. She tucked in its loose ends and those of her blouses in a series of pokes and thrusts which she had somehow converted into gestures supporting her conversation. For the rest, her manner was a compromise between physical drive and mental uncertainty, not yet, at sixty-three, completely worked out. Marvel had never said "I love you," but his marriage had survived many touched off by this ejaculation, and he still made fortnightly love between these sheets. Oh come to bed, for, supine, old breasts are young again, and point to heaven. He had had all the truly uxorious require – one woman. Now with his clobbered eyes he watched her reoccupy the rather hideously cheerful old chintz chair, absently probing her teeth with the match while smoke issued from her nose, or rather from one nostril, the result of a deviated septum. He became alert to a widening stain of melancholy there, in her still handsome profile, or at least of brooding introspection, and tried to hurry off to sleep.

He had not rushed into the hunt for another job, but after a period in which he did nothing but keep a Journal, in the old New England tradition, he had suddenly one day typed up several pages of his ruminations and shown them to an old schoolmate named Matt Shaw who by then owned and edited the Hickory *Blade*. "How about my writing a column?" he'd suggested. Thus began "Edgewise," twelve inches of free-cruising personal comment every other day for which Marvel got fifteen dollars a week, thanks to a "temporary arrangement" which they never somehow got around to discussing for revision. Among the "Yankee virtues" on which Matt Shaw prided himself must by all means be numbered his parsimonious treatment of employees. Marvel lived mainly by selling off acre by acre a profitable tract of land left him by his father, but that scarcely justified the Spartan wage he got for his column, and he had that very morning, prior to the maladventure at the supermarket, acted on his wife's breakfast-hour command that he go "straight to the horse's mouth and demand more money."

Matt Shaw had sat in his swivel chair with his hands locked behind his head in his favorite pose of a Man Who Is Always Available To His Staff. "Well, Ben, what can I do you for?" Ben pointed out that he was paid fifteen dollars a week, and then not always that. "Why, Ben, on that, we deduct for quoted matter, in keeping with our policy for all writers on space rates. Why should we pay you for something the Pope said?" He genially regarded a button at the touch of which a crisp old lady could be made to pop like toast from a doorway. His face clouded as he said, "You quoted a whole paragraph from that semantics fellow last week . . ."

Marvel reminded himself that, though the reverse of the scientific spirit that had cost him his last job, his present boss was an equally treacherous booby trap in another way, being an inflammable partisan of the old hat who fired people for harboring views inimical to his own. It was not necessary to express them or even for that matter to hold them, merely to be in his presence when his own prejudices were excited. Nor need your work bear any relation to the subject. Senility had shortened this ellipsis: finding himself to be shouting at you, he identified or confused you with the views being excoriated — and off went your head. "I think that stuff is hogwash, Ben," he said, tuning up. "How can you give it houseroom?" Many of his outbursts consisted in the defense of tastes and opinions whose relegation he equated with his own, as the semantics fellow would have been quick to point out. More. The vascular crises into which he worked himself had on at least one occasion necessitated calling the fire department, whose inhalators are of course at the disposal of victims other than those of conflagrations, good thing to remember. It was for both their sakes that Marvel must quiet him down.

"Values are going all along the line," he said, deriving the usual satisfaction from this observation. "Now you take I like to read poetry. Give me a good poem. They're the unacknowledged legislators of the world. So sometime ago with a train ride ahead of me, little trip down to Florida, I bought a couple of paperbacks to read. One of them was an anthology of modern verse. Brother! Ever heard of a guy named Ezra Pound?"

"I had forgotten about him."

"I threw the book down and deliberately saw how much of *Evangeline* I could remember." An eggplant flush deepened across Shaw's face as he recited in an ominous wheeze: " 'Silently one by one, in the infinite meadows of heaven blossomed the lovely stars, the forget-me-nots of the angels.' " He banged his desk with a force that shook a dish of paper clips. "That's poetry!" He took a suck on the single cigar the doctor allowed him a day now and finding it defunct returned it to the ashtray. He pushed some six or seven teeth up more firmly into their gums with his thumb, another nervous habit like running down to Florida. "The other book was about art. Do you understand the sculpture of Henry Moore?"

"No and I'd be a damn fool if I did."

"Clinkers!" He felt around behind his tie. "I tell you if we can't at least be intelligible we're through. Washed up. Kaput. I mean as a culture. Everything the dictatorships say about us is true — decadent, all of it. I tell you we can't afford people in responsible positions tolerating this kind of junk! Ben, I'm afraid we're going to have to let you go."

"But I didn't say anything about Henry Moore or Ezra Pound! You did."

"I did?"

"Yes. That isn't what I came in here to talk about."

"What did you come in here to talk about?"

Marvel explained as patiently as he could that he was sixty-five, a time of life when he should be making more than fifteen dollars a week especially if he wanted to leave a little something to his grandchildren, two of whom were also Matt's grandchildren. It always came as something of a shock to him that his daughter Evelyn had once been married to Amos Shaw, a tightwad chip off the old block whom Evelyn was well rid of, even though he only sent her seventy dollars a week alimony for the two children. Was Amos still hot stuff up there in the New Hampshire town where he owned a paper of his own, Amos with his open cars and sufficient pomade in his hair to stain his hatband like a doughnut bag?

"Oh, I forgot to tell you, I didn't get the raise, my dear."

There was no one in the bedroom chair. She had wandered off to drum up some support for the anniversary from Cotton.

Cotton's interest in such a wedding celebration would be secondary since he was not a party to the union but a product of it, and not a very animate one at that. He got splitting headaches whenever he had to look at anyone. He was their second son and fourth and last child. Alma had always cautioned her daughters against marrying for money though no stigma adhered to falling in love with someone who had it. It had been a son who had disappointed her by marrying money, and then once again a few years later, if anything more bitterly, by divorcing it.

It had been with Marjorie Worth's money that the newly-weds had built a modern house, and at her insistence, for contemporary architecture was not to Cotton's taste. They had had a child drown falling from a high chair into a stream running through the living room. This accent-on-living sort of thing had been only one of many bones of contention between them, and they had decided to call it quits shortly thereafter. Cotton had moved back into his old room. He did a little free-lance writing, including occasional newspaper feature articles, and was generally taken to be at work on a play. He had reviewed plays at the Smugglers Cove summer theater for two seasons for the Hickory *Blade,* but had been let go because of the Olympian severity of his standards. It was the trite and sentimental that oftenest drew his fire, particularly when so maudlin as to cause him to burst into tears himself. One of the first plays he had covered in the line of duty had been a story of a woman's faithfulness to a talented but alcoholic violinist.

"The briniest bit of fiddle-faddle to come along in years," he wrote, his eyes still moist from the experience. "But Cotton, we thought you liked it," said his parents who had sat with him. "Like it, that piece of tear gas?" "It seemed to me I heard you sniffle a time or two," said his mother. "That's what I mean," he said.

His mother had sat down blankly and for some time slowly moved her head up and down, willing comprehension from her depths as something that had to be pumped up from them. "Oh, *I* see. You mean . . ."

Another prior-to-Broadway production had been a dramatization of *Little Women*. One knew what to expect here all right, and it was early-along that the handkerchiefs began to come out and the hysteriacs to tune up. The death of Beth came in due order. Gazing from her pillow toward the sunlit window, she smiled wistfully and said, "My bluebird came again."

A sob racked Cotton's frame as tears welled to his eyes and down his cheeks, as they did down those of so many others in the house. The stage version ended in keeping with the book, with Jo becoming engaged to Professor Bhaer under the umbrella. He had nothing to give, he cried, "but a full heart and these empty hands," and Jo, slipping her own into his, answered, "Not empty now."

As Cotton stumbled up the aisle toward the parking lot, he excused himself to a party of friends he was with and hurried to the *Blade* office to hammer out his copy:

> *Well, the old chromo is back with us again, and it can be imagined that the adapters have missed few of the plenteous opportunities it offers for bringing in the well-known gusher. Muriel Dykes makes a fetching Jo, and the rest of the cast are properly endearing, but it remains for the most part the mawkish affair it always was, and the wary are hereby warned that, rather than plunk down their three bucks for this one, they can get the same effect by staying home and peeling an onion.*

Mrs. Marvel simply dropped her paper when she read this. "But you sat there and *bawled*. I was behind you."

"So? I said it was maudlin, didn't I? What's that got to do with it?"

"But—"

"Oh, my God, Mother, must we go through all that again?"

Yes, with Matt Shaw. The editor called him into his office the next afternoon. He attended all the openings at Smugglers Cove too. "I thought you enjoyed it as much as I did. That you thought it was good, and had heart."

"Please," Cotton said, wincing. "At least spare me that."

Shaw watched him as he struck a match and set fire to a cigarette. One of Shaw's blue eyes tended to avoid the other, and he nervously chewed a mustache like a wilted toothbrush. "I simply don't understand you. A person sits there blubbering, and then —"

"Oh, my dear Matt," said Cotton, "must we have all this again?"

"Yes, and not on my account." Matt picked up a sheaf of letters from his desk. There had been a flood of them protesting the austerity of the drama critic's notices, and he had no alternative but to take them seriously. "Cerebral block of ice" and "If he doesn't like plays why does he go to them?" were among the snatches Cotton caught in the samples Shaw showed him. Cotton put up a brisk defense, knowing his job was at stake. "There's a crying need for critical standards, in all of the art forms. If we can't maintain some kind of criteria, and do so honestly and vigorously, weeding out the meretricious wherever and whenever it raises its head, then what's the good of noticing anything at all? We cannot afford to let the second-rate slip through."

Shaw's head nodded somewhat as Alma Marvel's had. He weighed this fairly and hospitably, it being in its larger outlines a point of view to which he himself adhered, though in reverse: as a partisan of the outmoded he was equally strong in his invectives at the newfangled and the intellectual. He agreed to let the matter ride for a bit, having no replacement in mind anyway. Since there was nothing maudlin for the remainder of the season, Cotton finished it out. He started a second. Midway in that, however, there was another run of lachrymose entertainments, and again he gave them no quarter, writing with eyes still misted "sentimental slop," "the purest and most embarrassing hokum," and "more treacle than even Hollywood has extruded from this tired old theme." The last being a religious one, the howls of protest were conclusive. Shaw's desk was a torrent of mail. Cotton's stand was firm: "We cannot afford to let the secod-rate slip through." Shaw said that while he liked him personally and appreciated his integrity, it was increasingly apparent that Cotton was unsuited to a newspaper serving a community of homes. He must, regrettably, let him go. Cotton had flung out of the door calling his ex-employer a "cure for hiccups."

He had not worked since, except for book reviews in increasingly obscure journals. He was still known as the scourge of the obvious, whose standards were a mountain few could scale. "My but he's brilliant. He hates everything," they said.

Mrs. Marvel carried with her into Cotton's room this evening the firm hope that though no clatter could be heard in there he was working on his play—*The Seven Who Stank.* He was in bed reading a novel. He was eating coleslaw with his fingers from a plate on his chest. A sock was screwed into the carriage of his typewriter.

"Honestly."

He turned a page with unraised eyes as she passed him on her way to his desk chair, which she sat on after turning it around. She watched him a moment, unable to make out from this distance the title on the bright orange jacket of the book. "What are you reading?"

"It's a novel about a woman with three breasts."

"All this realism." She looked around the room. "I wonder what it gets us, carrying sex that far. And the false expectations it arouses in the young . . . You're what. Twenty-six."

"Actually it's a sort of symbolism of the devouring mother in our time. Want to read it when I'm finished?"

"Bllaach," Mrs. Marvel said, retching elaborately.

Cotton lifted another dripping tuft of coleslaw to his open mouth with his eye on the printed page. Mrs. Marvel reviewed briefly her relations with this son. She had reasonably enough not judged his ideas save by the emotional results to which they led: She wanted him to be happy, or as happy as one can be in this life. She had not even violently deplored his Communism, a system which she personally opposed because it "smacked of socialism." When that stage had gone nothing had replaced it. No end of opinions among the young, but no belief either. Ideas buzzed, a swarm without a hive. Cotton's humanity seemed both concentrated and nonexistent, like those extracts which are made without recourse to the fruits they simulate. Or another comparison sometimes came to her. He was like those poets he read — was Wallace Stevens one? — whose words reminded her of those highly seasoned dishes on which it is still necessary to sprinkle salt. *Something is missing here!* her own spirit cried.

"Why did you and Marjorie get divorced? It was never made clear to me."

"She was always standing at the window saying 'And yet . . .' "

"You had so much together. Losing a child in that awful brook . . . I hear she doesn't get a nibble on the house. Why? It isn't as if there was no money around."

"The real estate agents can't find it. It's too integrated with the landscape. There was a song about that in a revue, but this was It. We'd all have vanished if we'd stayed there."

"Well, it's all over now," Mrs. Marvel sighed. "The child's gone and so is Frank Lloyd Wright."

"I hate nature," Cotton ruminated away, able to read, eat and talk all three at once. "Human included. My own included in that."

His mother sighed again. Looking toward the window, she snapped the pages of a book on his desk, to which she was partly turned.

"Why don't you join a discussion group? You'd be surprised. One week with a good down-to-earth bunch like we have at church would cure you young people of all that therapy." She said after a moment of silence: "Why don't you go to church, Cotton?"

"There is no god."

"Don't split hairs with me, dear. You know that's not the point, but whether reverence is a fine thing. *Values*, the kind your father and I have had for forty years. They hold people together. So once again. Why don't you go to church, Cotton?"

"Because a day in his courts is as a thousand." He added after a moment, "The whole thing is a joke – life. It's all a joke."

"Is that why you never laugh?"

They seemed to have reached an impasse. If he didn't want to join a discussion group, then what about getting married again? Or painting the house? "Mr. Le Boeuf painted theirs in less than a week, and him with six fingers on one hand." She kept circling back to the idea of remarrying. Most of his old friends were family men now. George Lamont had married Nettie Wetwilliam last week. Yes, he knew that, what he couldn't understand was Nettie marrying George. "As Anthony Powell says, women may show some discrimination in the men they sleep with but they will marry anybody." "That another one of your rotten friends?" "He's a novelist." "Well, don't bring him around here. That crowd you've taken up with, they're all attractive fellows and all, Cotton, and, Cotton, I'm not strait-laced, but I don't want you sleeping with every Tom, Dick and Harry." "No, Mother." He spoke into his pillow, folding it into a sandwich around his head. It was this tableau of grief into which Marvel walked, or rather paused on the edge of, a shoulder to the doorpost, resembling slightly a drunk propped against a street lamp. One foot was crossed over the other.

"Look who's here." Alma beamed at him. "Glad to see you up. Ben, Cotton and I were talking about the big doings," she said, relying on a brief exchange the day before to lend truth to this, "and he sees no objections." Marvel tried again to forewarn his features that speech would be required of them but before any words could be effected she went on, "So why not full speed ahead? They'll all come. Bushrod I've written telling him about the anti-Semitism creeping into Hickory, so the Civil Liberties League will pay his way up from Washington — no problem there. Johnny and Evelyn know I've not been feeling well lately, so this visit could be their . . ." She took the telephone from the desk and put it in her broad lap. "And to make it complete, who dares me to phone the Trautwigs right this minute!"

Nobody dared her, but while she waited for the operator to get her through to Trenton, New Jersey, Cotton said from the bed in which he had not modified his slump, "What do you mean not feeling well, Mother?" "All in through here. It's — no I won't worry you. And Dr. Northrup says it's psychosomatic." Waiting for the connection she said, "It's psychosomatic and he still can't do anything for me. I'd like to see him with a patient that *did* have something wrong with them. But don't you go writing to Evelyn it might be serious — yet." She shook her head. "The doctors in this town." "What about Dr. Cahill?" "Bllaach!"

"But he fixed my nose," Ben bleated in the doorway, where he had been swaying from one jamb to the other with fixed feet, like a huge metronome. "Won't it be all right?"

"Oh, sure. You only had a cartilage break. Thank God it wasn't the bone. He patches people up like a lot of old crockery." She moved her head up and down to indicate the phone was ringing. "Well, if you want to frighten Evelyn that it may be an, oh, not growth exactly . . . I suppose they'll be out to the movies again and only Chester home." Father and son watched the single jet of smoke again under the prolonged frown. She bore little resemblance to those matrons pictured, in utility ads aimed at encouraging long-distance conversations, as happily keeping in touch. "Would either of you care to talk to Chester?" "Not if he still uses big words," Cotton said.

"Chester? This is Grandmother Marvel."

"Moo Moo! Nothing's wrong I hope?"

"Not a thing. Just thought we'd call and see how you all are. We're all fine. Your mother and father home?" She gritted her teeth at the *faux pas:* Art Trautwig wasn't his father, he was just his mother's third husband. A low laugh was in any case heard at the other end, and Chester in his changing voice, which croaked without warning among a variety of registers, replied:

"Scarce were those vessels washed on which we'd made our evening meal than off they hied them to that house of dreams, in whose enfolding gloom the cinematic phantoms weave their visual anodynes."

"Those two! When do you expect them back?"

"Not till the witching hour methinks, or worse. For no more will th'embattled hombres make their peace in the mesa'd West, their smoking armaments put by, than Cary Grant will post him through such feats as Hitchcock doth concoct."

"Oh, a double feature, eh?" said Mrs. Marvel, feeling rather proud of herself. "Next year you'll be a what. Junior in Central High. Your mother tells me about those straight A's in English Literature, boy. You keep it up, you hear? Look, Chester, Gramps and I have something we're sort of, oh well, it'll be our fortieth anniversary next month and, Chester, what would you think of a big celebration? That's what we're feeling the family out on. If that's what they want, we'll give it to them. A sort of Gathering of the Clan you might say. A real whing-ding."

"We'll come like swallows, and I'll bring a prothalamium."

"No presents. The reason —"

"For think. Twice twenty years have flown since first thy love's moon rose, till now when its red sun doth 'gin to set. Twice —" Alma put a hand over the mouthpiece and asked the men in a whisper "What's a prothalamium?" "A wedding poem, Mother. A sort of ode to a married couple." "Good God. I thought it was some kind of bottled gas."

". . . that span must sing which cloaks my years thrice o'er," Chester was saying in mixed trebles and basses, "which started ere that flesh to which thy flesh gave rise — my mother's — had thought of giving rise to mine. Long ere that breast whose young proprietor had given suck to her who gave it me — blest dairy of that unrememberable morn —" Mrs. Marvel reached to stamp out her cigarette, giggling nervously. "You modern kids. You going to talk that way at the reception, Chester? Will you read your poem out loud?" she asked in sudden alarm.

"Done and done. When did you say it's to be?"

"Well, now wait." Her smile had turned uncertain. "We didn't say we had decided — just sort of calling around to get the sentiment. We've got to make sure everyone can come then. I happen to know your — I happen to know Art has his vacation then. Well, anyway, we'll be in touch with your mother about it. But Chester, before we hang up, there's one more thing. Have you heard from Lee lately?"

Mrs. Marvel screwed the receiver firmly against her ear and listened attentively.

"Having wintered with our common father in New York, she's with him now in the agglomeration called Las Vegas, where nightly he disports himself in pools of light for pelf — much needed, I'll be bound, these days of alimony and the like. They'll be winging eastward in a fortnight, or so 'tis bruited in *Variety*, for him to begin work on his fall television series," Chester finished flatly, sometimes unable to sustain these Elizabethan flights, or suddenly getting fed up with them himself.

This was harder to decode but Mrs. Marvel had got the gist of it, well enough to relay it, on hanging up, to Cotton and to Marvel, whose path to rest was now strewn with news and comment raining on him at a great rate.

Lee, Chester's older sister, was with their comedian father Harry Mercury, Elsie Marvel's first husband, in Las Vegas, where he had a limited night club engagement. Custody of the children had been divided on the Mercurys' breakup, Chester going to his mother and Lee to her father, with complex provisions for switch visits at intervals inconvenient to everybody. "There. All accounted for. Come July 16, the Marvels will be reunited."

Cotton set his book face down on his stomach and sat up a little. "Mother, there's something I've got to tell you. Why you can't bank on Bushrod's being sent up here as a trouble-shooter for the Civil Liberties League. This Aronson they're trying to restrict off Main Street isn't a Jew at all. He's a Swede. Hadn't you heard? It's all a mare's nest. Some of us know but we're not saying. It's too rich."

She wagged a pencil in warning first at Cotton then at Ben. "Now look you two. I've settled this with my God, and the principle is the same though Aronson were a Zulu — even more so. The fact remains that prejudice exists in Hickory, for us to stamp out by every means possible. We've got to fight people like — Did you get the raise?" Marvel shook his head. "— skunks like Matt Shaw and his restrictive covenant crowd. And Bushrod knows how to do it. If either of you breathes a word of this to Bushrod or the CLL or anybody else I'll never speak to you again. If the promise that he'll find discrimination in his home town is all that'll bring a son of mine back to it in eleven years, so be it. He's coming. They're all coming home, from everywhere, once yet before — before they have to come for something besides an anniversary!"

She need not have tweaked her nose with a handkerchief on Cotton's account. The spectacle of a humanitarian who was mean to his ma riding his white charger to rescue a cowering Swede from anti-Semitism was too good for that student of the passing scene to miss. The siblings had a supposedly Cain-and-Abel relationship, though Mrs. Marvel could never remember which was which. The question was Ben.

He moved in from the doorway and sat on the foot of the bed. He thoughtfully stroked his chin, pulled his lip, his ear — everything free of contusion.

"I appreciate your wanting a do, but, my dear, wouldn't it be something in the way of a farce?" he said, trying to speak without moving anything more than his lower jaw, so that he mouthed a point he happened to feel strongly and even bitterly about, and which was his reason (and not an idle avoidance of a bore or a burden) for resisting the shindig. "Because look. Out of four children, there won't be one who won't be bringing his second, and in one case third, spouse, except for Cotton here who apparently just isn't interested any longer." Cotton though returned to the book was not absorbed in it a hundred percent, for he daydreamed as he read. He would show them all. He would get off a freight train and activate an entire town. "Why summon people for miles around to crow about something they simply no longer believe in? People don't care any more about their sisters and their brothers, let alone their cousins and their uncles. There's been a social revolution going on for just about the forty years you want to commemorate. The family is going and the clan is gone. Come to bed."

He went out abruptly, but as no one followed he returned instantly from the hall and continued:

"We're souvenirs, relics of a lost cause. We're hitching posts, we're coffee grinders somebody will make into lamps when we're gone. We might as well take our congratulations in the window of Cobleigh's antique store!"

He had put the case too well. He saw her broad back stiffen. "All the more reason to show them our ideals! These people who cry Reno at the first wave slapping their educated little bottoms. I'd like to tell them what I think of their pipsqueak sophistication. Trotting off to the divorce courts the minute the frosting is off the cake!"

"Yet posting with such dexterity to fresh arrangements."

"What?"

"They can't wait to get married again!"

"Right!" They were yelling fraternally at one another, crying out a common cause. "Children lining up for another ride on the carousel!"

"While their own children are shipped back and forth between one parent and another!"

"Do you realize, do you realize, Ben," she said, tapping the desk with one finger, "that now that Bushrod has been transferred to Washington, his first wife has to put the twins on the B and O the second Friday of every month in Baltimore so they can spend the weekend with their father? Why, that *judge* should be put in jail, the things that go on. It's disgraceful, and I for one will be happy to get them all together, up here in Hickory, and tell them so to their faces.

Not in so many words, the occasion will make its own point, which is 'What in God's name ails all of you? Marriages were once made of leather, what are they now, cellophane? Children were once given a Home, not shuttled among strange cities like pets under the guidance of train conductors and airline stewardesses.' Oh, you put your finger on something all right, Ben!"

It was a familiar sensation to Marvel, hearing his arguments marshaled against him. He was like those unfortunate military units which are routed by their own gas in a change of wind. He saw that frontal opposition was all wrong, as forty years of domestic diplomacy must have shown him; sabotage must be subtle, camouflaged in a show of compliance. And didn't fate put into his hands that very instant the means of doing so?

The telephone exploded in Alma's lap, where it had remained since her call to the Trautwigs. The familiar reedy voice that greeted hers was audible to both the others in the room, and even Cotton slid up to listen at this uncanny coincidence.

"Hello, Moo Moo," it buzzed all the way from Las Vegas, "how are you, baby? How's the geezer?"

"*Harry!*" she exclaimed, writhing on the chair and darting the two a look which dared them now to deny a pattern in human affairs. "We were just talking about you, and about Lee and just everything, and I'd love to talk to her if she's there with you." No, Lee was at the hotel, Harry himself being at the club rehearsing a number. "Are you having any fun? Are you meeting anybody?" Harry said, "Well, I've met Burl Ives, to name a few." She was in absolute hysterics at the gag and told him to hold the phone while she shared it with the others. Back on the wire again she asked about Lee. "She's at the hotel, listening to her living glanguage records. But she's why I'm calling. Moo Moo, she's been accepted as an apprentice at the Smugglers Cove theater there. I'm shooting her on East ahead of me. She'll be staying at the Hickory Inn there with the other kids, but I'd appreciate it if you'd look in on her. Not with a checking gup attitude, just casually."

"Of course! You know us."

"Because she may be eighteen but she's my daughter."

"She's nineteen, Harry."

"She is?"

"She was born the year we got struck by lightning, and that was forty-one. She was out of school a year with infectious hepatitis —"

"I'll be damned."

"— which is why she started college at eighteen instead of the usual seventeen. She'll be going back to Sarah Lawrence in the fall of course."

"Of course. You look in on her then, though she'll probably call you as soon as she arrives, and then I'll be up as soon as I'm through here in ten days or so."

"*Here?*"

"Sure. We'll all get together. Open the bubbly. Good night, Moo Moo, and best to the geezer."

"Wait."

She broke out her news, incoherent with excitement now. And Mercury, unstrung, homesick out there in Las Vegas, without even any home to be sick for, felt his blood stirred by tribal drums. "Will I *come*," he exclaimed on being asked. "Look. Listen. I'm thinking gout loud. Why can't I work my whole summer in with Lee's? I'm going on for Götterdämmerung Beer in the fall, maybe you heard, lots of material to get in shape before Labor Day, so if I could persuade my writers to hole in up there in Massachusetts with me . . ."

There was now no question of sleep. She plowed the floor, scarcely able to breathe, insisting it was a sign. If Harry, who was no longer an in-law really, came, surely the children would have no excuses. Then she had her first doubt. "Would his being here keep Elsie away?"

"I doubt it. It wasn't that kind of divorce," said Marvel, recalling a publicity shot showing Mercury carrying Elsie *out* of their apartment doorway to show the divorce was amicable, of which a clipping from a New York newspaper had reached them. "Well now. It's turning out to be a famous party. All this home talent. Besides Chester reading his ode, we'll have Harry doing an after-dinner turn —"

"We will?" She sat down again.

"Of course." Marvel trimmed and lit his first cigar since the one splayed against the supermarket door. "How could you possibly not call on him? I can hear him now, lining out jokes about hot pastrami and back taxes." He approved the coal of his cigar. "To say nothing of Yiddisher Mamas."

"Well, Ben, I didn't know you had prejudice."

"Me? God, it was the one marriage I had hopes for. That strong family sense of theirs. I'm afraid all the trouble came from our side. Ah, well," he sighed, "let's not dig all that up now. Let's think about our party, which is beginning to build up. It's none too early to plan. Harry might even m.c. it. Not that you could blame him for wanting to try out new material. Still, maybe we can get him to repeat some of his old routines. I always liked the one he did on television where he plays the bagpipes with a vacuum cleaner. A trifle obscene, especially where he milks the bag for a finish, but funny. And that butcher shop sketch where he pitches horseshoes with metwurst." She considered his back skeptically now, but it told her nothing. "So you can confidently get set to wow your D.A.R. and Mayflower Society friends. A night to remember."

She sighed, seeming to lose a little bulk among the folds of her robe, like a pneumatic toy expiring. "Playing quoits with metwurst I remember was kind of . . ."

"It has Freudian overtones of course," he called cheerfully over his shoulder.

"It does?"

He nodded, blowing a cloud of smoke toward the ceiling. "Especially when he makes a ringer."

"Does Harry know that?"

"That's hard to say. I can find out." She shook her head, deploring the fund of dirty erudition the world was bringing to her later years. "Now the food. Something like turkey Tetrazzini is always good for that kind of mass feeding. And of course champagne. Then a band. We'll have to have dancing," Marvel continued, raising to insane heights the costs he was prepared cheerfully to shoulder. "I assume you're thinking in terms of hiring the country club?"

She stared moodily at the telephone, then in the direction of the clock. "You're mad. It would come to over a thousand dollars. Probably throw your budget off for a year."

"The club fee is nominal —"

"It's nominal in name only." None of this meant, however, that his device was succeeding — merely that her mind was busy scaling them back down to reality. "We'll have what I said first, just a nice open house. Out on the lawn if it's a good day. Tables in the gardens. My gardens. Which you still, after all these *years*, haven't gotten around to wiring for lights. How beautiful they would look lit up at night, my rock garden and all." She was chiding him affectionately, dropping a hint for her present. Her broad face broke in its radiant smile. "It looks like an eventful summer all around, then, doesn't it?"

"And what will you tell the reporters this time?" Marvel asked, and shuffled quickly back to his bedroom before he could hear what she answered. He took a sedative in the end, and as sleep claimed him he was thinking of a man they both knew who had undergone plastic surgery for a new nose and who, as Alma put it, had never been the same since.

two

HARRY MERCURY'S broiled head appeared above a salmon-colored suit, borne on a tide of passengers moving along the train platform toward the gate. Nevada had tanned him well. His fingers were indistinguishable from the clear Havana cigar they flirted. He had hooded Oriental eyes and a fleshy, down-drooping nose like the handle of a derringer. In his left hand was a saucered cup from which he drank as he strode toward the station, the magnet of bystanders and porters trailing smiles. "Reminds me of my first wife's," he said, pulling a face at the coffee. "Grounds for divorce." Mercury cleared his throat after a gag in the arch manner of comedians everywhere; the Mesopotamian eyes loitered voluptuously over their prey as the tongue appeared in the cheek and the cigar rolled in the free hand. "She was a singer with a beautiful range, but I never saw her cook anything on it." A violent hiss of air from the locomotive brakes made him leap into the air. "Not so much soda in mine," he said, looking down behind.

Members of his retinue ducked among the crowd telling

who this was, for the benefit of those who mightn't know or recognize him. They included Chaucer, his chief writer; Nat Bundle, a press agent of almost Tom Thumb size; Butterworth, a man from the advertising agency handling the Götterdämmerung Beer account, and one more. Directly in Mercury's wake strode a dark-skinned youth of twenty-five in a plaid cotton shirt and a thin blanket around his shoulders. A bandanna folded into a fillet circling his brow was tied at the back in a knot from which an eagle feather stood erect. Straight as a pine, he ogled the onlookers on either side. "Rotten old him!" he said pointing an entire arm at the chattering Mercury. He was the most fabulous thing going, certainly in provincial Massachusetts, a writer Mercury had hired in Las Vegas and since been toying with the idea of grooming as something different in a stooge — a far-out Indian. Hence the obbligato incidentals he was lining out to try on the natives for size.

"Me have berth trauma. Ugh!" He felt his sore head. "All because boss begrudge couple bucks more for lower. Rotten old him!"

No, Mercury decided, reading the blank faces instinctively, he's too special. He signed almost imperceptibly for Prufrock, as the half-breed called himself, to knock it off, at the same time handing his cup and saucer to a gloved engineer leaning from the cabin.

"I like café au lait myself," he continued, the pack at his heels. "Café au lait hee — au lait hee ho, au lait hee ho!"

Moo Moo was hiding behind a pillar.

She had come down with bells on to welcome Harry and been about to dart forward in greeting when she had seen Mrs. Wetwilliam, local Mayflower Society luminary and regional chairman of the D.A.R., on hand to meet a nephew on the same train, and had instinctively stepped behind the nearest post. Mrs. Wetwilliam took the distraction in with the lofty frown that was her trademark. Who was this man who looked like one of the Hashemite kings but was cracking jokes? When she moved a slight distance off from the crowd, Mrs. Marvel found the courage to step out and acknowledge Harry, with open arms. That was when he started to yodel, and she stepped back again.

A loaded baggage cart interposed itself and she followed along beside it, listening to Mercury patter away on the other side, everyone heading into the station now.

"The railroads get these carts from the manual training students." Mercury grasped an upright of the vehicle which creaked as he shook it. "I'm a do-it-yourself man myself. Every time my wife tells me to do something I say 'Do it yourself.' Only way to get anything done." He was inches away from Moo Moo, who through the gaps in the luggage could see his satellites weaving among the crowd murmuring "Mercury. It's Harry Mercury the TV star." They looked like those furtive anonymous chief priests and elders who slink through mob scenes in religious dramas muttering "Say 'Release unto us Barabbas! Release unto us Barabbas!' "

When the chuckling porter drew the rig to a stop at the gate most of the baggage turned out to be Mercury's party's. The star made a humorous show of selecting a proper emolument for the porter on the basis of the pictures on the currency in his wallet. "Washington, Lincoln, Hamilton . . ." He removed the cigar from his teeth. "Ever notice women never get their faces on money? They don't have to. They get their hands on it." Mrs. Marvel smiled appreciation as she shook her head and shot, gaze down, toward the shelter of another post.

Concern for his health and the memory of a visit to Massachusetts in the winter accounted for Mercury's heavy tweeds and the topcoat now toted by Bundle. Harry combined hypochondria with business, no use denying it. He took most of his vacations in sanatoriums in order to deduct them as medical expense. He always emerged from these nursing homes and watering holes in top fettle, ready to plunge back into work at a clip that threatened to run his aides into the exhaustion in which he had, for the record and often more than half legitimately, enrolled himself. He had done less well in radio than he had before that done in vaudeville (and would later do on television) but he almost always managed to put in his thirty-nine weeks every year, getting squibs into the gossip columns to the effect that he was overworked as May drew to a close, sometimes missing a broadcast or two to bolster the credulity of the tax department, and with the arrival of June, having yielded to some summer replacement good enough to hold his audience but not likely to outshine him, entered some landscaped establishment as "acutely exhausted" or "suffering from complete nervous fatigue." Doctors not wholly shabby could be found to certify him as such, for Mercury did work himself to the bone when he was at it, living, eating and sleeping Humor.

By the early 1940s Mercury had himself slipped to a summer replacement in radio, so that now his disappearances into havens of rest occurred in the early autumn instead of late spring and began to acquire a basis in medical fact, though his hypochondria made that hard to tell. But Harry

Mercury was dated, and he knew it. Then came television, where the visual dimension restored to the ham his ancient birthright of thrown pies and exploding cigars, or, in its less visceral forms, cigars adroitly rolled in the fingers as the monologue unfolded. A few good writers — writers who not only had witty memories but could turn out new jokes as well as switch old ones, and who knew both his merits and his limitations — had helped keep him on top.

He was the latest Last of the Clowns. Along with the title, snatched for him by a quick press agent from the obituary of another comic with roots in burlesque, he was heir to the tradition that clowns are sad, and took to grooming that side of his nature. He digested the statements of intellectuals that comedy is the reverse of the mask of tragedy, and wore, for fashionable magazine photographers, expressions more lugubrious than Bert Lahr's. It was easy enough for a middle-aged man to get depressed God knew: catching glimpses of yourself in a restaurant walled with mirrors, eating in triplicate; remembering your poverty-stricken childhood and your mother chewing the juice out of the rib-roast strings; the time you went into a delicatessen for cold cuts and were waited on by a rabbi emerging from the curtained back room, where the proprietor lay dying. When seeing any mortality, misery or defeat, or a bevy of curvaceous cuties.

He became suicidal. At least there was a period when unsuccessful attempts at suicide were reported, by the ever sympathetic and alert Nat Bundle. Once at a weekend party on Long Island he was found in the kitchen trying to cut his wrists. He had snatched up the first object in sight, a butter knife, and in his distraction begun sawing with the dull side of that, plenty of time to rush in and stop him. He jumped out of a second-story window, ruining that hostess's lilacs and spraining an ankle. Once in a fit of valid desperation over the dropping of an option he had run out of his own country house, Dim View, and thrown himself into a stream that flowed behind it. Luckily it was a dry summer and the water only a foot deep. But he was susceptible to colds, and on that occasion had caught what his mother-in-law would have called his death.

Harry had dismissed the crowd with "That's all for free," and his entourage moved in loose formation toward a station lunch counter carrying the bags. A woman in a shawl who spoke no English and who had been watching from a distance held a sick child up to be healed. Mercury then hurried after his boys, turning now and then to look around for a face.

Mrs. Marvel ran up breathlessly, and was about to call a greeting when through the closing plate-glass door of the coffee shop she saw Mrs. Wetwilliam having tea in a booth next to one being pre-empted by Mercury's mob. Grips were flung into a corner and there was a great deal of muscling appropriation including the acquisition of an extra chair for the fifth man, Nat Bundle, who was parked in the aisle. Mercury autographed a menu for a waitress. Through the plate glass Mrs. Marvel noted the gingerly absorption of all this by Mrs. Wetwilliam and again her spirit failed her, and the cock crew. Something about the way the woman steadied the lid of the teapot with one finger, as she resumed pouring for her Ivy League nephew, palsied Mrs. Marvel's arm and froze her at the door. Looking through which in exile she resembled a wretch in a Kafka rigmarole symbolizing Guilt . . . Yet wasn't a sixth at Harry's booth out of the question and weren't the five there now deep in a business huddle it would be impolite to interrupt? Of course. She slipped in and perched unobtrusively at a counter stool, there to nurse a cup of tea of her own and compose the report on Lee for which Harry would certainly ask.

What on earth impression could you give of that sweet bundle of nerves? Lee was high-strung even for artistic pursuits. On a factory job briefly held the summer before, she had been ill on the assembly line and had with a mop cloth pursued her sickness on the conveyor belt till it disappeared through a hole in the wall into the shipping department. Seeking her out backstage the other morning Moo Moo had found the thin thing huddled with needle and thread over Shelley Kelley's wardrobe, nearly in tears. Theater in their blood indeed! She didn't look as though she had any blood for the theater to be in. What, specifically, did she want to do in this medium? Lee had sucked at a pricked finger. "Direct." The term "broken home" rolled like a punctual tramcar through the uncomplicated township of Mrs. Marvel's mind, bearing its simple freight of trouble and uncertainty. The attraction was a drama of the Dust Bowl by a promising young exponent of the new "twisted" theater, touted as a sort of Tennessee Williams without hope, in which Miss Kelley played the mother of four sons to all of whom the land was poison. She had had one breast caught in a potato-digging machine they didn't even own. Eying the loaded piperack, Mrs. Marvel had asked, "But if these are poor people, why does the mother have so many clothes?" "Well, it's a character part and they're all cheap dresses. But here's the thing," Lee went on, her brown eyes hollow with fatigue, the arms looking paler than ever under the pushed-up sleeves of a black sweater, "the mother's lost weight in the rewrite, the author's made her sickly for more conflict, so now I've got to let all these things out before dress rehearsal tomorrow morning. I've never sewed a stitch in my life."

Mrs. Marvel had gathered everything up and marched Lee home with her to run it off on her old Singer. The blowzy chintz of the long unused sewing room gave out a burst of welcome as the door opened. Mrs. Marvel was soon bent over the Singer herself, her feet pedaling briskly, the needle bobbing along the seam of a let-out Mother Hubbard.

"Here's what Moss wants," Lee called from the couch on which she had been ordered to stretch out in stocking feet. "The minute she shuffles on stage in that thing you're doing, he wants you to know this is a sick woman." "I know. Drink your eggnog." "It's a fine line. He doesn't want a laugh when she comes on, *he wants a nervous titter.*" "Don't worry. Are you drinking?" for Mrs. Marvel's back was to the couch. "Yes. I've never seen one of these before, but I've heard of them." Mrs. Marvel shook her head at the thought of a generation to whom eggnog was unknown. She chewed her tongue as she guided the garment along its new seam. "I figure if this fits me, it'll hang on Shelley Kelley about the way it would on a woman who's lost thirty pounds before the curtain goes up. That what Moss wants?" She pulled her own dress over her head and wriggled into the Mother Hubbard. Since it fitted her to a T, it would no doubt convey the baggy effect required for the star in this character part. Sitting in her shift she began on the next dress, and got down to brass tacks.

"Now, about your father and mother, dear. That year before the divorce, did they fight a great deal? I don't mean to pry, but if you're still troubled —" Mrs. Marvel substituted a more modish term — "if you're emotionally disturbed, it's far better to talk about it than keep it bottled up."

"I'm not emotionally disturbed. Why should I be? Most kids my age have something like this. Parents divorced or separated."

"Don't try to fool me, or be brave. The more a person tries to hide it the more it shows it's eating them. Now, you say they fought bitterly in front of you —"

"I didn't say bitterly, I said *freely*, to show they had nothing to hide," Lee said with her quick, whispering laugh. When she laughed or smiled she thrust her tongue out over her upper teeth, a shy mannerism that charmed boys it did not annoy. "Chester was bothered by it more than me. I think that Elizabethan talk of his is an escape. A defense mechanism."

"Now we're getting somewhere. Go on. It helps to talk about it."

"But I'm not upset, Moo Moo."

"Nonsense," said Mrs. Marvel firmly, "and the way to get rid of these things is to talk about them, not keep them to ourself and never let our devoted Moo Moo in on anything! Is that the way?"

"Right at the moment I'm ecstatically happy," said Lee hugging a pillow.

"Because you're letting it out. I know you. Remember it's my daughter we're talking about as well as your mother, so we can speak frankly. I know Elsie was shattered by the divorce and you're like her exactly — the same delicate feet and that snapdragon mouth she had as a girl and kept licking when she laughed. Now, was the conflict as far as you could make out — I was never told — ever about money matters?"

"Mother is a cheapskate and Father is a spendthrift," said Lee, plucking the fringe of the cushion which was yellow and said BANGOR. "Daddy throws it around like confetti. On us kids, Mother, friends. Probably on people in Las Vegas right now."

Mrs. Marvel wheeled in her chair and pointed a triumphant finger. "There, you see! You're worried stiff your father will get himself mixed up with some divorcee out there, tramps they call them, in that — that mess of baited fishhooks!"

"Gee. I never thought of that."

"So now it's coming out! And let it." Moo Moo grew flushed in her excitement, drawing up a slipping shoulder strap. "Do you think it right, child," she said, tucking a snipped end of thread into a wad already collected in her underlip, "for a girl to go to her father and the boy to the mother? At least *that* could be the other way around."

"Oh, what's the difference?" The girl was in tears now, and Moo Moo rose to put an arm around her, comforting what she had known all along would have to be comforted. "There, there. You've come to the right place. Go on," she said, returning to her work. "What were you going to say?"

"Girls don't get along with their mothers anyway, or boys with their fathers, so what difference does it make? Were you and Mother ever any closer than she and I? You don't answer. Well, Daddy and I are absolutely insane about each other."

Then why aren't you here to meet him? Mrs. Marvel thought, looking over at Harry from the station counter where her tea was growing cold. And where was Cotton? He had promised to be on hand and help welcome Harry. Mrs. Wetwilliam was gone. The men were deep in discussion over a feud Nat Bundle had proposed Mercury have with another television comedian, yet to be selected. She honestly felt she had been fair to Harry that day they had altered Shelley Kelley's clothes. "This is something girls don't learn any more," she had cried, indicating the Singer set militantly whirring again. "If they did, instead of taking courses in semantics and listening to swamis lecture, they might make better wives and stay married. When your father came home from a hard day at the studio, what would be waiting in the oven? A nice roast? A chocolate soufflé? No, a statue! Something she had done in clay modeling class that afternoon. Oh, I'll be truthful, even though it's my own daughter. Result, here you are."

Lee drained the last foamy dregs from her glass and set it down. "Aren't you thinking of ceramics, Moo Moo, not semantics?"

"Yes, that probably says it better. And now she's married to a man who doesn't know the one from the other." Mrs. Marvel rose, shifting the hoard of thread-ends under her lip like a pinch of snuff. "The same thing isn't going to happen to you if I can help it. Come over here and I'll show you how to sew. Maybe if you keep at this apprentice thing long enough, who knows, you may wind up a fit wife for some man."

"Benny and Allen, Hope and Crosby — name your own. The fact that so many comics have used it with success makes it wurt considering," Nat Bundle said. "Eminently wurt considering. The great feuds have all been radio — television has never had one. So medium-wise the idea is fresh. The public in my estimation is ready for another feud. Provided it ain't a rehash of the old. Provided it's done wit wit — wit wit and a certain *panache*."

"I agree," said Butterworth, coming in with the agency's point of view. "That Thursday night timeslot is going to be a brute. I've just broken the news to Harry that *Blood All Over Everything* will be on then. The top crime show on the air is going to be hard to buck. Believe you me, Götterdämmerung Beer is going to have to look to its Trendex. I kid you not. Any publicity will help. A good feud would be good for both Harry and the other comedian. Now I'll give you my idea who that should be."

They had all stopped the foolishness now and were serious. Prufrock had dropped his blanket and removed the headband and eagle feather. This was important. Mercury had an air of grave waiting, trimming his cigar into an ashtray shoved toward him by Nat Bundle, who was simultaneously striving to accelerate service by firing expressions of inquiry and impatience high over both shoulders. Chaucer leaned across the table raking his red hair, his pickle-green eyes bright with interest.

"I suggest Lew Pentecost," Butterworth said. "Lew is also — He's been slipping lately and I'm sure he'd welcome the idea." They nodded at one another, taking this in. "Another thing in favor of its being Lew Harry pick the fight with, you boys can get to work on it right away. Lew's touring *Waiting for Godot* this summer, and by God I'm not sure it isn't at the Smugglers Cove barn next week."

"Meaning we might very well find Lew at the Hickory Inn when we blow in there," Harry said. "Since he's got his own series to get ready for fall, his writers are probably up here too."

"You mean," said Prufrock, raising his eyebrows, "we'd have to collaborate with his writers on this feud?"

"How else? The way Benny and Allen worked it—" Harry turned around, hearing his name called. "Moo Moo!"

"Harry! How *are* you? I got here earlier," Alma said, bearing down toward them as best she could along the cluttered aisle, "but you all seemed to be having such a solemn discu-hu-husion," she laughed. She was beside herself at the pleasure of seeing him, and he drew his arms around her with "Baby, how are you? Id'z good to see you. You're looking like a million."

"Not quite that old, Harry," she said, straightening her hat. There was a great rising and stumbling of the experts to meet this woman whom Mercury introduced with an arm still circling her waist as the Dean of American mother-in-laws. Just then she turned, seeing someone come in the door.

Cotton burst in daydreaming. He would show them all. He would have solid worth. He shook everyone's hand in an upstanding way and with a word of welcome to each like a mayor greeting a party. Then immediately the resolve ran out of him. He fell in with the writers, whom he had wanted especially to meet.

"Is Prufrock your real name?" he asked as they went out the door.

"No, it's a translation of my Indian name—Rolling Stone. Me not Chippewa off old block. Me know. Me shape of things to come. Me awfully sorry," said the Indian, adjusting the stole around his shoulders with a roguish air.

Cotton threw his own shoulders back at the other's example and began to walk with something of his grace, emulating his fluid gestures as well. Mrs. Marvel noticed this as the pair fell back, seeming to have come to an understanding with one another quite quickly. She smiled. That young man seemed awfully nice. She hoped that as writers they might have something in common, that the newcomer might have enough influence on Cotton to keep him from running around with those terrible girls he'd been seeing.

She and Harry got into a cab of their own, and Harry lost no time in raining questions on her about Lee. "She's nuts about you," he said. "She wrote me about the dresses you helped her with. Look, from what you could see, is she mixing gall right with the group?"

"Mmm, well, I'd say she's mingling fairly well. From the little I've seen of her. I took her a malted milk backstage the other day, get some flesh on those bones, and she was having a sandwich with a middle-aged man named Weintraub."

"One of the owners. That's the connection I got her in there. Weintraub's O.K. He's got a hobby that I don't know which takes up more of his time, it or the business. He's a famous philatelist."

"I suppose the theater is full of those. More so than the other arts. Well, in that case I suppose a girl is safe from him at least . . . Tell me, Harry . . ."

Mercury's eyelids came down as he brooded and dreamed over a sketch based on the old talking at cross-purposes idea, thinking what a mine of material dear Moo Moo would make for a writer like Chaucer. "You say he's a philatelist. Has he ever undergone treatment for it?" "It's hopeless. He's up all night with the things. Some rare specimens in his collection." "I can imagine. Can you tell me something about his background. Where is he from?"

"Walla Walla. His father was the town podiatrist." "Then it runs in the family. My, this sort of thing is on the increase." Finally she gets it all straight, or thinks she does, so that when someone informs her that So-and-so is a well-known pederast, she says, "Tell me, does he have a large practice?"

But it wasn't for television, certainly for the Götterdämmerung Beer people, Mercury thought, coming to and laying a hand guiltily on Moo Moo's. ". . . so while I can't vouch for the company she keeps at the theater, Harry, I can assure you I've let no grass grow under *my* feet in thinking about an eligible boy for her."

"Oh?"

"One of our local products. Malcolm Johnsprang. He's a fine clean young man with a very flourishing real estate business. He's been out of town but will be back I think tonight, and I'm going to get them together at our house. Probably mean breakfast, the hours they keep at that barn. Breakfast, it's beginning to sound serious already. And Harry, after they've met I want you to find out from her what she thinks of Malcolm. Because he's a sort of protégé of mine."

"Leave it to me. Lee knows in matters of the heart she has her Daddy's ear. Thank God that's all of him she's got, eh, Moo Moo?" They laughed like fools at that, squeezing hands as a swerve in the traffic flung them together on Harry's side, and Mrs. Marvel wriggled with joy. How good it was to have Harry back. You couldn't ask for a better beginning for the Gathering of the Clan.

three

MALCOLM JOHNSPRANG was a naturalized rather than native Yankee but no less chauvinistic a one for that. His exact birthplace was known to be below the Mason-Dixon Line and suspected to be Mississippi or Alabama, but no one knew for sure as the subject was taboo in his presence. He had left his home state in early manhood making his way deeper and deeper into his "beloved Nawth." He had lived for short periods as a real estate broker in both Connecticut and Rhode Island which had failed his (by now) rigid regional standards on both scenic and human counts; only Massachusetts satisfied them fully. There were times when Alma Marvel wondered whether even she came up to snuff. Malcolm hewed with uncompromising purity to the old New England values, preferring his bicycle to his car, his horse to both, and being in favor of hearts of oak. In winter he aggressively organized sleigh rides, coming to life in the subzero weather and flapping his arms while he breathed vapor to indicate to his frozen subjects that they were having a better time than might appear to be the case.

There were stories that he tried to take clients house hunting on the handlebars of his bicycle, but they were probably what Mrs. Marvel called prophylactic.

Seeing him prop his bike against the carriage block this morning Cotton ran up the stairs to his bedroom two at a time, bathrobe flying, while Mrs. Marvel went to the door. Malcolm removed the clips from his ankles and advanced up the walk. He was a great believer in pineapple chunks, Alma remembered too late. Malcolm was what. Twenty-five. The difference between that and Lee's nineteen vanished somewhere down the long perspective of Mrs. Marvel's sixty-three, like parallel lines meeting in infinity. For the rest, he had the erect carriage and apple-cheeked archaic decency of young men who "wait."

"Alma Marvel as Ah live and breathe!"

But he was not all that happy. Behind his exterior spirit lay a note of disquiet which Alma was quick to detect and he not loath, presently, to reveal, for the exchange of confidences was a cardinal element in their bond. "It's Mama again," he said pacing the parlor floor. "Where does a man have to go to get away from his kin – Alaska?" "Let it out. Now what?" "Now what not? Oh, damn. She phoned me at six o'clock smawnin' about that girl down home they think they've got handpicked for me? Ah've made it clear as Ah could that it's no sale – we simply not *simpatico*. We too dissimilar in taste and temperament. Ah couldn't live anywhere but up Nawth, it's where Ah belawng, but Betty Lou'd stick out up heah like a soah thumb." Malcolm flung himself into a chair very nearly in tears. "It destroys me to war with Mama, but Ah just can't make that woman understand."

Mrs. Marvel was about to offer a deploring cluck of agreement about meddling elders when the knocker sounded on the open door and Lee entered with a deferential smile, bearing an armload of things wanting tidying.

Malcolm's bow reminded Lee of a clown she had once seen loosen his shoelaces with his teeth. The brown gamin's eyes, coltish legs and flickering smile above the silk scarf knotted at the pulsing throat had struck him to the quick. He lost no time in declaring his eligibility.

"Your grandma and Ah just discussing a very sweet old thorn in the flesh, mah mother," he said, drawing out a chair for Lee at the dining-room table to which Alma promptly herded them, for Lee must get back to the theater in an hour with the things pressed. "She's that eternal nuisance, a matchmaker." Mrs. Marvel trotted back and forth between dining room and kitchen bearing objects germane to breakfast, beside herself with pleasure. She resembled a contestant in an egg-and-spoon race.

"You can't really blame her for that," said Lee, lifting her orange juice from its cradle of crushed ice. Moo Moo had been up since dawn and now looked ready for bed.

"No you can't, but after a point you give up, don't you? Mama dies hard on the subject of the gal you probably overheard us talking about, so you might as well hear it all, lest darker suspicions than necessary breed in that lovely head. The thing is, it can't be got through Mama's brain that we're hopelessly incompatible."

"Where is she from?"

"The Deep South."

Alma poured them coffee from her best silver pot, tilting it adroitly by its teak handle. Bacon and eggs materialized while the acquaintance blossomed.

"What's she like?"

"Mama or Betty Lou?"

"Well, I was thinking of your mother, but describe Betty Lou if you'd rather."

"One description will do for both. Betty Lou is what Mama once was, Mama is what Betty Lou will one day be, for womanhood is of a mold in that part of the country, where its role is still mainly that of wife and mother. You surely agree it should be more than that."

"It would be terrible to be regarded as a child-bearing machine."

"A barren prospect."

"What do you do?"

"Handle selected properties." He swallowed some coffee, watching Lee spread jam on a muffin. "Ah must be excused from understanding the Southern mentality, ma'am. Knowing very well where Ah have put down roots, she wants me to marry a gal who was Miss Cawn Pone of 1958, with an accent you can cut with a knahf." He sighed and looked away. "The South is ouah cross."

Lee sipped her coffee with a melancholy air. "I don't want to get into an argument with you about that, but as for your mother aren't you taking it a little, um, harder than you ought? I mean lots of people have Mama trouble, or Papa trouble, or something like that. I mean that's standard equipment."

"As we don't need Mr. Freud to tell us, eh, Miss Lee?" Malcolm answered with a rich wink. Lee finished gulping a mouthful of muffin, gesturing before she had begun to talk.

"But Freud did show us how complicated a little nest of neurosis the family is. Maybe it's got to go. I really wouldn't know. I mean it's too close quarters for anybody's good." She glanced at the kitchen door behind which could be heard the thud of a steam iron on Celeste Holm's skirt, and lowered her voice. "That's why lots of people start another family — to get away from the first."

"Ace a hell of a reason for grinding out another generation!"

The door was punted open and Moo Moo entered bearing fresh hot muffins, which she set down with a scrupulous regard for the conversation. Instinct would tell her when to join it. "Alma, you're a wonder. Everything is so good. But here's something interesting, Miss Lee. Psychoanalysis is supposed to have taken the romantic illusion out of love by reducing it all to libido. Yet Freud himself was very romantic in his co'tship. Old-fashioned romantic."

"Viennese schmaltz and all."

"Yes. So you could say on that basis that Freud who killed romance was himself the last romantic. He got his co'tin' in before psychoanalysis."

Lee laughed appreciatively, the tip of her tongue flickering out in the way that set Malcolm's blood to seething. Her mouth was that flower from which a pink stamen issues when squeezed. As for Moo Moo she could scarcely breathe — the thing was going so well. Such table talk! She slipped into a chair with the feeling that now was the moment to join it, which she did with the air of one positively presiding at a salon.

"Lee is a little older than you'd think from her having had just one year at Sarah Lawrence, because she missed a school year when she was a little girl. There's a story, doubtless prophylactic, that they hold classes in students' cars they're so small. It might be fun to hold seminars riding around in Bronxville like that but there's probably nothing to it. Lee's an apprentice at Smugglers Cove, staying at the

Hickory Inn. No wonder the theater's in her blood. Her father is the noted comedian Harry Mercury."

"One of the great clowns of ouah day," said Malcolm making a mental note to catch this man's stuff with no delay.

When the parlor clock struck eleven Mrs. Marvel said, "Lee, I know you're due at the theater. Those things are ready but I simply must be here when the plumber calls. Oh, dear. Malcolm could you —?"

"Delighted," said Malcolm with a smile behind which he seemed to gain weight. "Ah don't happen to have mah car, but if Miss Lee will do me the honor of —"

"No, you can use mine," Mrs. Marvel said quickly. She couldn't see a girl squatting in the antlers of a bicycle while her ear was being stertorously breathed into. It was too high a price to pay for regional worth. "It's got the same shift as your Dodge. Little more coffee then before you go?"

"The thing about Papa," Malcolm said as they drove to Smugglers Cove in the Marvel Buick, "was his sudden disintegration. He just up and fell apart. He was riding up in an elevator in the county co't building one winter morning when with his teeth only, not using his hands, he lifted the derby off the head of the man in front of him and set it on another man's head. There was nothing for it but to settle him in a comfortable sanatorium, where he died two years later. All Ah inherited from him are these sound teeth, in which there hasn't been a cavity in ten years, and which Ah hope to pass on in as good condition as Ah got them." He stole a sidelong glance at Lee. "In the accepted fashion of course."

"Have you known Moo Moo long?"

"Three years. We met in an antique store browsing, shortly after Ah moved to Hickory. No wonder the theater's a dying form. Look at these roads. But here we are. Look, how about having lunch with me some day?"

"Well, we have such crazy hours. I never know when we . . ."

"Understand perfectly. In that case we'll have to make it dinner."

"Ah like austerity in a landscape."

It was after dinner and Malcolm had parked his Dodge on the bluff which formed the eastern limit of Smugglers Cove, a small town said by geologists to be in danger of sliding into the sea. It clung precariously to the precipice which overlooked a rock-and-saliva bay, into which a narrow river boiled away there. The dramatic landscape fell away inland into gentle billboards anouncing productions prior to Broadway or summer-stock perennials. Lee had not yet shed the sense of being personally out of key here, especially when dusk came on, that hour of day that seemed so much gloomier than night. Samples of the theatrical fauna drifted by in the half-light; girls in bright shorts and scarves eating hot dogs and laughing up the path off which the car was turned; then three youths in tight jeans and open shirts who floated away on the balls of their feet, gesturing freely.

"And Prufrock? So it was only a question of time before the police arrived and there they all lay — in one moist heap."

"And everything went beige."

What on earth were they talking about? The accident they had been routed round a while ago? Lee felt ill at ease, the more so because of Malcolm's arm which stole with massive nonchalance onto the back of the seat, and threatened to become protective.

"Ah love this stern and rockbound coast. Those pines. The stubborn fields . . . You don't say much."

"Ah'd rather — I'd rather listen." She leaned her head wearily against the doorpost and giggled nervously, with the glimpse of pink that drove Malcolm mad with dreams of pigeon kisses.

"Ah have a theory that what a man likes in scenery he likes in his women," Malcolm said, edging closer. "Ah love restraint in a woman."

"I like it in a man."

"Another point on which we agree."

Malcolm's hand had ended its long and circling flight to her shoulder, on which it came to rest like a wary bird. With his other hand he reached over and turned her by the chin. The smell of bay rum thickened, and with closed eyes she compared this sensation to that when the conveyor belt had come out of infinity and gone on into infinity bearing its implacable parade of packing cartons to be tarred with a stencil: something that could not be stopped. His lips on hers were like the touch of cool, spotless bologna, and then she thought for some reason of the bubbles bursting forever in the river down below. Malcolm knew it was too soon to think of luring that pink stamen from its chalice, and he began to draft a mad letter to leave at the hotel desk with a dozen roses. His own tongue eluded the checks of reason and, despite all he could do to control it, sent out a patrol into deliciously doubtful country. He was not surprised to feel her pull away. To save the situation he claimed the withdrawal as his own. "Better not get too close. Ma's sore."

"Ma's sore?" she said softly.

"No, *mah* ah." He pointed to his right eye. "Lots of pink ah going around and there's nothing more catching. Can't have you going around backstage like a taillight." As she explored this thought, frantically raking her hair with a comb, he said: "Yawl ought to go for the likes of me, if the theory is true that we seek ouah opposites. Ah mean Ah know Ah'm the impulsive outgoing type — which Ah personally can't abide." She vaguely sensed herself to be in some kind of jam, mixed up with an interesting bore, an intelligent ass. He let a silence blossom following this, planning to recover the broken trance and starting from scratch avoid his error in strategy. He stroked the back of her hand reverently with his thumb while he was wrecked by a flash of thigh. She murmured thanks for the dinner while peering at her wristwatch, lifting, in order to do so, his hand along with hers. Later he threw his head back and like a dog howling in pain cried out:

"Down to the Puritan marrow of mah bones
There's something in this richness that Ah hate.
Ah love the look austere, immaculate,
Of landscapes drawn in pearly monotones.

"Ever read Elinor Wylie?"

"No, but I've always wanted to."

"Be a copy at the hotel desk in the mawnin'. Now Ah know you've got to get along. We'll discuss the merits of Miss Wylie another evening."

Lee laughed helplessly as she climbed out, ways and

means for meeting the threat of another evening already agitating her mind. The device by which fate enabled her to cope with it was one which in even her present distraction she could not have imagined.

She edged warily into the theater parking lot early one evening a day or two later to see what cars were there. They were three sports jobs, a jeep, and a balance of more rational sedans. None of them, thank God, was the Dodge. As she took note of them a voice behind her said, "An actress can't be too careful in her choice of vehicle." Turning around she found herself looking into a pair of black eyes under a shock of even blacker hair, glossed and parted on the side. It was a moment before she recognized Prufrock, whom she had met once. What was he doing here? Just calling on some apprentices who were friends of his, Goof Walters and Georgie Meticulous the Greek boy, she probably knew them, though he realized he should be at the Inn batting out stuff for rotten old him. Well actually he was worrying up a sketch on the American Primitive fad, would she mind his trying it on her for size? Mercury owned a farm going to rack and ruin because nobody plowed or planted anything any more, they just folk-painted. The Department of Agriculture might have to put canvases on price parity. "Well, your father sits in a rocking chair in overalls and a beret," he said, sad to note her attention wander off to the driveway, "and leafing through an *Art Digest* he rocks and says to his wife 'Maw, I see Dali's having a restrospective at the Knoedler.' 'Yes, Paw, I know. Don't you think his stuff is a little precious?' 'It's precious, Maw, but 'tain't valuable . . .' There is a famine in the land . . ."

The vehicle of which she stood in fear rushed to a stop

and in a cloud of dust Malcolm was seen coming forward waggling a book. Without hesitation Lee looped an arm through Prufrock's. "Bill — isn't that your name? — you're just taking me to dinner. I'll explain later, or you can duck when the coast is clear, but I'll say when that is." Prufrock's mind a jumble of thoughts about woman the aggressor, he found himself being marched by one of them toward the man she was running away from. "Oh, Malcolm. We were just going to dinner."

"Ace all rot, Lee. Ah have a client to meet out this way and just thought Ah'd drop the book off."

Now Prufrock collected fools. It was not his most attractive trait, but he collected and classified fools as a lepidopterist does butterflies. Under that liquid gaze paraded all specimens of the genre, unconsciously competing for distinction as the perfect find. Mercury had in two weeks at Las Vegas revealed to the satirist he had hired certain notable and cherishable facets of human *folly*, but then so would most of us; what Prufrock hunted down was the pure distillate, the prime and irreducible Ass. He recognized the Real Thing instantly in Malcolm. He invited him to join them. Lee, harboring the lewder forms of disgust, wished them both in hell. Malcolm had enough form himself to decline the invitation, but they did chat a moment all three there on the path, in the late afternoon light slanting through the pines; of Elinor Wylie, of the theater, then, when Malcolm learned what Prufrock did, Harry Mercury. "Ah am hoping to meet Mr. Mercury very soon," he said, with a glance at Lee. She was sketching with the toe of her shoe in the dust. Prolonging the encounter a moment, Malcolm spoke of trends in humorous entertainment. "What yawl think of the sick comedians, Mr. Prufrock?"

"They won't live."

"Well, they a disturbin' lot, and that's a fact. A disturbin' phenomenon. Tom said something about it last week."

"Tom who?"

"Tom magazine."

Sighing that this man must be let go, Prufrock took his leave and walked his Lee up the drive to the main highway, where they flagged a cab and did race away for something to eat. It was necessary to go to the Hickory Inn so Lee could change into something long. It was opening night, and she had to dress because she was ushering.

four

PRUFROCK asked Lee if she knew the theme of the restaurant they were in was nautical. Their table was illumined by a mass of rope shellacked into a unity with a soft pink shade on top. Other lamps were gasping fish into whose mouths bulbs of varying wattage had been screwed, with an occasional outright ship's lantern. Through a door opened by a person in a sou'wester you "boarded" this establishment on a gangplank contrived to sway realistically, giving some arrivals the sensation of *having* eaten. All this was in honor of the region's great whaling past. The two young people were drinking Martinis at their wits' end with one another, under a figurehead at whose outjutting bust Prufrock cast uneasy glances. He had gotten into a business suit himself. He looked out through a rounded pane over his chair.

"Through my porthole I can see them parking cars, Mother. I'll mail this when we touch the Falkland Islands and you may get it by Christmas, but oh, Mother, it'll be years before I come rolling home to you."

"It was nice of you to rescue me," Lee said, turning the stem of her glass in her fingers. "It's because he's so nice that it's such a problem. He comes tooling up the drive like that all the time, sometimes on his bike, thinking it looks like Lochinvar out of the West I suppose, or maybe it's just the pleasant old custom of dropping in. Anyway, he never phones beforehand."

Prufrock shifted his gaze to her without exactly removing his face from the porthole. A self-conscious Indian is a rather disturbing thought, she thought. What are we coming to? Prufrock's efforts to attract the waiter were in direct conformity to the many jokes cracked on the subject, but his gymnastics were a sort of diversion in their constraint. He scribbled a note on a pad he always carried and passed it across to a woman at the next table, thereby reversing a famous cliché, for the note was for *her* to pass to the *waiter* and read "How about dinner tonight?" The waiter nodded when he got it, and vanished into the galley.

This humor hadn't been altogether fair. There was trouble behind the scenes. A new fire-preventing sprinkler system had been installed in the kitchen which at the suggestion of flames would release torrents of extinguishing water. But it proved to be even more sensitive than claimed. The heat of the ovens and deep-fat stoves themselves had proved sufficient to release its corrective streams, so that the chef and other kitchen help now stood in a steady downpour, into which the waiters also made sorties to snatch what undrenched food they could for the hungry patrons. Some had donned oilskins such as those affected by the doorman: even his own had been impounded. Those who say that the Age of Conveniences has rendered obsolete the pioneer spirit, the calls to hardihood, are wrong then aren't they? The young people's waiter having departed in natty blues returned in a dripping slicker, a hat shrouding his face. The motif was growing; never again would the place have such atmosphere.

"It's a sketch I've been trying to work up for your father, actually."

"Oh, tell me about it. Daddy often tries things out on me. It's fascinating to be in on the, um, genesis of ideas."

"It's a takeoff on all this chichi telephoning in restaurants, actually." These boys say "actually" too much, Lee was thinking. And spread their fingers across their chests like we do, and what else? Yes – they move their eyes without moving their heads. She'd learned the natives called Smugglers Cove in the summertime Queer Cove, which she thought neither very witty nor very nice. She was already developing a deep professional pride.

"Nobody gets anything to eat. The waiters serve only telephones, which are borne aloft on trays in a bustling manner. Your father is a big shot trying to reach another big shot – through his New York office, his London office, Maxim's in Paris, Lisbon. Finally he locates him, as we know when the waiter trots up with another phone. It's the man at the next table."

"Oh, I like that. Bill, have you shown it to Daddy yet?"

"Not yet."

The waiter came at last with menus behind which the two took shelter for some minutes. Prufrock cautiously lowering his met the doe's eyes watching over hers. "How about this? Your old man's with a babe he's trying to impress. She says 'How's the cuisine here?' He says, 'Superb, my dear, they do it with a wine sauce I'm dying to have you try.' " Prufrock, a tireless student of nervous behavior, noted again the girl's attempt not to laugh, to pull her lip down over her teeth, cover them with her tongue. What caused this inhibition in people with perfectly good teeth? It was a mystery.

They ordered the mixed fisherman's platter, a split of sauterne and, for Prufrock, one more Martini. She had twisted her cocktail napkin into a tight wick and was now leaning with her elbows on the table and the knuckles of her fingers dovetailed into one another. She asked him where he was from and he answered Saginaw, Michigan, which she had a suspicion was the first thing that came into his mind. His mother was a French-Englishwoman named Sally Mockridge who had taken up with this lumberjack Indian, with whom she had several children. Here the wicked light returned to his eyes and he said, "There was a woman who knew how to take care of children. Parents these days stew and read books about it, but she knew! The way she would do, she would sit in her favorite chair with a box of candy and a book, a bowl of water and a washrag on a table in front of her. And the minute any child came near her she'd grab him and wash his face. That kept us away."

His Martini came, and after drinking liberally of it he set it down and resumed:

"She wanted to be a singer. A Valkyrie who carried clear to the gallery where the people who had saved their nickels and dimes and walked through slush to hear her sat. Without a voice, that was a little tricky. She ended up belting out hymns in the church choir, growing more bitter by the year. She deserved better — who doesn't? Poor wretch. It's all a sorry swindle, really. Anyhow, she had breakfast in bed every morning out of a determination that she had it coming to her. Except that we had no servants so she had to get up first and fix it for herself. Can you imagine? It is my story that this woman crawled back between the sheets with a tray she had to pretend there'd been a maid to fix. There she'd lay, eating it on that basis. She had the figure of an earth mother but she was as cold as a fiddler's bitch," Bill said, getting a little savage now. "Her eyes were like hailstones. I do not now recall their color. Maybe they had none, like hailstones."

"Bill, you ought to be a writer." Fine *faux pas* that! she thought closing her teeth on it.

"I can see her on her fat back yelling at us to be quiet, and I always noticed something. She kept her face absolutely composed when she screamed. Not to get any more wrinkles into it, you see."

"Bill, you're much too perceptive."

"Curse of our time. Everyone a tortured bundle of acumen, eh? After such knowledge what forgiveness. And the night comes down and, oh, Mother, I'm only a newsdealer on sabbatical. I'm not what you want. I'm not what you were looking for but, oh, Mother, what grievance were you nursing when you should have been suckling me?"

Lee became uneasy. She had heard these boys scientifically blamed their mothers — not the Oedipus thing, just the opposite: they'd never had that and gone on to the next chapter — something like that. A schoolmate whose brother was one had tried to explain it to her. Was Prufrock joking? Or was it one of those moments when an outcry escapes, a filament of honest yearning disguised as nonsense flashes out of the careful shell.

"Father say you bad Indian. You lollygagging around late-nineteenth-century poets. You *fin de siècle*. Ugh! Go. Never darken cabin door again — you sample of overspun human organism." So self-consciousness made him slip into this talk as it did Chester into Elizabethan. We need to keep our nerves sheathed from one another. "Basic dichotomy adding to subtle biochemic tensions already racking individual. Ugh! What about *your* mother?" Feeling she owed him a confidence or two she fabricated a few. Her mother buttered the bread for the birds who wouldn't slice it for her father. She — "Oh, she'll be up here in a few weeks. Maybe you'll meet her then." Their food came, then a skinker swathed in leather drew a cork from a split of sauterne as though he were pulling Excalibur from the rock. "Everyone's coming for my grandparents' anniversary. The Marvels. *There's* a marriage worth celebrating." He remembered meeting her grandmother at the station. "What did you think of her? You with your acute perception."

Prufrock was watching three men rise from a corner table and leave: Chaucer, Butterworth and Nat Bundle. Despite disparities of size and gait the trio had an organic unity imposed by the cut of their clothes and the gravity of their conversation as they picked their way among wet waiters. Butterworth and Bundle were returning to New York that evening and were cleaning up with Chaucer a last bit of business. Finally they walked three abreast to the door, linked in a series like the lights on a Christmas tree, and, like the lights on a Christmas tree, they went out together. Not by the gangplank but by a side door leading into the lobby where they were joined by the sudden chimera of Harry Mercury. In a moment of further solemn talk Bundle said something that made Mercury turn his head and look through the glass doors into the restaurant. After blessing the departing with hands on their shoulders Mercury came in. Prufrock prepared a face as he bore down toward their table.

Setting his firewater aside he smiled and said, "Me disintegrating with the group."

"I can only stay a second," Mercury said, sitting down. "So who goes out with sigzteen-year-olds?" Since the question applied almost equally to either and Harry was brushing his vest down as he spoke there was no certainty as to whom it was addressed to. "Everything O.K. at the theater, sweetie?"

"Swell, Daddy. I came down for a bite when I bumped into . . . Ushers have to dress for opening night, hence this thing. Going to see the play?"

"I want to catch it sometime this week. We've got work to do tonight. Lahr's spoiled it for me, but then Lew'll do all right. Nobody claims to know what *Godot* means so who'll say he done wrong?"

Prufrock that emotional lock-picker knew what Mercury was thinking. Mercury longed to follow, not Benny into a famous feud, but Ed Wynn, Bert Lahr, and Zero Mostel into the ranks of clowns who had Shown They Could Act. He wanted to play the doomed principal in *Godot*. He wanted to be asked to Yale or Bennington to analyze humor. He also knew Prufrock was one of those bastards who know everything from a clue, from one word of unguarded comment or the self-betraying flick of an eye, who are floating over you in a glass-bottomed boat. Prufrock drew back, but Mercury had not cocked an arm to sock him, only to consult his wristwatch. "Got any monologues yet?"

Prufrock held a finger aloft while he swallowed a mouthful of hot fish, eager to begin. "Colleges open the week you do. So what about you do a reminisce about your own schooldays? You had one especially beloved professor. Roentgen — his first name was Ray. He was past his first youth, being very nearly eighty. He'd lost a leg in the Spanish-American War. There is a saying that when the Barbary apes leave Gibraltar it will cease to be a British possession. So every Sunday night you went up to his rooms and sat at his foot, while he talked about Life. He would fix us with an eagle eye — the singular being quite in order as the other had been plucked out by a condor in the Andes —"

"Isn't this a little far out?" said Harry holding up a hand like a traffic policeman.

"Wait. Professor Roentgen has friends from the four quarters of the earth. One night the Pope dropped in, to shoot the papal bull."

"God."

"The Catholics will love it."

"I also got Protestants to worry about."

"It's a *non sequitur,* Daddy. You say you want some off-beat stuff for the show. It's like putting Poulenc on the program along with the standard Brahms and Beethoven."

"What else?" said Mercury, glancing at Prufrock's glass. "What do you build to?"

"Why should you build to anything? It's your mid-program monologue. You just ramble on like Mark Twain. For a finish if that's what you mean you might tell the story of the space salesman who turned out to be not from Madison Avenue at all but a funny little . . ."

Mercury screwed about in his chair, frowning into the lobby. "Kick it around with Chaucer then. See what he can throw into it."

The poor Indian got a firm grip on the stem of his wineglass. He cleared his throat and said, "If you give it to Chaucer he'll make him a history professor who thinks dates are important, so you have one every Saturday night."

"Hey, you just make that up?" said Mercury, smiling a little as he reached for pad and pencil. "Look," he said as he scribbled, "I don't want to rush you but we've got work to do and Lee's got to get to the theater anyway. By the time she leaves Chaucer'll be back from seeing those guys to the train. We'll meet in my room say in twenty minutes. Because we've got an awful lot of work to do on the feud. Waiter, the check."

When Prufrock arrived for the conference Mercury was in bed, where he could think better than on his feet. The order of business was for his writers first to outline suggested material they had been working on which would then be kicked around in open and usually fruitful conclave. Chaucer did the talking while the half-breed sat in a chair watching Mercury between the footposts of the bed, on one of which hung Harry's green Tyrolean hat complete with whisk. He was fascinated by Mercury's hair, a meticulously glossed and parted residue falling grievously short of the sides to which it aspired, the skull gleaming through it in a way that heightened its resemblance to the skeleton of a small fish. He had once known a man with hair like that who combed it with a toothbrush, or so it was said.

"It's Bill and my's feeling," Chaucer said, choosing his words carefully as he rambled among the furniture, "that hypochondria is a natural for a twit. It's psychological and will therefore mirror our times more than Benny's Maxwell or the bags under Allen's eyes, valuable though those were in their day. Ours is an eminently foolish age that cries out for satire." Mercury nodded, a faint preparatory smile playing about his lips as he toyed with the tassels on his pajama cord. He was not smoking at the moment but cigar stumps lay everywhere like ordure.

"It will lend itself to gags like this," Chaucer resumed with the most covert of glances at the half-breed, meaning they had cleared the first ticklish hurdle, their master's feelings. "He's in the hospital with symptoms for which no organic cause can be found. Oh, he is? Yes. I'm on my way to visit him now. Oh, you are? What's that you're taking him? The most appropriate thing I can think of for a psychosomatic patient — a basket of wax fruit."

Mercury's smile broke into open amusement. He chuckled. "Swell. I like it." He smiled again. "He such a hypochondriac? Pentecost?"

Out of sight of Mercury but visible to Prufrock, Chaucer clapped a hand to his brow and with his expression said "Oy oy oy!" Bill cleared his throat to speak but Chaucer cut him off with a warning shake of his head, at the same moment snatching from Mercury's hand some penciled notes he had picked up from the bedside table.

"What'll we rib *me* with?" Mercury asked, lowering his eyes with maidenly modesty. "Have you guys thought of that?"

"Later," Chaucer said. "Pentecost and his boys are expecting us upstairs for a session in the morning and we'll have more of it firmed up then, so we'd better work tonight on the Western skit and the Progressive School one so we'll have them ready to show Tallulah. Butterworth said he'd try to make her definite for the guest shot, but he needs something to show before it can be firmed up."

Chaucer was still shaking his head the next day as Prufrock followed him up the flight of hotel stairs to Pentecost's headquarters. "God," he said. "Well, as my grandmother used to say no one recognizes the shoe that fits them. Imagine Mercury not — God." He gave up. "Bear in mind we're walking on eggs with this cluck even more," he cautioned as they approached suite 312, "despite the good reviews he got. So be careful. Let me do the talking. I hear he's paranoiac on some subjects."

"Let's kid him about that."

"Look, he's sued two people that I know of."

"What happened?"

"They settled out of court."

Bill studied the back of Chaucer's red head as Chaucer rapped on the door. Sometimes Chaucer seemed worth adding formally to his collection, then again he blurred away as not quite the Real Thing. Would he ever see that Malcolm again? A sentence boomed in a hearty voice beyond the door trailed away as the speaker neared and opened it. They were greeted by a man who might have torn it from its hinges.

He was the tallest and most heavily upholstered man Prufrock had ever seen, and the upholstery was muscle not fat. "Hello, hello, hello." His conviviality was more shattering today as he expanded under the rave in the *Blade*. He wrung hands and took note of names, then shooed the callers in like ducks to meet his writers, a sorry-looking duo. They were a man of forty in a plaid shirt, named Abe Gonsil, and a much younger but scarcely less eroded one named Jerry Bemis who wore a crumpled pair of Bermuda shorts that matched the shirt Gonsil had on. He received the newcomers' congratulations, then clapped hands to get them to order.

"Now this is supposed to be the foreign ministers meeting in preparation for the summit level, but I don't suppose you guys mind if I sit in and kibitz for just a —" He plucked a ringing phone with a ham of a hand. "Oh, Julie, thank you. Thank you, liebchen. You know how much your opinion means to me . . ." He watched the others while he made his impression on the caller, a ton of debonair style. Prufrock had seen him on television once or twice but had not been prepared for the Gargantuan scale of the original. There was something almost maniacal in the ogle, obviously lost to its object, with which he finished, "In that case I'll come earlier. See you in an hour and don't light the candles till I get there. Heh heh. Toodle-oo."

Prufrock let escape a giggle it had gone beyond his nervous powers to contain. Luckily it was lost in the clatter of the returned phone as far as Pentecost was concerned, but one or two of the others looked at him. He screwed his gaze resolutely into the rug pattern while Pentecost came back rubbing his hands and resumed chairmanship of the meeting he'd said he had no part in. He scratched his nose thoughtfully, drawing attention to the organ it was perhaps most necessary to avoid if composure was to be maintained in the beholder. It was that luscious asymmetrical strawberry the grocer places on top of the box. His girth was equatorial and his shoes were like violin cases. There were so many targets one feared to draw a bow.

"Now the thing to decide on first is what they call in politics areas of agreement," Pentecost told the diplomats now disposed in a meek ring around him. "What can we rib each other about that's not only of human interest but will stand up week after week as a vein of humor? This idea is only as good as the material you chaps come up with. Forget it not, my hearties."

"It could lay an egg or it could be pay dirt," Jerry Bemis said.

"It could be pay dirt or it could lay an egg," Abe Gonsil said.

"Righto. And of course we have to bear in mind that humor is a release for people's cruelty," Pentecost explained. "That's true more than ever today with the tensions they live under. Poor people. Hence the popularity of bowling."

Bemis nodded. "People have to let go. They don't want any more soft soap — they want honest satire."

"People want honest satire — they don't want soft soap," said Gonsil. It was evidently his role to repeat, more mournfully and in reverse, what had been stated.

"Righto." Pentecost clapped his hands again with an air of really getting down to cases. "Now what can we kid each other about that'll meet these requirements?"

The gazes of the ministers scattered in doglike dismay as Pentecost walked into their center, dragging his load of grotesqueries. "Think of the great feuds that have gone before; that stood up week after week and even year after year," he continued. "What have Mercury and I got to be ribbed about?"

"Have you got a sports car, Lew?" Chaucer asked, avoiding the seat of the other's trousers.

"No, I haven't, but it would be too close to Benny's Maxwell. Just the opposite in the sense of new as against old, but basically the same. But keep going. Keep throwing them at me. Jerry?"

"The other day I noticed the lavish tip you left the waitress," Bemis said, looking away in shame from the others. "Could we work that up with a modern psychiatric slant? You tip generously because you're basically a skinflint, chase women because you're a Puritan at heart."

"Too subtle. Abe?"

Gonsil had walked toward the window wearing the expression of a man who intends some day at any rate to throw himself out of one. He spread his arms along the cross ledge and laid his chin on his fist, gazing out like a loyal old hound dog. "What about a series where you deflate one another's egos?"

"Why, what do you mean by that, Abe?" Pentecost asked, scrutinizing his nails.

"Somebody tells you you hadn't ought to run Mercury down the way you do — he's a top executive. You say, 'Yeah, I know. I saw him selling tops on Broadway.' Next week it'd be, 'Mercury's a key figure on Broadway.' You say, 'Yeah, I saw him in his hole in the wall, making keys.' Something people will look forward to every week. Make them turn their sets on."

"Too corny. We don't want it all meat-and-potatoes but it should be subtler than that. *Subtle jibes at physical stuff* — that's the golden mean. Let's keep it concrete! Let's get back to personal traits. Has either of us any outstanding physical characteristics?" he said, presenting to each a yard of rump in turn. "Some physical detail that might lend itself to derision?"

Here Prufrock lost control of another giggle, a bubble of hysteria that he had with difficulty kept bottled up that long even with his eyes on the rug. As he laughed his knees went up and his head down, leaving him in the position that is recommended for quieting heart palpitations.

"I was just looking at your feet, Mr. Pentecost," he said. "They're not exactly dainty, are they? A little on the he-man side?"

Pentecost pondered them tolerantly. "Well," he said with a smile, "feet are O.K. but they don't lend themselves to this sort of thing. Not because they're not a legitimate subject for humor — they are — but picking them up with the camera all the time would get too cumbersome. Keep trying though. I feel you're warming up, all of you." In the silence that followed, he scratched again the red sumptuosity they were all dying to get on the agenda but to which none dared risk the first allusion. Prufrock, his system temporarily cleared of hysteria like a Leyden jar of its electric charge, studied it openly. Bemis caught his eye and gave a warning shake of his head.

"Dum de dum de dum," Gonsil hummed, his chin still resting on his fist and his gaze directed to the street. "I hear you leave your clothes on in a Turkish bath to get them dry-cleaned free, Lew."

"Swell. But too close to the tightwad angle done by Benny. But keep going all of you! Keep concrete like this with subtle overtones."

Gonsil tried again.

"He's pulling the Kleenex out of the box to see if there were five hundred sheets like it says, and now he's having hell's own time getting them all back in again."

They all laughed at the joke, and Bemis threw pleasantly over his shoulder "Maybe you ought to work for Jack Benny, Abe."

Gonsil sighed and turned from the window. "Yeah, maybe I ought."

There was another silence, longer than before. They frowned into their hands, into the air, at one another. At last Chaucer stirred. "I'm talking off the top of my head — and maybe I'm even off my head — but what about this switch? We take cracks at one another's sponsors."

They all paused to think. Nods and pushed-out lips indicated the idea to be either insane or sheer inspiration.

"It could put us in the almshouse or it could make history."

"It could make history or it could put us in the almshouse."

"How would you go about it, Chaucer?" Pentecost said. "Could you give us a for-instance?"

"Well, if you kidded Götterdämmerung Beer — in a way that would result in increased sales not harm business — we'd come back at Krak-Oats. *Is* it really as slenderizing as they say? Why don't certain parties use it then?"

This was coming close. They were on thin ice now. Which was where Chaucer had used the sponsor device to get them; they had to find out how close to where Pentecost lived they could venture. They avoided looking directly at him now, humming "Da de dum" and making thoughtful clucking noises. Some thought they sensed a dangerous vibration from Pentecost as he turned to the window. In the silence the heavy leather belt around his trousers could be heard creaking as he breathed, like a ship's timbers.

"Of course it's not as though it hasn't been done before," he said in somewhat lowered tones. "Ed Wynn kidded Texaco gasoline for years — that *was* the commercial. I'll grant you it was his own sponsor's product. Where we'd be breaking ground would be kidding one another's. As such it might work if you got up the proper material for it. Theoretically I can see it building up and building up through the season, with both of us on either my last or Harry's last show of the year, maybe with the sponsors on hand too, ending in a blaze of adult satire."

"So that if television lasts a thousand years, men will say this was its finest half-hour," Prufrock said.

Chaucer had sent the dog out on the ice. He now crept out on it himself. Drawing a deep breath, he said:

"As writers we can say the star is a heavy responsibility."

Pentecost turned back, now frankly amused. "That's pretty good. Heh heh heh. Is Harry putting on weight again?"

Gonsil broke open a roll of fruit tablets and passed them around the circle, prying one loose with his thumb for each of the diplomats in turn, to each a different flavor. "Well, let's all think it over," he said, "but meanwhile I'll say this against Pentecost. The sonofabitch is always late for a date. The dames seem to love it. But if you told this one you'd be there in an hour, Lew, don't you think you'd better get on your horse?"

That was how they got rid of him. When he was safely out of the room and the elevator door had been heard clattering shut, the four broke into animated dispute. Differences were sharp and often heated over just how much they had learned from Chaucer's courageous feeler about weight. Some said Lew's amusement indicated less sensitivity on the subject than they had feared, others that his having thought the jibe referred to Mercury showed a blind spot that was absolute. Not even his own writers could speculate with any degree of confidence. All agreed that at least some preliminary material might be drafted on the subject to be kept between the four of them till they were surer of their ground. Chaucer and Prufrock agreed to work it up, and took their leave.

"Could you take a crack at it?" Chaucer asked him as they traipsed back downstairs both measurably worn by their ordeals. "I'm so damn tied up with the sketches."

"I'll try," Prufrock said, trailing by his usual step. There was a new gem in his collection.

"And we must keep echoes of others out of this. Mercury doesn't want to be another Milton Berle or another Red Skelton. He wants to be himself."

"Which shouldn't be aiming too high."

"Pentecost is unpredictable, more so than Harry. He may be a good sport or he may be ugly about it."

"He may be ugly about it or he may be a good sport."

Chaucer whirled on him. "Damn you! Can't you take anything seriously?" He spoke with a vehemence that surprised both of them. "Well, I mean it's our bread and butter after all," he said, relenting. "So anyhow, swell, you knock something out and we'll let those guys have a look at it. They seem O.K. And let's keep our fingers crossed and hope Pentecost won't be too touchy. Because it stands to reason you can't have a feud with a goddam sorehead."

five

LEE sat with her elbows on the table and her face cupped in her hands. Her fingertips applied a pressure at the temples drawing them back in a manner that increased delicately the slant of her eyes. Prufrock often noticed older women doing this and understood the need to exorcise forty-year-old slack, but what gain did this goose count it to convert eyes intended by nature to be luminous orbs into exotic slits? While he spied on her she picked his brains about Harry, alert to signs in his face of mendacity.

"Did you ever see any of these women he ran around with in Las Vegas?"

"I didn't say he ran around with them and I didn't say 'women.' All I know is this one. You've seen her yourself on television. She gives those voluptuous weather reports. Pants 'Dallas 42°, Spokane 38°' on a chaise longue."

"I vaguely remember. What's she like?"

"Oh, God. What's anybody like? I only saw her once in the flesh, and I can say that again. She was getting into a hotel elevator with Harry."

"Up or down?"

"What difference does it make?"

Lee's head bobbed in its pale chalice. "Daddy's essentially domestic. He needs a home with a woman in it."

"A piece-loving man," said the rotten Indian, looking away from that trusting nod.

"He really is. He needs peace and quiet and emotional security *as a person*, though of course it's the *Sturm und Drang* that makes the artist great, clowns included."

"Harry has many things that make him grate." Prufrock in whom the pythons of pity and self-pity forever writhed always winced for his victims, thus becoming the butt of his own cruelty. He really should stop this; the twinges of compassion he felt for the lamb could lead to anything. Shifting some unused cutlery around his smoking coffee he begged her to tell him more about what the artist was like at home, and dissolving her pose at last Lee refilled their cups from a pot stamped with the tumbling-bell trademark of the Town Crier restaurant. In stitches she told some more about Mercury's hypochondria. "On a winter's day, you'll see him at the window reading one thermometer with another stuck in his mouth!" Prufrock filed the image away for future reference.

Dinner over, Lee was presumed safe from Malcolm's more ardent attentions, but it was such a beautiful night she dreaded returning to her empty room. It was Sunday and she had the evening off, being scheduled for publicity the next week and unneeded at the tech rehearsal going on now. They drifted down Chestnut Street to the Spitachunk, and the ferry being about to leave then for New Lambeth across the river, they impulsively boarded it.

As they stood at the railing the engine could be felt throbbing through the soles of their feet, like those machines in men's washrooms onto which you step and for a dime receive a massage through shoe leather. Lee could not remember having seen any in ladies' rooms, though they must be there since women as admitted are notoriously foot-conscious, constituting the bulk of a podiatrist's practice. They discussed all this.

A faint evening wind ruffled their bare heads as they stood gazing out at what there was of water. On the benches behind them were another young couple; an old woman with a parcel from which protruded the claws of a plucked fowl; several laborers bound for the night shift in a New Lambeth factory. They were joshing one of their number about the brand of cigar he smoked.

"Ferries can be fun."

Prufrock glanced at Lee skeptically, wondering if she were dishing him out a dose of his own word game. Her enchanted face ruled out any likelihood of that.

"We used to ride them to Staten Island and Hoboken when we went to New York, my roommate and I and our dates. Her family are very rich. They have a yacht they carry a Volkswagen on, for shore visits." She turned around and put her back to the rail. "I had too much to drink."

"In that case hadn't you better stay facing the water?"

"Oh, it's nothing like that. I just mean I'm talking too much. Look, why do you always seem at your wits' end with everything? As though you've got a key in your back and are wound up as tight as can be?"

"Why do you?"

"I asked you first."

He said he was sorry, he was not allowed to give out that information.

When they disembarked, a head in a stocking cap called

from a comic-strip wheelhouse-window that the boat would return in half an hour for its last trip of the night.

They wandered away from town toward the sea, for the river was tidal here, removing their shoes and socks on the shingle. Prufrock carried them all. "Feel the mud between your toes," she said. They were breathing heavily when they gained a flat boulder to which an instinct, perhaps self-preservation, took them. It was four feet high and though he helped her up with his free hand her foot slipped, her ankle bone striking the edge. She sat down with a howl of pain, nursing her foot.

Prufrock dropped everything in the slime and joined her. She laughed, letting him take her leg on his knee and inspect it with morbid curiosity in the failing light. "It's bleeding," he said. He produced a handkerchief and dabbed it, bandaging it snugly when it had stopped trickling. "You'll surely be able to walk back?" he said, anxiously evaluating the distance they had come.

"Oh, sure."

She sighed, looking around with an effect of pleasure. She did not remove her leg from his lap nor he his hand from her shin. It rested just above the bandage. Gazing about, she wondered, Is he testing his sensations, seeing what he feels, if anything? What's going on in his own bloodstream?

"Low tide," he observed, taking it in. "Me can tell. Have kinship with nature." They had wandered past the limits of New Lambeth and were now closer to Smugglers Cove, whose few lights could be seen spilling off the bluff into the sea. The Spitachunk muttered sluggishly among the rocks, in neap tide tonight.

Bill's hand moved up her foreleg to her knee, where it paused. They both lowered their eyes to take note of this.

The back of his hand was brown against her pale skin. It had a glaze like a pretzel. "You have very long legs," he said, as though measuring a journey. His hand made another short trip, this time stopping at the hem of her skirt, like a large spider approaching shelter of which it is wary.

"Yes, they're long," she murmured, drawing her skirt up a little to expose a more inviting expanse of flesh than his palm tarried on. They sat motionless a moment, stranded on an interval of consciousness having no apparent connection with their existences. They seemed to be waiting awkwardly for some kind of clue.

"Bill?"

"What?"

"Are you, um . . . ?"

They regarded his stalled hand together, as though enlightenment must proceed from it; a little as though at the same time it were being mentally encouraged to "Go in and win." It slipped along her skin to softer flesh, to where both thighs came together. His other hand pressed her back down on the rock, on which they both lay with their legs dangling, like castaways getting their wind after climbing aboard a raft. After some time, his hand ascended clumsily into silk obstructions, whose folds his fingers explored till his palm rested at last on the curve of all legend. Then they remained absolutely still.

Lee was performing with herself the experiment of which she accused him.

In her few previous skirmishes, she had always bridled at this point. Tommy West had made her mind clamp down with hostility, Georgie's eyes when he tried to set her up with a little stale Swinburne were like buttons coming off of old shirts, Malcolm seemed to think he was an anteater on the first kiss. And she could still not recall her exact sensation when Betty Markham slipped an arm around her in bed, over the no man's land between pajama top and bottom. Now she could describe herself as feeling nothing. This was progress, in that it was at least void of distaste. Was some boy managing to defuse Sex for her? Glory be. She drew back her head a little to take in his face. His eyes were shut tight, otherwise it was as blank as stone itself.

What about inside him? Inside him the demons of derision were loose. So that when he opened his eyes to the sight of hers he was all set to laugh — and did. She looked so as though she were going to say, "Oh, Bill, what'll we do?" His mind issued a steady flow of such romanticisms: "This thing is bigger than both of us," "Her eyes sought to plumb the depths of his," "Their lips met in a kiss," he formulated antiseptically. These clichés were like the phagocytes that tumble into the bloodstream like firemen out of their beds at the first threat of infection. They were the Keystone Cops of his guardian farce.

Their lips met in a kiss. A smile twisted his mouth as he felt hers cold and moist against his, twisting too, like a key in a lock. He tried his best to Feel Something. So did she. Neither knew each was trying to do this, to wring something from the other, and so they lay kissing on a rock, two lovers in a seascape, clasping and clutching one another the more passionately because neither of them felt a goddam thing.

An old man watched from a cottage window, his heart torn with memories of his youth.

They missed the ferry, letting its whistle moan unheeded knowing they couldn't make it anyway. Bill said he knew a short cut through a patch of woods to Smugglers Cove, where they could get a cab back to Hickory over the bridge. It was blacker than they'd thought after plunging into it, and Lee in her muddy slippers stumbled in actual fear through the snapping brush behind him. Wild plum bushes caught at her skirt; branches whipped her cheeks and stung her eyes, so that once she lost sight of his lithe back and she scrambled over another stone calling for him to wait. He glided in a bent-over fashion, with a stealth aimed at making himself look authentic but managing only to frighten her further. He peered for tracks, off the lost path, held a wet finger in the air.

"Rolling Stone guide you safely back. He commune with wind and sky, speak the language of the elements. Many moons ago his fathers walk upon that very beach. Leave no tern unstoned in their pursuit of food."

"I notice the tribe keeps changing. Aren't Chippewas from the Middle West?"

"Me belong to Algonquin bunch, actually. Famous scalper, feared around all Broadway. Name to conjure with in box offices."

The upshot was that they stumbled with sore and even bleeding feet in behind the railroad station, where, a train being due in, they found a taxi around. They tidied themselves in the back seat, puffing and laughing. It had been a lark after all.

When they got back to the Hickory Inn, however, there was a note for each of them from Harry Mercury. Lee didn't tell him what hers said, but his read: "Where the hell have you been all evening? Come up to my room the second you get in please. Urgent."

SIX

MERCURY was back in bed by the time the poor Indian had closed the door. "Lock it again," he ordered, on all fours.

Bill did so and walked to the center of the room where he stood appraising the bed's troubled occupant between the footposts on one of which again hung the green Tyrolean hat complete with whisk. Mercury's red and white striped pajamas were buttoned up the side like a dentist's tunic. "Well?" Mercury said, composing his hands on his stomach and returning Bill's gaze with the stern one of a magistrate. He sat propped on two pillows.

"The feud's off," Mercury announced.

"Why?"

"He's sore."

"Who?"

"Who? Pentecost. He's fit to be tied. Something you razzed him about in the samples you sent up. Chaucer says you wrote them."

"What's the bone of contention, in particular?"

"Something about his fat can, or the size of his beak or

some goddam thing. Don't you know any better than to kid him about some point you might know he'd be sensitive, being as how he considers himself a ladies' man and all? He assumes *I'm* behind it, or at least approved it, and now he's going to knock my block off the first time he claps an eye on me. He may even come to get me. That's not to be ruled out." Bill checked the door again, making sure it was locked. Mercury hitched himself up on the pillows. "Why the hell didn't you show me the stuff first, or anyhow show Chaucer? He's up there now trying to smooth it over. Which I doubt if he can. I know Lew and his temper. He *will* take a sock at me if he sees me before he simmers down. He double dog dares me to come out."

"Is that why you're eating in your room?" Bill saw the debris of a meal on a tray.

"That was certainly uncalled for. What do you think I am, a yellow belly? That's from lunch. But is that your idear of meeting the situation – adding insult to injury?"

"I'm sorry. I only meant, is it that bad?"

"It's that bad. He's going to knock my chump off the next time we meet." Mercury sighed and looked away. "So the feud's off."

Bill walked to the window corner to absorb this, to think it through. He had counseled himself to the need of meeting unexpected turns and concepts in his new position, but had not foreseen the possibility of hamstringing a feud by enraging one of the principals. Both, if it came to that . . . Let's see, today being Sunday Lew Pentecost had no performance, and tomorrow would be off to Ogunquit with *Godot*. They would have to hold their breath till then. "Pentecost is a sorehead," he said, recalling Chaucer's warning.

Mercury spread his arms like the wings of some great frantic bird.

"That's what I'm trying to tell you! *And* a ladies' man. You ought to know if he fancies himself that you can't send him for his approval ribs about the width of his can or the length of his nose. Common sense ought to tell you that. I told you we had to feel our way around this thing carefully, that the ribs were on spec and show me everything first. I told you an ounce of prevention is worth a pound of cure."

"No you didn't. You told me the ribs were on spec, yes, but I distinctly don't remember you saying to show you everything first." Bill perhaps thought that lapsing into Harry's style of speech would establish some sore of rapport between them and lessen the tension. "Neither did Chaucer. If he told you he told me that . . . I mean you both told me to work up some samples myself because you were both too busy with the regular material to be bothered, and now look, another thing. The agreement with his writers was that they were to see it first, and only them, till we thought it was safe to pass on to Pentecost. If it fell into his hands that's not my fault."

"Well, it fell into his hands, and now—"

There was a knock on the door. Mercury shot the Indian a look and drew the covers up to chest level, prepared to do better should the need arise. Neither moved after that. The knock was repeated, louder. Mercury swallowed, nodding to the Indian, who took this as a sign to creep up to the door, where he dropped noiselessly on one knee and put an eye to the keyhole.

The key was turned just enough to afford him a squint into the dim corridor. He saw nothing first. Then he made out what seemed a brown trouser leg piped with white. He turned and soundlessly shaped the words "Room service?" over his shoulder. Mercury got up. "I forgot. I ordered supper." He thudded toward the door muttering "Goddam solitary. Meals shoved the hell at you. I mean really!"

The waiter trundled in the new and out the old. Mercury locked the door and strolled back to the bed, running a palm up his long brow. "I'll eat it later," he said. He wheeled on Bill. "You want some?"

Bill shook his head. "No thanks. I ate. Besides I don't feel like eating. But look. While you're eating, or thinking of eating, maybe we can —"

"We're waiting to hear how Chaucer made out, mainly. That's the main thing. We're waiting for that report."

"All right. While we are, maybe we can go over some of the other material. I've been doing a good deal of work on that ramble of yours about your relatives, Harry."

"What ramble of mine about my relatives?"

"The one I've been working on, Harry."

Mercury sat down on the edge of the bed, frowning. "I'm not sure people will get that it's satire *on* the family memoirs everyone's writing." He crossed his legs. "So I've got one eccentric sister who works in a banana mill —"

"Wait. That's only the beginning. You have a brother named Ishmael Purchase. He's a dentist who fixes people's teeth while they wait." The poor Indian traversed the foot of the bed, running his fingers through his hair with an effect of impromptu creation. "You have another brother named Frank Sodarocket, who's a painter, who's being hung in the Guggenheim."

"In the morning?"

"His prize-winning entry is a huge arm in gouache seen

throwing rice at a woman in white and a pile of cubes, symbolizing the union of form and content, of tradition and experiment." Mercury smiled modestly at the floor, smoothing down the knee of his pajama trousers. Bill drew a deep breath. "We pan to you in the Guggenheim coasting slowly down the ramp on roller skates, inspecting the canvases one by one. You float on out the door without comment, skating across town to Sixth Avenue where you drop into your favorite delicatessen chair and gasp out to the waiter, 'Sardines in oil.' "

The brown eyes were great with reproach as Mercury rose and darted into the bathroom, where he reached into the medicine chest. The clock on the wall stood at eleven sharp, time for his pill.

"That's great," he said, emerging. "Just great. And I can tell you what I'm coasting slowly down to in the Guggenheim, if you're curious. To the lowest Trendex I've had in sixteen years of broadcasting. And don't give me any more Poulenc. The subscribers are leaving in droves, the Philharmonic is broke."

"You have another brother."

"What's this one's name?" Mercury asked, fair warning in his voice.

"You forget. Riboflavin, Slocum, something like that. He's ninety-three, and wise for his years. What Graham Greene has called chicken sandwiches."

Mercury was shaking like a leaf. He stood at the window in his striped pajamas, graphically like the awning visible just outside it in a bath of neon light, gazing down into the street. He shook his head for some little time.

"You say you want something that'll hold up intellectually."

"Not that well."

Bill would not give up. "The art of Complete Chaos is a delicate and difficult one. Who in our time has the courage and talent to explore for Humor the possibilities inherent in utter Meaninglessness?"

There were footsteps in the hall, causing Mercury to thrust one leg back into the frazzled bed. They vanished. Mercury got the tray and carried it to his nightstand, stirring brutal memories of Saginaw. Bill watched him crawl back into bed and prop himself in a sitting position against the pillows again, settle the tray comfy on his lap and start to eat. Once he made a face that Bill imagined to be like those his mother used to make. Having swallowed a mouthful or two of his meal, which he called "claptrap" and offers of ill-defined portions of which the half-breed declined with shakes of his head, Mercury took a gulp of coffee and became didactic.

"Offbeat, sure, all very well. But even a *non sequitur* must have a grain of logic to make it go." He used the gesture that sufficed him for most occasions. It consisted in joining the fingertips and thumb of one hand in an upward-pointing cluster. "A seed of meaning." These were all things Bill had once told Mercury. On "seed" Mercury's teeth bared and the cheeks went up in an echo of rabbinical entreaty or Bedouin pride. "That's what makes nonsense — the grain of sense inside it."

Bill nodded apathetically. They were both silent, listening to a muffled persistent thudding going on in a room overhead. Mercury looked down at his tray and instantly looked up again.

"Like that line in the sketch you started where the wife comes home from town with a mink coat and he says,

'What did you buy a mink coat for?' and she says, 'Because I was cold.' He's flabbergasted. Because she was cold! Who-ever heard of that for a reason for buying a fur coat? It's the most unheard-of thing he ever heard of. *Non sequitur*, you see, with the grain of sense in it."

"Do you think we could work that up into something for you and Tallulah, Harry?" Bill had risen from the chair in which he'd been slumped during the playback of his analysis, and now stood again at the bar of justice — the foot of the bed — looking (to alter the metaphor again) between the goalposts on one of which hung the hat which gave the room a vaguely collegiate air. "The whole thing a mad exercise in ratiocination. Meaning slipping through the interstices of meaning, the void between two atoms in the brain, as Conrad Aiken says."

Mercury took a bite of roll, tearing his head away from it rather than the roll away from his teeth. He chewed a moment, looking sadly toward the window. He had the air the Psalmist of old might have had when he wrote, "How are they increased that trouble me!"

"Maybe I shouldn't of hired you."

Bill now felt a chill of fear. Of memory laid like a lash across his guts in which the years lay twisted and coiled. There, but for the technicality of Harry's being a man and his not having actually cooked the food he had served himself in bed, was his mother, sprawled on her fat back. Mercury frowned across the waste of brown chenille and suddenly changed to one's father, threatening to drive one away from home, a decadent, out alone into the cold. "You have friends at the theater here. Your coming up wasn't a total loss. And getting expenses paid and all . . ."

Another sharp rap on the door. By now they were both

nervous wrecks. Chaucer's voice was heard in a loud whisper, "It's me," through the rattled knob.

Bill let him in, getting a glare for his pains as Chaucer hurried on by like someone cutting you on the street.

"How is he?" Harry asked as Bill twisted the key in the lock again.

"Not cooled down much. He may demand satisfaction."

"What do you mean?" Harry asked in a treble register.

Chaucer turned to Bill. "I suppose you've heard. The feud's off."

"Why?" He wanted to hear Chaucer go through it all now, through the rigmarole which put them safely in Lewis Carroll country, out of real harm's way.

"Why he wants to know," as of one for whom the very rudiments of reason had to be spelled out. "Because he's sore as a boil, that's why. I just came from that hornet's nest — he may even fire his writers. That crack of yours about all wool and a yard wide, that's fine to begin with. And then you see in him not just one ham but two. More brilliance. I told you to go easy on physical characteristics. I told you expressly it was all on spec and to go easy on physical characteristics. Didn't I, Murk?"

Murk's shutters were lowered as he nodded, drawing a piece of string from his mouth, which was busy with roast beef. He was disintegration itself. "You can't ride roughshod over people you want a feud with. Benny's stinginess, Crosby's horses, these are one thing. But physical traits you got to be careful."

"Fred Allen —" Bill began.

"That's a nasal *quality* in the voice, not the nose as such, for the living love of God."

"Hope's nose as such is poked fun of. Ski slide, old apple

core. And come to think of it, Benny did the bags under Allen's eyes."

Splitting hairs with half-wits was going to be the Psalmist's undoing, judging from the rattling disarray in his lap as he jerked upward against the pillows. He again pinched an imaginary piece of fruit on its underside. "Benny ribbed the bags under Allen's eyes and Crosby does Hope's nose because Allen and Hope ribbed themselves about it first, thereby giving notice it's O.K. It's fair game. Pentecost hasn't done that, and anybody fancying himself a lady killer you should know damn well his appearance is going to be off limits. From head to foot he's sensitive areas. He's not like me."

Observing him, Bill wondered whether he would relish having his hair likened to a smelt's skeleton or his mouth to a toy piano. He had a wild thought of asking Pentecost to hire him, to square accounts. "Can't we give it another try?" he asked instead.

"How? How are you going to have a feud with somebody you're at swords' points with, will you tell me that please? He's going to hang one on me the first chance he gets, if it's the lobby of this inn. That right, Chaucer?"

"That's right." Slumped in the window chair, Chaucer shot Bill another blame-assigning glare.

"I simply hammered out a trial sample of what we agreed on, for a starter," Bill said, "with no expectation that Pentecost would see it before we'd all checked further. If you deny that much I'll call you a goddam liar."

"All right, all right, you guys now," Mercury said, putting the tray back on the nightstand. "Knock it off."

"How *about* that ladies' man angle? Pentecost's in Hollywood, so's Mercury, they've both got the local disease—

starlet fever. They're rivals for the same dame. Pentecost finally gets her, a super-blonde, two years in the making . . ."

"It's Pentecost we want a battle with, not the morals office." Chaucer with his pink hair and pickle-slice eyes remained a study in angry gloom. "It could have been such a good thing for everybody. Not just the five minutes of every script taken care of, the thing *itself* could have been good. Urbane and witty. Somebody ought to hang one on *you.*"

"Care to step outside and try it?"

"All right, you guys, all right. Let's not get in a pool of blood ourselves," Mercury barked from the bed where he was trying to light a cigar. This was one of a box of five-cent rum-soaked crooks — uniformly misshapen stogies which he was thinking of switching to for his monologue spot; a trademark as crooked as Harry Lauder's stick . . . "We're not in such shape material-wise that we can afford to squabble among gourselves."

"All that travelogue stuff we were kicking around and couldn't get a story line for," Chaucer continued, "we could have unloaded it all into the feud. A running routine about two American tourists outdoing each other in vulgarity." Mercury's eyes watched him through smoke and flame. "That gag of Bill's for the Greece part. Pentecost is so dumb he thinks Contantine's Arch is a foot disease. Then my gag for England 'Did you visit the Cotswolds?' 'Oh, yes, and found them a charming couple.' "

"Yes." Bill would wait till they were alone to tell Mercury that Danny Kaye had done that gag with the Himalayas. "Loved him, loathed her." Time enough, too, to explain that Constantine's Arch was in Rome. He never committed his malice to the knowledge of the victim, let alone in the presence of a third party. Only secretly, for his own delectation. Some might consider this worse than open cruelty, an onanistic vice, but the fact remained it hurt no one else. Harry's clod of a gagman got the same mercy as his flower of a daughter. Neither dreamt he was being spared derision — which was some morality on his part.

"Can't we patch things up and still have it?" he asked, one foot in Lewis Carroll country while with the other he tried to keep his balance somehow in the real world, whatever that is. In the former he had but to give fools their heads to exist, but in the other were numerous traps of the fools' laying, into one of which he seemed to have stepped. "I'll be glad to apologize personally. Go up and say it was all my fault. Then we can let bygones be bygones and have the feud."

The trap tightened painfully in the form of the expression with which Mercury now turned to Chaucer: an intimation of business to be resumed without him; with him already out of the room, pocketing whatever severance pay — He now began to fight.

"Getting back to what we were saying a minute ago, Harry, yes, I have friends up here." Harry closed his mouth and turned back. "So don't worry too much about that. Not just those at the Cove."

Bill cleared his throat in a way that gained their joint attention.

"I've also got a friend at the Writers Conference — you know, the one at Winooski College? It's only a few miles north of here." Mercury nodded, appraising his serpentine cigar. "Well, this guy is in charge of the evening lecture series they have in addition to the daytime classes and workshops, and they're put to it for speakers. I should tell you this before I go. In case you get a phone call from Mickey you'll know what it's all about. Harry, I'm afraid I talked out of turn. I told him you might lecture for them."

"Me?" Mercury's eyelids went down like little awnings.

"I told him of your interest in the psychology and philosophy of Humor. The thinking you do on the subject. Why we laugh. That sort of thing. I know they'd love to have you."

"Me?" Still lowered.

"I mean the sort of thing you did just now so brilliantly with the *non sequitur*. That could be one category you'd analyze. Then others, with illustrations as you went along. Hell, you'd have them in stitches till midnight. It'll take preparation, and you're busy with the show, but I'd be willing to help." Bill waited till Chaucer had closed the door of the bathroom to which he'd gone, grumbling "Now for the opener we'll have to write a whole nuther script." When he and Mercury were then alone, Bill went on: "I could discuss it all with you informally, draw you out, maybe get you going into the tape recorder with stuff I could then copy the meat of into a speech. I came up here to work, and I'll be damned if I'll leave here a loss to the firm."

Harry gave a grunt. He reached to the table to drop ash from his cigar. "That's the damnedest thing I ever heard of."

"The Anatomy of Humor. That could be your title. Look, I think it's your duty. The whole purpose of these summer conferences is to get *creative* people in their respective arts. Writers teaching people to write, painters discussing painting, why not comedians on comedy. Rescue the world from chalk dust!"

"It's an eminently analytical age," Mercury observed. "Every subject goes under the microscope."

"Right! You'll be a riot."

Bill left the spot to which he had all this time been rooted, moving toward the door. "I'll send down some books on the subject. Essay of Meredith's on comedy, and also Bergson's treatise on 'Laughter.' You probably know them, but you might care to brush up for the lecture."

At the door he paused and turned.

"Oh, by the way. Bertrand Russell is speaking tomorrow night, in case you'd care to catch his stuff."

seven

FILLED with remorse over her betrayal of Harry Mercury in the railroad station, Mrs. Marvel vowed to make amends. Chief among her plans to do so, at the moment, were reprisals against the woman who had made her act as she had. It was the Mrs. Wetwilliams of this world who legislate the standards in which the occasion had been permitted to become enmeshed, the false shibboleths of class and "sort," and it was time they were brought to book.

Restitution was first of all to consist in the acquisition of information leading to the admission of Mrs. Marvel to the circle over which, locally speaking, Mrs. Wetwilliam queened it – the Mayflower Society. Mrs. Marvel had hunches, kindled by the discovery of mementoes in the attic (particularly an old letter), that an ancestor of her own had come over with the first shipload of Pilgrims. The letter was now in the hands of a Boston genealogical firm for authentication. Mrs. Wetwilliam and her social elite were a crowd with whom she wouldn't have been caught dead, which made her doubly determined not to be barred from their company, for who of us can bear to be upstaged by his inferiors? One thing would make her happiness complete: getting the credentials in time for the Anniversary.

That was going swimmingly. None of the children were here as yet, but all had been heard from, all promised to come. The event gave promise of snowballing into quite the greatest of Mrs. Marvel's life. She sat at her open bedroom window this afternoon in a dreaming dither. Beyond distant treetops soared the white pillars of the Wetwilliam mansion, in which even now some caller might be preening herself on a forebear who had sailed perilous seas or fought in the Revolution that matters might come to this. (Ben Marvel had a grandfather who had been blown to bits at Antietam, but of course he cut no ice here: it was the wrong war.) Well, Alma Marvel would yet produce the right antecedent, if not in time for the annual Fourth of July Ball the Wetwilliams gave for the Mayflower and D.A.R. aristocracy jointly, then in time for her own Fortieth Anniversary. Having brought the town to her door in one smashing glory, she would be content to retire forever to her garden and her crossword puzzles. But having gained the privilege of those other doors she would disdain entering them, thus striking a blow at the Mrs. Wetwilliams of this world who went about snubbing their equals and sometimes their superiors. Still the glory in the Marvel annals would give just cause for pride in their family, which Harry had of course married into.

Mrs. Marvel knew that priggish coterie well. She had in early womanhood, during a spell of domestic service, once waited on table at a Wetwilliam "Fourth," and as she would say in lieu of words and with a pantomime of throwing up, "Bllaach!" Looking at the castle now, Mrs. Marvel uttered the sound, letting her tongue well down over her chin in a graphic accompanying moue. It was what she really thought of those women with their ancestors long turned to worms and their stuffed-shirt husbands many of whom were also worms, and she would not rest till she was one of them.

The phone rang about half-past two.

"This is Mr. Sligh," said a young man's voice. "From Genealogy Incorporated? I drove out from Boston and I'm having a sandwich at the Hickory Inn. I wonder if it's convenient to drop in on you in about half an hour. I have information for you."

She could hardly bear the wait. Thank God Ben, from whom she was keeping all this till it materialized, was out. She paced the empty house for fifteen minutes of the thirty, then plunged down the street on an errand that would take up a few more. She took a warming pan to Cobleigh's Antique Shop for repair. When she got there the door was locked with a sign on it reading "DEATH IN FAMILY. BACK IN TEN MINUTES." The Colonial spirit! Returning she saw a blue convertible stop in front of the house and broke into a gallop. A young man with a figure like a furled umbrella and hair as black as licorice sprang out and mounted the stairs.

Mrs. Marvel reached her front porch panting. The caller was about to rap the knocker a third time when she rumbled up the steps behind him.

"I'm Mrs. Ma-ha-harvel," she laughed, puffing. She shifted her possession and added, "I've been running."

"I see," he said, flashing the whitest teeth and the blackest eyes imaginable. She tidied a strand of hair and poked her blouse into place. "My name is Sligh. Neil Sligh."

She gave him her hand, noting his glance at what she was carrying. "I was just taking this to be mended," she said, extending it by its long handle.

"Collection plate. I guess that goes far back!"

"No, no. It's not a collection box."

He studied it frowning, with the air of one "guessing again." "Popcorn popper?" said the youth whose familiarity with Americana seemed not to have too broad a base. The price of specialization no doubt.

"It's a warming pan."

"Ah! They had to keep food warm those days all right. Men coming in from the fields late, one thing and another."

"Not their food—their *feet.* They put coals in these things and slipped them between the sheets to warm the bed before—"

"Before popping in themselves." He looks Spanish she thought, leading the way into the house. That would be on his mother's side, with a name like Sligh. Confusedly she stamped over the vestibule rug, as though they were bringing in snow.

As they entered the living room, emotion began again to shorten her recovered breath and to quicken her pulse. "Would you like a cup of tea?"

"I think not. I've just had coffee," said the young courier. Oh, of what! "Unless you want one."

"No." She shook her head, sinking onto a deacon's bench of great authenticity, the austerity of which was relieved somewhat by a foam rubber pad and bright cushions flung onto it over the years. Neil Sligh turned to a wall and studied a small oil. It was a primitive showing a Maine woman, her face framed in a faded blue kiss-me-quick, shelling peas with obvious disapproval. The peas cascaded, thumb-pushed, into a saucepan clutched tightly between her legs, its handle protruding forward. The face seemed to anticipate the construction that would be put on all this by Freudians to come, and there was censorship in every line of it.

Mrs. Marvel was physically ill. Why didn't he out with it? Yet instead of coming to the point herself she murmured some delaying comment on the portrait, nursing a moment longer the probabilities at stake, hoarding a moment longer her furious hopes. Those roared within her like a furnace. Propped on a nearby table was a dim pencil sketch of a young man with a bulging forehead and fanatical eyes, which had been in the discovered letter. The subject was almost certainly Archie Spry, her putative link with glory, and a gesture to it would introduce the business on which the stranger had come. But her hand lay palsied in her lap while the suspense killed her. She would, in just a second, inhabit a windswept eminence or a sliding dungheap.

Sligh drifted over and pondered her genially, asking permission to light a cigarette through the flame of a match already pretty much applied to it. *He knew something.* He was a dazzler, all right. He had dimples and a smile of the kind Harry Mercury called "a peck of popcorn." He inclined his head as he contemplated her, at the angle at which a violinist secures his instrument under his chin.

"Well, tell me about it," she said, her tongue like a piece of cardboard that had to be bent laboriously into the shapes and positions necessary for speech. "Have I an ancestor who made a certain voyage to Plymouth?"

He dangled her a moment, the doll boy. This was like waiting for the report on a test for a disease which the odds of one's having may be statistically negligible but which the two possible answers, positive or negative, seem to make fifty-fifty.

"Yes, you have an ancestor who went to Plymouth."

She knew that she was turning pale, as one does, in security, from the shock of a danger narrowly averted—paler perhaps than if one had been struck. "In 1620?" she said, looking away.

"In 1620."

She settled over slowly, and for a moment listened to the beating of her heart, to which was added the creaking of the deacon's bench whose framework her agitation reached. One more agonized move, as a jump in hopscotch, and she would be "home."

"On the *Mayflower?*"

The youth laughed, making an impulsive gesture that if completed would have brought his hand tenderly to her shoulder. "Forgive me, Mrs. Marvel, but it's just that you're so wonderful."

In addition to a feeling of resentment something else tainted, now, the receipt of news for which she had so long sickened. In getting it, she had been tracked to her secret like a beast to its lair. It is this kind of attendant exposure that makes a compliment one of the hardest things to hear gracefully, and why people are so often sheepish when congratulated. They have been found out, curled up there with their egos. To make a man look silly, praise him.

"If all our ancestors were like you there wouldn't have been so many chickens among them," Sligh remarked in what was certainly an odd turn. "Because though you don't find much about it in the schoolbooks, Washington's army was shot through with cowardice."

"That is certainly no concern of mine. It's not the D.A.R. one would join on the strength of it but the Mayflower Society. Shall we get back to the subject of the Pilgrims?"

"Ah, yes." Sligh frowned at the coal of his cigarette. He gave the impression of saying and doing things carefully rehearsed. "You realize, of course, that all the actual passengers on the *Mayflower* are known to us because of Governor Bradford's history."

"My dear boy, of course I know that. I've read the history and I know Archie Spry's name doesn't appear among the first settlers of the colony. The question is whether an ancestor of his does. Because he is an ancestor of mine."

"Then it is with mixed feelings that I must tell you what we have found out about him. Or about his father who had the same name, and of whom this is more likely a picture than of the son." Sligh indicated the pencil sketch, which his office had seen and then sent back by registered mail, keeping the letter in which it had been found, for further research. "Because the handwriting is awfully dim there in the letter, but we've looked at it under X-ray and by some other methods we have of restoring pencilwork, and it seems to be saying it's a sketch of the writer's father, a maker of barrel staves. All right." Sligh took a seat in a deep chair across from Mrs. Marvel, hiking up a trouser leg. "While faintheartedness existed in the Revolutionary army it was unheard of among the Pilgrims, that is after it had been weeded out, because when the two ships turned back to England after the *Speedwell* sprang a leak — you remember all that of course."

"Yes, but not as though it was only yesterday," Mrs. Marvel said, managing a little smile while the other laughed responsively and said again that she was terrific. She rose and wobbled toward a table. She asked across it, "Why are you telling me all this? What has the *Speedwell* got to do with it? It's the *Mayflower* we're talking about. Wasn't he on that?"

"At first, yes." Sligh coughed, and waved off a cloud of smoke. "Archibald Spry *père* went to Plymouth all right, but it was the Plymouth in England, that they turned back to for repairs. The *Mayflower* went back with her, as you know, and while they were waiting for the leak to be fixed everyone was given a chance to reconsider. The voyage of which they'd all now had a snootful would be dangerous, and after they got to the new world, *if* they got there, there would come cold, hunger, disease, sickness, pestilence and howling redskins in a strange land. Anyone who wanted to back out could do so." Mrs. Marvel closed her eyes and drew a long breath, with that expression of rapture which is seen on the faces of opera singers losing themselves in their roles. "No questions would be asked. Nothing would be said. He need have no reason to be ashamed."

"That a few remained behind history tells us," Mrs. Marvel said, moving toward a chair.

"Several remained behind because of age or infirmity. But one did so because he got cold feet. His name was Archibald Spry."

"It's a lie."

"I'm afraid not, Mrs. Marvel. I'm sorry to bring you news of this kind, but our job is to give the facts. Your ancestor came over later when the going was easy, settling down to a soft life in the Massachusetts town where your letter about him was written by his son — also something of a poltroon. You notice the whining tone about the cold, whereas the records of the time indicate a fairly mild winter as those winters went. He carried on a lumber business, making a good thing of trade with the British, whose side the family moreover favored during the Revolution —"

"I will not sit here and be insulted."

"He was, from references in the letter to the prices he was getting, a shrewd businessman. But he was a profiteer and a coward. He did not come over on the *Mayflower*. He got *off* the *Mayflower*. In August, 1620."

It had not been Mrs. Marvel's impression that the youth's necktie was polka-dot, but both it and the expanse of white shirt behind it seemed now to be swimming in that design. The area of black spots grew until the entire room appeared to be swimming in a speckled mist. Her head rolled back and settled in a corner of the wing-back chair in which she had seated herself just in time.

She was spared the knowledge of how she got to the couch in the window embrasure on which she came to, but inference left no possibility but her having been hauled to it by the stranger. Cold water was splashing on her face from a teakettle cocked in midair by Sligh who was standing over her, himself a little pale but managing his ministrations as objectively as if she were a philodendron about to be given another dollop. Seeing she was all right, he set the kettle on a nearby tavern table, placing it on a copy of *American Heritage* so as not to soil the surface.

"Are you sure?" she breathed.

"Positive. But please, you must lie down." He forced her gently back among the cushions he had piled under her head and got some brandy from a cabinet to which she directed him with a weak hand. Sligh poured himself one too, after which he sat down and they discussed the whole thing like two intelligent people.

"A Pilgrim with cold feet is not a very pretty thought, and having one for an ancestor could, I know, finish you socially in these parts," Sligh said. "But there is no need to go to pieces. Your secret is safe with me."

"We would have to leave town if it ever came out."

"Disgrace we can live down, ridicule not."

"We would have to sail for another world," she managed with a brave smile.

"That's the spirit! You're worth the lot of them," Sligh exclaimed with a wave intended to embrace the whole of regional snobbery. "That's why I'm going to see you through." He laid a hand to his breast pocket, which bulged tangibly. "Would you care to see the records I examined? They're photostats of documents recently uncovered in the basement of a museum in Plymouth. I mean, again, the one in England." Mrs. Marvel shook her head, or rather averted it definitively.

"Spry," she murmured. "He was well named."

The other sighed charitably. "Who are we to judge him? We might have jumped ship ourselves, after that dose of open water. I know I would. Frankly, I'm not one of those who have what it takes."

"You seem to have what it takes to assemble evidence." She sipped her brandy, settling herself in a slightly more upright position against the cushions. "You said a minute ago you'd see me through. Just what did you mean by that? What does that imply?"

Sligh knit his brows and rose, walking away from the sunlight pouring in through the window.

"Ours is an old and established firm, and you pay for our discretion as well as our research. But while you can count on me, how do we know we can count on every Tom, Dick and Harry into whose hands this information might fall? Clerks seeing it in the files and so on, now or in years to come. Who could use it against you in an unscrupulous way, if you know what I mean. Only one way to safeguard against that. For me not to turn it in. I won't let it be filed. It's strictly between you and me, forever. How's that now? Wouldn't that be worth something to you?"

Mrs. Marvel moved her head in order to bring his shifting form within her line of vision. She found herself appraising the distance between his eyes. She sat up more erectly on the couch, on which her legs were still stretched out. She laid an arm along its back for support.

"You mean you want us to settle this — between us?"

"How could I turn a fee in without filing the data? I'll just stamp your case N.F.A. No facts available. Dead end." She saw the back of his shoulders shrug and his arms spread. "Can you think of any other way of doing it?"

"And this private settlement — between us, as you call it — is to involve a little more in the way of cash than the office fee would have been?"

Sligh laughed and turned around. He pinched his nose

and looked to the floor, where with his heel he tidied a hooked rug over which he had so unceremoniously dragged her.

"Are you trying to blackmail me?"

"Mrs. Marvel, I'm afraid you're a little overwrought. Who said that? I can understand your feelings. You learn of a family skeleton you'd *give anything rather than have get out of the closet*, so in your hysteria you start using words that . . ."

But she was not hysterical. He noticed her hand slip slowly along the top of the sofa as she fell back once more among the cushions.

This time it took longer to revive her, and when she awoke there were two people standing over her instead of one. Lee was chafing her wrists while Sligh again held the teakettle poised over her head, ready to tip the spout another time if need be.

"No," she said, pushing it away. The cushions among which she eventually sat up were as sodden as she.

"Moo Moo, what's the matter, Moo Moo? What *happened?* Are you sick? Or what is all this?"

"What are you doing here, child?"

"I came to town for a prop for next week's show but couldn't scare any up, so I thought I'd see if you could help. It's a period piece, but never mind that now. I walk in here and find a strange man pouring water on you."

"She'll be all right," said Sligh, again putting the kettle by. "Let me introduce myself. My name is Sligh, Neil Sligh," he went on through tentative mumbles from Mrs. Marvel as she organized her matted hair. He glittered from head to foot when Lee introduced herself. He was a changed boy. "I'm from a brokerage house handling certain of Mrs. Marvel's investments," he improvised fluidly, "and the shock of hearing what happened to one of them was too much for her. It'll come back, she mustn't worry. Now let's give you a chance to ask your Moo Moo what you wanted while we all have that cup of tea she offered a while ago. Something about a prop for a show? What prop? What show?"

He winked at Mrs. Marvel, and the popcorn smile broadened and the dimples deepened as he heard all about Lee Mercury, daughter of the famous comedian whom, of course, he never missed. There was no doubt of his being what an earlier generation — Mrs. Marvel's — called a "rapscallion."

What Lee had been sent shopping for by the prop department was a table known among antiquarians as a "tilt-top," the kind with the top that folds down. Of this it had to be the subvariety called "bird cage," the tops of which rotate as well, when up. It was for a scene in an Early American comedy in which the lovers ate together at a table which they could revolve in a way that would keep humorously interchanging their suppers. None of the antique stores on Main Street had one.

"I have," said Mrs. Marvel, and, quite herself again, proceeded to haul from a corner of the room a table the weight of which compelled her to accept aid from the rapscallion. She tipped the folded-down top up, and then, the other two seated as audience on the sofa, began to expound the article's merits.

"Of the five basic varieties of the American tilt-top, this is known as the piecrust — note the scalloped rim, like a pie. The workmanship and the carving together with the patina of the wood vouch for the authenticity of this piece," she said with a glance at Sligh, who was giving Lee the scrutiny invited to the table. "These legs," she went on more loudly, rapping them with a knuckle, "are typical of the period. They never vary in your true tilt-top: a tripod pedestal with three arching cabriole legs ending in either claw-and-ball or snake's-head feet. There you have it. Any carving will be of foliage, on the knees, which is sometimes repeated on the knobbed element of the shaft. Now the top! You see that it turns. Mr. Sligh?" She stood over it, manipulating it, like a steering wheel. "This is a first-rate article, to which you're welcome, Lee dear, if you're careful. I inspected this minutely before I bought it, as any collector does, and it's a collector's item."

"I could never take it, Moo Moo. It's too valuable."

"No, you take it. These things are like character," she went on, looking sharply at Sligh. "There's always someone out to fool you, and an amateur can be fooled. But you can always tell a fake from the real thing in the end."

Lee rose and came over to examine the object more closely, as did Sligh now too, bending his head with hers, caressing the carvings with fingers as gentle as hers.

"The telltale signs are in the out-of-the-way places, the corners and joints. You can fake surfaces and maybe even the patina, but you can't fake handiwork. You'll find no marks of your modern buzz-saw up in there!"

Lee again refused to take the table, at which Mrs. Marvel freshly insisted it was all right provided there was no roughhouse in the scene in question, where it would give her personal pleasure to see her treasure of use. It was insured, as were all her valuables. The problem was one of cartage.

"I'll be glad to drive Miss Mercury over with it," Sligh offered, "and I'll be careful."

"Oh, would you?" Lee said.

"Sure. That's my car outside, the convertible. We'll put the top down and she'll ride upside-down fine in the back seat. Want to come along?"

"Just a minute! We were going to have tea," said Mrs. Marvel, who proved herself a match for him. "Lee, will you go into the kitchen and fix it? Mr. Sligh and I haven't quite finished our business yet. There's the kettle."

When the kitchen door was safely shut with Lee behind it, Mrs. Marvel composed herself on a chair directly across from Sligh, who was lighting another cigarette on the sofa.

"All right. Now then," she said in low tones. "How much do you want?"

"Want?"

"The blackmail – remember? We were discussing terms when we were interrupted."

A mouthful of momentarily held smoke broke from Sligh's mouth in the gasp of astonishment with which this was met. "Blackmail! Why Mrs. Marvel, what on earth are you talking about? I meant no such –"

"All right, Mister Convertible, shall we stop this folderol? I can read you like a book. You came up here to pull a little extortion, then one look at her" – she jerked her head toward the kitchen –"and you decide to change your mind. She looks better to you than the thousand dollars or whatever it was you were going to milk me for, with another installment six months from now no doubt. Shh! Let me finish. I saw that look in your eye when you sized her up. You'll drive her to the theater, make a date, maybe another, then –"

"Oh, my dear Mrs. —"

"Be still. Then another. Because unfortunately she had a look in her eye too. She's as innocent as the day is long and you're as slick and handsome as they come. One never knows what these things will lead to, but let me tell you right now so we understand each other. If you think your having me over a barrel, as they say, will keep me from opposing the match you have another think coming. You know what you're down for in my book, and you'll never turn on enough charm to change that."

"My dear Mrs. *Marvel.*" He threw up his hands. "This *match.*"

"So you don't intend to do right by her, eh? Well, we'll see about that too. A stitch in time saves nine. These things happen quickly. A sigh, a glance, and instead of selling me your silence you've got to buy mine. Well, it's not for sale. At any price. If exposing you means making a public disaster of myself, so be it!"

"But I've only just met the girl!"

"That was enough, judging by the way you called off your dogs. You're smitten."

"I am?"

She nodded, mouth a taut line, eyes closed. "You're drooling. It stands to reason. Otherwise why would you change your tune and become nice as pie to me? No dirty work at the crossroads now, eh, *Mister* Sligh? You make an impression on the girl, next you must make one on the family. Well, no granddaughter of mine is going to marry the likes of you. Why, what do we know about you except that you work for a Boston firm into whose till you're not above putting your filthy paws, and that you're a potential criminal. Well, that's not enough in these parts. We like to see solid achievement. What do we know about your family?"

"That's a subject I wouldn't bring up if I were you!"

"Hush! You'll be hot stuff at tea, then go on with your, what do you call it, snow job afterward. So I'll say this now. If you think I have no more in me than to sit by and watch something develop you are sorely mistaken. Besides she's spoken for. One of our local boys."

A shrill whistle from the kitchen indicated the water had come to a boil. Mrs. Marvel's eyes were all but invisible and her voice all but inaudible as she quickly brought out what she had yet to say.

"When it comes to those we love, we're quite ready to show you the Spirit of '76!"

After tea which went substantially as Mrs. Marvel had foretold, with Sligh being hot stuff and laying it on and having loads of personality and all that, she stood at the window watching them drive off with her piecrust table. The scarf around Lee's head fluttered as she turned to Neil to say something, while the car vanished around a corner.

After letting the curtain drop from her hand, Mrs. Marvel stood a moment in the silence. Then she began to tidy the room. She cleared the tea things back onto the cart. She propped the picture of Archibald Spry on the mantel from which it had been removed. The foot warmer stood on the floor against a chair. She picked it up, carried it to the mantel and set it down in front of the picture.

"Here," she said aloud to the face, "you're the one who seems to need this."

eight

MALCOLM marched once across Harry Mercury's hotel room and turned around. Facing him squarely, he announced his news.

"Ah don't know whether you are aware of it or not, suh, and if you are you must forgive me for emphasizing what must distress you. Ah take that risk in order to bring to your attention what it is mah duty to, in case you are not. I shall come to the point. Youah daughter is mixed up with a queeah."

Now Mercury had been roused from a sound sleep by a stranger phoning in the lobby to ask to see him "on a mission of some delicacy," and was even now not fully awake. In addition, the term Malcolm used was one for which the original existed in such quantity in the world in which Mercury moved that there was little call for its use, especially disparagingly, and which was recognized, indeed, only after being unswaddled from the thick layers of accent in which it lay muffled. The intruder was moreover dressed in the military jacket and breeches of the War for Independence and was carrying a musket, fife and drum.

His head was encircled by a bloody bandage. Some flash of resemblance to Chaucer in his high coloring and greenish eyes had furthermore seized Mercury with the wild thought that Pentecost had roughed up one of his boys and was coming for him — till the Southern accent owned by the caller explaining that he was on his way to a Fourth of July tableau ruled out its being Chaucer, heavily disguised, without completely restoring Mercury's sanity. His confusion could hardly be exaggerated.

"What did you say?" Mercury gathered his dressing gown about his knees in the chair into which he had dropped.

After introducing himself, Malcolm had set his paraphernalia on the bed. He now retrieved the fife which had rolled to the floor and propped the musket, on second thought, against a footpost. Then he resumed puffing out the information about Lee which was a good week out of date, about as much out of date as the news had been which Moo Moo had rather more happily regaled Harry with in the taxi, that Lee was seeing Malcolm.

"Ah debated with mahself whether to bring this grievous matter to youah attention. Finally downstairs in the bar, where Ah was killing twenty minutes till the parade starts, Ah got the courage to phone you. Ah have wanted to meet you ever since making Lee's acquaintance but have so far been denied that privilege, and regret keenly it must be under these circumstances. You may think that mah warning you of the nature of the person with whom she has become emotionally involved has an ulterior motive. Once it would have; now Ah am out of the running for her favor, therefore you may consider mah intentions purged of jealousy. Ah have nothing to gain. Ah am not, suh, a snitcher. Is that quite clear?"

Mercury nodded, crossing his legs the other way, and waited in a daze that was not clearing any too fast. Malcolm eased the bandage at his brow and moved off from the mantel against which he had paused to lean.

"When Ah say the young man who is winning her heart is doing so fraudulently, Ah do not do so on the assumption that you are not aware of his make-up, for you must be, since he is Mr. Prufrock, one of yo' employees." Malcolm paused for another nod from Mercury. "Ah do so because she herself may not know he is and you may not know they are involved with one another. She is an innocent girl who stands to have her life ruined by an attachment which could be brought to full bloom before she quite realizes that it can come to naught. That is to say, to grief. Ah cannot stand idly by and see that happen. And since neither can Ah with the delicacy called for by her youth and sex broach the subject mah duty as a friend requires me to, why, Ah have no alternative but to broach it to you, that you may discharge yours as a father. The subject is a painful one to me as it must be to you, so having done mah duty as Ah see it — and having had the pleasure of meeting a great clown under circumstances Ah would give mah right arm to undo — Ah will, with yo' permission, suh, bid you good day."

"Wait."

Mercury, now reasonably alert, had several reasons for wanting to prolong this encounter. Anxiety for Lee was not one of them, though he was anxious for her; not because he had seen her dining with Prufrock whom he regarded as harmless for the same reason Malcolm considered him a threat, but because of the other black-eyed slicker he had seen her drinking with in the bar. Mainly he was loath to cut short a visit by a character who could not have been more extraordinary had he descended from a space ship. He was doubly fascinated for the substance hidden in the asininity, for like Lee he had detected the slab of worth, like a gold ingot carved with absurd and archaic embellishments. It was as though the space ship had discharged a character from a costume novel. Another reason for detaining Malcolm was the wish to satisfy his curiosity about something.

"May I ask how you and Lee met?"

Malcolm bowed, as it were, from the neck, executing a ceremonial nod which acknowledged Harry's right to ask that question as a father.

"It was at the Marvel house. We were introduced by Lee's grandmother, properly, at breakfast."

"Ah."

"Alma Marvel is a dear friend, and Ah deplore the matter on her account too."

"She speaks very highly of you. She's very devoted to you."

Malcolm, already excited by the pressures and tensions of the meeting, turned away with emotion. He brushed at an eye as streaks appeared in his sooted cheek and grease-paint wounds. Mercury was touched himself.

"She's very fond of you, as I am of her," Harry went on. "Don't let anything happen to your friendship with her. She needs you . . . We need one another. Life is so short."

Malcolm turned completely to the window where he stood a moment drawing a handkerchief from the Colonial sleeve. Mercury paced behind him, shaking his head. What a screwy world it was. He had come up here for peace and quiet, to work in a normal, healthy, small-town atmosphere. The fact was that he was mixed up with a constellation of freaks.

Malcolm turned from the window, his emotions brought under control.

"At least Ah have done mah duty as Ah see it, and Ah hope you take it as intended."

"Oh, Ah do, Ah do," Mercury said, lapsing emotionally into the other's speech as he grasped his elbow. "Yo' sincerity is appreciated, don't worry about that."

Mercury would have liked him to stay, but they both had things to do, and he shook Malcolm's hand with the reassurance that he took the information given him in good part and expressing the hope that they might meet again.

"Oh, we will. At the Marvels' anniversary. They were good enough to invite me. It makes me very happy to be considered a member of the family. So we shall see one another there no doubt, suh, and Ah'm sure you join me in the vow that, for their dear sakes, that is one occasion when jaw will be unconfined."

"I certainly join you in that."

Mercury helped him to the door with his musket, fife and drum.

"You going to wear all three of those in the float?"

"No, no. Just the fife is me." He struck the pose for Harry, who smiled. "There's three in the traditional tableau, as you know. Ah just mind the things from year to year. You must try to see the parade. It begins at noon."

Mercury closed the door after him, half wishing the world were a better place to live in. Of course if it were, according to the intellectuals, there would be no Laughter, so in a perfect world he would starve to death. Then how could it be perfect? Another paradox. He was getting to be a philosopher. These reflections, pursued as a sound of firecrackers broke out beneath his window, made him think of Prufrock, and that made him think of the smooth article he had seen Lee with in the bar. She had introduced him. What was his name again? Some quality that fitted. Cunning, clever — sly, that was it. Must be spelled Sligh.

He consulted the local telephone directory, without finding it. Feeling more and more unstrung, he rang the desk to ask whether a Mr. Sligh were registered there. He was. Leaving his hand on the phone a moment after hanging up, Mercury thought, Then he's an out-of-towner, not one of Moo Moo's protégés. But he called the Marvel place anyway, for a chat with Moo Moo that might somehow yield fruit. Nobody answered there.

He took off his robe and threw it down on the bed, one sleeve reversed. Then he climbed into the bed where, feeling suicidal, he got to work on a draft of the speech Prufrock had written for him. "Comedy is the umbrella of tragedy turned inside out," it began.

A lecture! How in the name of God had he ever let himself in for anything like that?

"Ah have come," Malcolm told Mrs. Marvel, "on a mission of some delicacy." He paused in his circling of the laid-out teatable and shot a glance at the ceiling. "Is Ben home?"

"No." Ben was never home these days when things were boiling up into a mess all around her, and the Anniversary only ten days off. Leave it to Ben to be safe in the dusk of a movie house while she coped with it. "He's not here. Go on."

Malcolm sat down and braced himself with a swig of the strong tea she had poured them. This was going to be harder than telling Mercury: Alma was a lady.

"It's about Lee. You know the young man she is currently going with?"

"I certainly do." Alma nodded, closing her eyes as she conjured up all too vividly the wrong form and face as far as Malcolm's tidings were concerned. "What about him?"

"It's your business to know what company your granddaughter is keeping while on her visit to you, so heah we go. The young man she's seeing is a queeah."

"A what?"

"A queeah. A nance. A flit."

She shook her head; she was still unenlightened.

"A homosexual, Alma. A pervert."

"Oh, my God!"

Mrs. Marvel was split as by a bolt of lightning, but split so cleanly down the middle as to leave her emotions rather neatly divided. A malicious pleasure in the charges to be added to those already brought against the rapscallion for the moment overshadowed her concern for Lee. That customer one of those? Well, you could never tell they said, and he was unnaturally handsome, that was sure. She had read in one of the more esoteric journals, perhaps it was the *Reader's Digest*, that effeminacy was no requirement for inversion—indeed the "manliest" men were often so blighted. Athletic coaches in their shower rooms etc.

"How about that?" Mrs. Marvel took a bite of cookie and a sip of her very favorite Lapsang, composed now that she had the problem in clearer focus and now that it did not, for the moment at least, pose the threat of exposing her own secret relative to Mr. Convertible. "What could come of it?"

"Come of it? Nothing! That is precisely the tragedy, Alma. The Nothing will happen to her that happened to the hero of *The Beast in the Jungle*. The beast that will at last spring out and claw our innocent to bits, the realization that nothing can come of it. She will be led up the garden path, through dreams and expectations, to that vacuum which nature abhors."

"Are you sure?"

"Having gone this far, I can spare you nothing. To spare your feelings is to betray them. They were seen on the beach together — in the altogether."

"By who?"

"Yours truly." He looked away to the curtains, chewing a macaroon with an expression of dashed despair that she had never seen on his face before. "Ah *think*."

"Just swimming? Or did they —?"

"Ah am not a spa."

"No, I know." She looked hopelessly into her lap. She was not holding up too well under the rain of intricacies and surprises. The look of dazed uncomprehension returned as she shook her head, like a boxer rising on the count of nine. "Then is Lee homosexual too?"

"No, no. She is heterosexual."

"Oh, dear." It was getting too much to cope with. She preferred to table, as it were, these aspects of the matter till she felt stronger. "What can we do about it? Two ordinary citizens."

"Individually perhaps not much. But together, maybe something."

Malcolm rose, after another good mouthful of the sturdy tea, and resumed circling the table.

"Ah propose that, standing shoulder to shoulder, we make it clear to the person central thereto that we know that fraud is being perpetrated in ouah midst which we shall deal with as we see fit in these parts if he does not immediately cease and desist—that is, withdraw his attentions. Mah motive here is free of jealousy, as you know, mah dear Alma. Would it were otherwise, but Ah am out of the running for Lee—"

"Oh, Malcolm, I know. And I'm so sorry and wretched about that. And angry!" Mrs. Marvel said, swerving miserably in her chair.

"Never mind." He held up a hand. "Ah know. Say no more. So be it." He continued his travels about the room. "But Ah still have enough feeling for Lee to see to it in a perfectly disinterested way that no wool is pulled over her ahs. Are you with me in this?"

"I am, but let's make sure of one thing before we move—our facts. Are you?"

"What's there to be sure about? A dog's a dog, a cat's a cat, we don't bother to make 'sure' of those things. Just so a flit is a flit. Lee may not know it but Ah do. It's always apparent to another man."

"It is?" Mrs. Marvel said, the wonder growing. "Anyhow let's make sure we're talking about the same man? What's yours' name?"

"Prufrock. . . . What's the matter, Alma?"

She was shaking her head again. "I didn't know she was seeing him, and I still think they may be just friends, but in any case he's been replaced. I'm afraid I'm going to have to bring you up to date." When she had, she poured them both some more tea, and wondered should she tell him everything. She emitted a long, long sigh.

Could she rely on her closest friends not to laugh, not just aloud, but at all, at her? She had dropped hints to him about Archie Spry and as a New Englander he had responded with instant excitement at the possibility of her having an ancestor who had come over on the *Mayflower*. Would he not respond proportionately at the news of her disgrace?

"What's the matter, Alma?"

She had turned her head and was gazing between the curtains at the maples waving beyond the window. They touched her with a sudden fear of the town from whose eye they screened you but from whose mockery and malice there would be no refuge. She felt alone. Doubt of even a dear friend's kindness once one's quivering heart lay bare was cause for despair. Yet this very fear bred a need to prove him. It was now certain she needed an ally. Her husband would not do in the role – forty years of intimacy told her that. Ben was an intellectual; he would find an ancestor who had deserted the *Mayflower* uproarious – refreshingly antiseptic in a belt of patriotic cant. And as for Cotton! What Ben would not understand was that a wife had to be *one* of these women he called "dragons of sweetness and light" to outwit them. These gossips, Furies of the beauty parlor, Medusas under the hair dryers, call them what you will, had to be beaten on their own terms. *You had to be one of them to be free of them.* Ben would not understand this or if he did would understand it again intellectually, not sensing her woman's nerves rooted like a mile of ivy in the social soil you called home. But Malcolm would understand it. He was an intellectual too, of sorts, who analyzed things, but there was something else in his nature, something warm and feminine that made him take tea with you and chat about subjects. Yes, she decided, he would be sympathetic. She would tell him *if* the time came when she needed a confidant or an ally.

Her eye moved from the window across the wall to the mantel where a snapshot of Lee caught it — or to which the snapshot had like a magnet drawn it. The girl was a year or so younger than now, in shorts and a halter, laughing as the wind pasted a strand of hair across her cheek. Mrs. Marvel felt a burst of shame. How, that face asked, can you sit there and worry about your fat old self? Even now that innocence and that gaiety might be in peril, falling in love somewhere along the beach or in the front seat of a convertible with a charm as fake as the fakes you had to watch out for in the best antique shops. What kind of grandmother was it who wouldn't think first of the safety of a lamb like that and second of her own fat old dignity? For a week she had hesitated inquiring around, to see if Sligh had stayed in town longer than the two days she knew he had, from Lee's having admitted seeing him then — for fear of finding that he had.

She rose and went to the phone. She called the Hickory Inn.

"Is a Mr. Sligh registered there?"

He was.

She hung up and returned to the table. Malcolm sat watching her curiously. She took a good look at his face. He was always described as moon-faced yet in reality she thought of his cheeks as more solar, radiating good will and honest warmth. He was her friend.

"Sligh," she said, standing behind her chair which her

hands gripped, "is something worse than what you say Prufrock is. He is a blackmailer."

"A *what?*"

She told him the story, sparing nothing once she got into it. She brought it out rapidly, watching his features as the tale unfolded. He coughed once into his napkin but there was no sign of a smile, certainly no sound of a laugh. When she finished his face was grim, and also calculating. Perhaps he weighed the advantage to himself more than he did the embarrassment to Alma: ammunition against a second rival more tangible, therefore more usable, than he possessed against the first. He could hardly be criticized for that!

"Where are you going?" she asked when he had drunk off his tea and was fastening his bicycle clips around his ankles.

"Attend to a little business."

"You won't do anything . . . ? I mean rush headlong into this with Lee or anything? We don't want to frighten the girl out of her wits."

"Don't worry." He straightened and rose. "It's this Mr. Sligh who bears a little looking into. Ah'm pretty good at research mahself, you know."

She watched him worriedly as he mounted his wheel at the carriage block and wobbled away into the afternoon traffic. She would give anything to know if she had done the right thing. Sometimes she wondered why she had ever gotten married.

nine

"JUST WHAT do you mean by that?" Neil Sligh asked, stooping to retrieve a pin fallen from the folds of a new shirt he was opening and dropping it into a wastebasket. He apologized to the caller for continuing to dress after admitting him to his hotel room, explaining that he had a dinner engagement within the hour. "What do you mean by a mission of some delicacy?"

"That you have behaved in an unseemly manner toward a lady. That you have abused a confidence, undertaken blackmail, and in general betrayed a professional trust by threatening slander to the name entrusted to your care. None of these things are lightly regarded in these parts, suh," Malcolm continued, speaking as his father might have done before him and his father before that, in their time and place. "Chivalry is something of which you appear ignorant, in which case Ah am prepared to teach you its rudiments, suh. Family is held in sacred respect here — present as well as past, perhaps more so. Living kin being something that we balk at no ends to seek the welfare of — including all ages and descendants." Malcolm's left eye contracted slightly, like a clam under lemon juice, as he fixed the other with a steady glare. "Ah think you know what Ah mean."

"Just what has all this to do with you?" Sligh asked, masking any anxiety he may have felt by turning away as he climbed into his shirt. "Who are you? How do you come into all this?"

"As a friend of the family whose honor you choose to regard as a football for your personal gain. As that friend, Ah have come to demand satisfaction."

Now Sligh was hearing terms he more emphatically didn't like the ring of. Malcolm had arrived carrying under his arm a small black case, oblong in shape, which now stood on a table beside the door. Sligh glanced at it uneasily.

"I think I can explain this. You've got it all wrong, or rather Mrs. Marvel has. Wonderful woman. Why, I wouldn't harm a hair of her head! She simply misunderstood what I said. In outlining her plight to her — I assume you know all about what that is — I was trying to use, well, hell, euphemisms, so I suppose she thought I was being evasive, or saying things where she was supposed to read between the lines. So she jumped to conclusions. Blackmail! I had no intention of any such thing. Why, she's a wonderful woman."

"On that score we agree."

"But she misunderstood, I tell you! It's all in her mind."

Malcolm waved away these circumlocutions as though they were a cloud of tobacco smoke. "Please, Mrs. Marvel has told me the whole story. You simply changed your tune — or maybe tried to change your spots — when you saw a plum that looked better to you than the money. Knowing her also, Ah quite understand your wish to reform, to give it the better construction. But it's too late. The truth had out before then. By a matter of minutes, maybe seconds, but out. Too late for you to qualify for that family! You had put yourself on record as an extortionist."

"But I tell you she misunderstood me!" Sligh confronted Malcolm with his loose cuffs flapping, the tails of his shirt still out, in an attitude of entreaty. "Does she remember what I said? *I* don't. But I do know that I only meant that I'd keep it *sub rosa* — off the record — on the q.t. That's all. *Absolutely positively all.*"

Oh, was it? Mrs. Marvel was wondering that to herself that very instant as she plowed the parlor floor trying to recall exactly what he had said, racking her brains and sometimes physically clutching her head in the effort to reproduce it. Oh, if she had a tape recording of that interview! But even then would the evidence be definitive? Would the evasions and ambiguities — which she certainly could remember the tone of — permit any clear proof one way or another about his character? How could you *prove* that his interpretation of what he'd said was just a story he switched to after getting an eyeful of Lee, against his protestation that it wasn't?

Malcolm was swayed by no such doubts, his emotions being those of a firm resolve to act on intelligence unequivocally issued him.

"Any defense for yourself must be based on the possibility that Mrs. Marvel lied to me, which mah personal knowledge of her puts quite out of the question. And Ah shall come to the point and say to you what Ah came to say. That this town isn't big enough for both of us," Malcolm said, thereby evoking the parlance of still a third section of the country.

"And if I don't get out I may live to regret it?"

"That Ah can't swear to," Malcolm said, cryptically. He walked over to the carrying case which he now opened, revealing a brace of pistols of the kind in use during the Civil War period or thereabouts.

"Family heirloom?" said Sligh, tucking in his shirttails as he drifted over to inspect them. "What are you going to do with them? Why did you bring them here?"

"Give you your choice. Unless of course you specify other weapons entirely, which it is your privilege to do as the challenged."

"You're mad."

"Hopping. Hopping, suh, and Ah advise you to listen closely to what Ah have to say, because chew mah cabbage twice Ah will not. We can settle this with these or anything else you name, but settle it we shall. Unless you are prepared to meet mah other requirement as stated. Leave town by sundown tomorrow evening."

Sligh walked to the dresser. Sliding open a drawer he selected a tie with hands kept hidden from view.

"Are you in love with her?" he asked, knotting the tie.

"That is neither here nor there. This concerns Mrs. Marvel, whom Ah do love as a friend and will not see dishonored."

"Where are you from?"

"Hickory, Massachusetts, is mah home."

"But it's a handy cover-up for the other, you'll admit. I mean if you *were* in love with Lee you could use this chivalry business about Mrs. Marvel as a neat ruse for letting daylight into me, thus eliminating me as competition. Hell of a good excuse both to scare me off and play the White Knight for everyone's benefit. She has mentioned you, you know. Lee has."

Malcolm stiffened as though he had felt a pain, or were steeling himself to.

"In the most favorable terms. You may think me a rat and a sonofabitch and everything else in the book but I'm not rat enough to play fast and loose about all these intense things. You're not competition, but she likes you. So do I. You have a way of making friends, and inspiring confidence. And can you keep the conversational ball rolling! That's why I hate to see you going at this in a way that might land us in the morgue or in jail, besides putting the clock back a hundred years. Of course that's the threat you're using against me, isn't it? That I might wind up there. A kind of blackmail in itself." Neil Sligh smiled as he turned around and drew the collar of his shirt down. He smiled richly, the dimples Mrs. Marvel admired appearing in his cheeks like a pair of jewels and affording Malcolm with brutal charity a glimpse of what Lee saw in him.

"Are you in love with her?" Malcolm now asked.

"Yes, I am. Very much. I want her for my wife."

Malcolm closed the lid, fastening the catch on the black case.

"In that case Ah must emphasize doubly that Ah mean business. There are now two people to protect from a villain, one from extortion, the other from the danger of not seeing through him till it's too late. We heah up Nawth do mean business when we talk it. So when Ah wawn you to keep yo' cotton-pickin' hands off Miss Lee and her grandmother both, Ah advise you to heed what Ah say!"

Malcolm tucked the case under his arm and moved to the door.

"Ah shall telephone this hotel at eight o'clock tomorrow evening. If you have checked out we may consider the matter closed. If you have not, Ah shall arrive at dawn the next morning, with these pistols, which will then be loaded, and knock yo' good-for-nothin' block off! Good day, suh."

Toward nine o'clock of the next evening, Malcolm propped his bike before that house at which he was ever welcome, pocketing his clips as he approached the stairs while Cotton and Marvel both fled upward to the safety of their bedrooms. Alma let him in, her face drawn and her eyes dark with fatigue. "Well?"

"It's all settled, honey. Ah called on him yesterday and delivered what let's just call an ultimatum, to spare you the details. Ah phoned just now and it worked. He has left town. Ah think we've seen the last of Mr. Sligh."

"Yes, spare me the details. Because, oh, Malcolm, now I'm not at all sure . . . I mean I'm so mixed up and my head is such a mishmash of . . ." She clawed her hair a moment at a wall glass. "What I look like, that's how I feel."

"What do you mean, you're not at all sure?"

"Of his guilt. How could I prove it in court?"

"The fact that he's flown the coop proves his guilt. And is another index of his character. Who but an opportunist would take that little gaff for what he wanted? We've smoked him out, honey, don't you see?"

She turned around and smiled simply at his simple logic. "Of course. Dear old Malcolm, straightening everything out like that." She dropped with exhausted relief into a chair, her legs stretched out, her head back. "Don't tell me too much about the ruckus, just that you had a showdown and it worked. Go on."

"There's nothing to tell but that. Ah just called on him and demanded satisfaction in no uncertain terms. That appears to have done it. Thank God he was the opportunist you suspected him of being. It meant he had less fight in him."

"You kept Lee out of it I hope? She doesn't know anything about this sordid squabble personally?"

"No, she knows nothing about it personally. Wouldn't think of dragging her into it."

"Because we don't want to give her a birth trauma or something."

The occasion called for a little refreshment, perhaps a cup of coffee, for which Malcolm politely pled. Mrs. Marvel felt she could do with another too, and off they trotted to the kitchen.

"I hope I can get myself pulled together a little," she said as they drank at the table there. "Get over these headaches I've been having, this nervous stomach. Dr. March doesn't seem to do anything. There's nothing organically wrong with me and he still can't fix me up."

"How about Dr. Broome?" he said and great was her regurgitation. "You're just worn out and unstrung from all this to-do, Alma. It's perfectly natural. There'd be something wrong with you if there *wasn't* something wrong with you."

"I suppose you're right. Worn out and unstrung is the truth all right. Worn to a frazzle. Everything is such a shambles." She sighed as she took the cream pitcher from Malcolm. "Everything is a shambles and the family haven't even begun to arrive yet."

part two:

BED OF ASHES

ten

BUSHROD was the first to arrive. He reached Hickory early one afternoon the Friday before the festive weekend, in time to investigate the anti-Semitism his mother had promised him faithfully he would find in his home town, in which he had found little enough to lure him back in the years since he had married and left it. The Civil Liberties League of which he was secretary paid his travel expenses but he did not abuse the privilege. As they crossed the Spitachunk River bridge into Hickory proper, their tires singing familiarly over the grillwork, he watched for a drugstore remembered as serving decent sandwiches (having settled with his wife that they shouldn't descend on the Marvels at lunch time but grab a bite first).

"Used to be somewhere in this next block," Bushrod said, screwing his snub face into an expression of lookout. He scratched his head without noticeably disarranging his hair, which was like steel wool. "Sandwich or salad O.K. for you, Clara?"

"Perfectly, Bushrod."

Clara Marvel was one of those women who are content to be reflections of their husbands, having no identity of their own. As the wife of a tool and die manufacturer she had held opinions of a reactionary stripe, which Bushrod had promptly reversed on marrying her a year after her first husband's death. Bushrod's ventriloquism had transformed her into an active and even militant liberal. He quieted her fear of labor unions, taught her whom to vote for, what charities to support, what nations to boycott. Within a year she was purged of every toxic trace of conservatism. She gave herself a civil liberties test regularly featured in one of the weeklies that now came to her house, modeled on those quizzes run in more banal publications that tell you whether you love your husband or are an extrovert. Questions were: "Did the President act rightly in the steel strike?", "How was the Supreme Court split on the Frobisher case?" and the like. For the answers one turned to page so-and-so, and tallied one's score. These tests were like booster shots stabilizing her fitness as a wife for Bushrod, one whom he would not be ashamed to introduce to his friends and take to parties. Her last grade had been 85. She now rebuked merchants, as bellicosely as her meek nature permitted, for displaying advertised brands to the detriment of superior but untouted ones. She did occasional picketing, shouldering her placard with a deferential smile as she milled in the cold with other insurgents, and she never bought anything without consulting *Consumers' Reports*.

Bushrod found the drugstore, Larrabee's, but was another three blocks finding a place to park. That landed them smack in front of the Second Congregational Church, stirring memories of a more abrasive sort. It was there that

Reverend Korn had baptized him Bushrod. God, he thought again, with the resentment off which the years were apparently not to take the edge, couldn't they give you a better name than that? His mother had found it in a historical novel she'd been reading at the time. Bushrod was what Washington's favorite nephew, the son of his beloved brother Jack, was called.

Bushrod Marvel, who believed in taking people as they are, cranked his window down and spat his gum into the street. Backing the soiled Chevy in beside the curb, he looked into the rear seat where his own son was.

"Going to feed the inner man, Beaumont. How's that sound, eh? Feel like a bite to eat, Beau boy?"

A glance at Beaumont would have indicated the absurdity of the question. At the age of eight he weighed a hundred and forty pounds and he was not tall. He lay on his back, his hands folded on his stomach, over which he could not button his blazer, feigning sleep, as he had for the past fifty miles as a means of securing immunity to conversation.

Mention of food revived him, but he took care to conceal the fact, knowing that as an official problem in obesity he was kept under strict surveillance. Confections and starches were barred from the Marvel household while his parents sought the psychological roots of his gluttony. If they wished on the sly to indulge a sweet tooth of their own, they must outwit an almost ethereal sensitivity to food. Vibrations of eating reached him from distant rooms and through closed doors; he would stroll into their bedroom and find their guilty mouths, as they turned the page of a book too carelessly or lay with one hand under the quilts. A box of candy given them as a gift posed a major crisis; in whatever bureau drawer or behind whatever closet shelf they hid it he would root it out and polish it off, exercising something like that telepathy which is often the subject of parlor games. His parents were ineffectual in the reverse of this: evidence of goodies smuggled into his own bedroom was discovered usually only in the form of debris — empty cookie cartons, fruit or sardine tins, candy bar wrappers, even chicken bones. These were generally unearthed by the cleaning woman from the depths of the closet or the bottom of a drawer, once even from between the mattress and bedspring. Sometimes they were simply chucked out of the window, where they would collect among the bushes till found. Once a box which had contained a pound of glazed fruit turned up. "Why, we haven't had glazed fruit in this house," Clara told Bushrod. Their first inkling that he had other sources of supply, perhaps neighbors' houses when the neighbors were out. He learned of one with a deep-freeze in the garage which was never locked, and from it helped himself to flavors of ice cream of which the Marvels had never heard.

The fact that he made so little effort to conceal the evidence seemed to their pediatrician, a man with a wistful interest in the emotional problems of his patients, significant. "It shows us he wants us to find out, and do something about it. Well, we will." Pills were prescribed, a diet drafted, and plans instituted for weekly weight checks. They indicated no loss for three weeks but no gain either, which the doctor counted progress since the lad was growing and a static weight was a relative reduction.

The regimen was blown sky-high by a visit from Beaumont's half-brother and half-sister, twins of Bushrod's by a former marriage whom their mother, now also remarried and living in Baltimore, put on a train once a month for a weekend with their father in Washington, as Moo Moo had bewailed. The twins were by contrast thin and puny and had to be plied with rich desserts and drowned in cocoa. The crisis was discussed with the doctor and a decision reached. The psychological hazards of exclusion from the siblings' largesse was greater than the physical one of backsliding, so Beaumont was given holidays from his diet for the duration of custodial weekends. That was how matters stood at the time of the family's own visit to Hickory, for which, of course, further complications were anticipated.

Bushrod settled his family at a table in the drugstore and scanned the menu for something calorically worthless. Having ordered cottage cheese and fruit salad for all three of them, he stepped over to the pharmacy section for a chat with old Mr. Larrabee, who remembered him from high school days. After a moment of reminiscence, Bushrod came to the point.

"I understand there's some feeling about a new merchant trying to move into Main Street. A fellow named Aronson who wants to open up a liquor store in the Bon Ton Block."

Mr. Larrabee hemmed and hawed, but finally admitted that yes, anti-Semitism had crept into Hickory. Petitions were being circulated mainly among shopkeepers requesting the Better Business Bureau to "oppose the debasement of this choice row by a type of merchandise alien to its traditional tone," which had been set by high-grade clothing and department stores, book and gift shops, an outlet for Rosemarie de Paris candies and another for British Woollens, etc. Citizens of a contrary temper were busy signing counter-petitions, so a storm was in the making of which little Aronson was ill equipped to be the center. He could not have broken a lance in the *cause célèbre* even if his initial stood for Aaron, as rumor by now had it, instead of Axel, which was the case. He was at this moment a very confused man, scratching his head over a letter he had received that morning from Bushrod, written on CLL stationery:

Sir: Wind has reached us of the discrimination to which you are being subjected, which by now may very well have attained persecution pitch. But never fear! Even now forces are riding to your rescue, and we shall see with every resource within our power that this disgrace is aired, if necessary on a national scale, to the end that your liberties and rights as an American be not in any way endangered or abridged. Forces leagued against you are also leagued against me — that is how I consider it. So courage! I shall arrive on Friday next, and promptly come to see you in my capacity as traveling secretary of the above organization, in which capacity as well as that of fellow American I salute you, and sign myself,

Sincerely yours,
Bushrod Marvel

This communication frightened as well as baffled Aronson. It was the first hint of any hostility against him in the town, and he had beyond this no idea what its author was talking about.

"Ay tank Ay go see Larsen," he told his wife, meaning his lawyer. "Ay yust don't understand. Ja, Ay better go see Larsen."

He was mounting to Larsen's second-floor office on

Chestnut Street at about the time the Marvels were finishing their drugstore lunch. Bushrod left a tip of two quarters, one of which Beaumont abstracted as they rose to go, and which he spent on candy bars with the same speed and secrecy after leaving his parents on the sidewalk to run back for his sun goggles, which he had left behind on purpose. By the time he rejoined them at the car the five bars were distributed imperceptibly about his person.

There was nobody home when they arrived at the old Marvel place but a note pinned to the front door by Moo Moo said she was out on an errand from which she would return in ten minutes and for them to make themselves at home. "Take your old room, Bushrod, and Clara dear, your choice of those across the hall for Beaumont — Hi, Beau! — and then I suppose you'll want to freshen up et cetera. Plenty of food in the kitchen. See you soon."

While Clara unpacked, Bushrod dashed off to look up Aronson. The address he had led him to a small cottage on a dead-end street he could remember playing roller-skate hockey in, using branches for sticks and a tin can for a puck. There were children playing hopscotch in it now.

The visit to his lawyer had hardly stilled Aronson's apprehensions. Innocent of the agitations going on at the other end of town, Larsen was as perplexed by the letter as his client. Neither could make out the signature, which, together with the high-flown contents, led Larsen to the suspicion that the note was the work of a crank. Phrases like "forces leagued against you" and "also leagued against me" as well as "riding to your rescue" suggested an unstable and possibly even deranged mind, in view of which Larsen wondered if it oughtn't to be turned over to the police. In any case he would like to keep it for further study; he wanted to look up the organization on whose stationery the ravings appeared, of which he had never heard; his secretary was good at deciphering illegible scrawls and he would give her a crack at this one as soon as she returned from lunch.

"Have you any enemies that you can think of?"

"Yumpin' Yiminy, why anybody want to be after me?"

"Are you a citizen yet?"

"Not yet, but Ay going to night school and Ay learning plenty American history you bet, and in eight more months —"

"Well, don't join any organizations, especially patriotic ones. Anything may put a crimp in your case and hold your papers up till God knows when. I see this outfit is located in Washington. Have nothing to do with them, steer clear of any crackpot organization. If they put the bee on you about joining, say no. We don't want you being investigated. All this is important, you hear now, Axel? *Keep your nose clean.*"

"Ay do yust dot," Aronson assured him, and went home to lie down. He composed himself as best he could with a little nip of Akvavit. When the doorbell rang he answered it in slippers. A tall stranger with eyes like match tips in a fanatic's face was out there.

"Mr. Aronson?"

"Yes."

"I'm Mr. Marvel."

"Who?"

"Bushrod Marvel. I wrote you that letter. From the Civil —"

Aronson tried to push the door shut, against firm counterpressure from a large foot and then its owner's elbow.

"Ay don't want to yoin anything," he said, glancing at the briefcase.

"I don't want you to join anything. I'm here to — Don't you see that —?"

The Swede's agitation indicated to Bushrod how thorough was the victim's intimidation. He had come to investigate prejudice and found terror! This excited him to redouble his efforts to get in, which in turn further heightened Aronson's panic. So that when the little Swede heard the word "persecution" from the stranger's lips he instantly recognized a psychiatric term used in newspaper reports of maniacs and tried to shut the door with one last violent heave. He was no match for the madman, who pushed back inch by inch, till the Swede was pinned against the vestibule wall under a disarranged etching. The madman stepped inside.

"My God, have they got *you* scared. But don't be afraid. We're in this together."

"We are?" Aronson gulped, his eyes bulging with alarm as he tried to impress on himself the importance of keeping calm, to humor the intruder till he could slip into the kitchen and call the police. "You like drink?" he brought out.

"Why, that's very nice of you. Yes. Don't mind if I do."

The nut followed him into the tiny parlor, where he stood watching him pour out two glasses of white liqueur from a bottle already opened. The man didn't look like a Jew, he was thinking . . . and that accent . . . No doubt some variant of Yiddish with which he was unfamiliar, and which was probably distorted by the poor devil's hysterical state.

"Now, what has been the nature of the threats so far? Any hints of physical violence? Or is it still all verbal? Has your family been threatened?"

"Not yet," Aronson said, watching the nut's reflection in a wall mirror as he corked the bottle.

"No swastikas painted on the doors I suppose?" Bushrod asked, almost hopefully.

"No."

"Any poison pen letters?"

"Yust yours."

After handing the madman a glass, Aronson half turned toward the back of the house where there was a sound like an icebox door closing. The lunatic raised his glass and proposed a toast to democracy, to which they both drank. Having tasted the liquid, he looked at it and asked a question.

"What is this?"

"Akvavit."

"I see." Bushrod dropped his briefcase on a chair. "Some foreign drink?"

"Ay take it along from old country. Yust dandy drink. Yust a minute, Ay go see if my wife — Ingebar!"

"Never mind that. Are you a Swede?"

"Oh, ja."

"I see. Then Aronson can be Swedish too. With one 's'?"

"Two first, in old country. But we here try to Americanize."

"Causing great confusion if I may say so," Bushrod said tersely. "Great confusion to everybody. Do you realize how much of people's time and energy you've been wasting? All those petitions — Look. What does the initial 'A' stand for, if I may ask? What is your first name?"

"Axel."

Bushrod put his drink down. His eyes narrowing, he took the other in as though he were an impostor.

"Don't you realize the trouble you've caused? Haven't you been aware of any opposition to your liquor store?"

"Why, no . . . Lease take long time, but . . . You mean people against me because of that?"

"That's just a subterfuge, man!"

"What?"

"A cover-up. They say they're against a liquor store in Bon Ton Row as a screen for the real reason. They're trying to restrict this town. They wouldn't mind a neon sign saying Ballantine's or Old Crow if the name on the window was McGillicudy or Hathaway. They're trying to keep you out because they think you're a Jew. Is this the first you're aware of all this propaganda going on behind your back?"

"Well, Ay swan." Aronson sat down.

"Yeah, Ay swan too. Let's both swan. Haven't you ever been taken for a Jew before? Haven't you ever suspected your name might be taken for that, spelt with one 's'? That's Jewish in most metropolitan areas. All this going on here — here in good old Hickory — while you sit drinking Akvavit and waiting for the lease to get ready. And I come several hundred miles to help you."

"Ay real sorry to cause all that trouble. Over nothing."

"Nothing! The situation hasn't changed just because you're a Swede, man! *Think*. The fact is that prejudice exists, here in your home town. I advise you to be more alert to present-day currents. What's your opinion of this hullabaloo now that you've been told? That your lease has been held up because they don't want Jews on Main Street."

Aronson cocked his head, looking away. "Well, people think they pretty sharp to deal with, you know."

"Aha! Race prejudice indeed! I see I've come to the right place after all. My work is cut out for me. So you yourself, once the misunderstanding is cleared up and you're safely settled among the downtown merchants, will do your loyal part to discriminate against minorities. Is that the situation?"

Here Aronson looked at him narrowly. "You a Yew?"

"Why, you—! I'll thank you to keep a civil tongue in your head. Do I look like one, for heaven's sake?"

"No . . ."

"Well then."

"Ay yust wondered. You so hot on the subyect."

"And I advise you to be too. Oh, good God, what's the use." Bushrod flapped his arms, turning away.

He picked up his briefcase and went, leaving the chastened Aronson to go back to the kitchen and clear it all up with his wife, over a glass of Akvavit. They were sorry about the whole thing, and decided that the least they could do would be to join the Civil Liberties League.

Though the evil in question existed none the less, proving itself in fact the graver for being fosterable under conditions of pure fantasy, and though the cogency of Bushrod's mission remained therefore undiminished, he was deflated and out of sorts when he arrived back at the Marvel place.

"Mother, this Aronson isn't a Jew at all. He's a Swede," he told her accusingly. "The whole thing is a mare's nest."

"A Swede! Good heavens, not really. What a terrible blunder. Oh, Bushrod, it's not my fault. I just wrote you what I'd heard . . . A Swede, imagine that. Will some people's faces be re-he-hed."

"How about mine? How do you think I feel, coming all the way up here for nothing."

"But Bush, it doesn't change anything. There's still anti-Semitism, dear. Fight it!"

"How can you? How are you going to smoke the bastards out now? They'll all say they knew all along he was a Swede, so that proves it was the liquor store they were objecting to, not him."

"You're right, Bushrod," Clara said, laying a hand on his arm. "Oh, what a nuisance."

"But surely you can write some kind of report? Then relax and have fun. Come, let's have a cup of tea, or a drink if you'd rather. Come on, all! I want to show you how we've done the kitchen over. And to meet Ruby. It was her I was fetching from the bus stop when you arrived."

After showing them the kitchen, freshly decorated in bright red and blue wallpaper with small fruit and vegetable figures, she introduced Ruby, a handsome young colored woman who worked for Mrs. Marvel now and again and was here to pitch in for the Anniversary. Ruby fixed tea while Clara mixed Bushrod a highball, which she gave him with another understanding pat. They all sat around the kitchen table. Bushrod poured the tea, including a cup for Ruby, who he insisted must join them. Ruby consulted Mrs. Marvel, who signaled with a nod for her to comply. Bushrod told her where he worked, and asked if she were a member of the CLL. She said no, she couldn't afford things like that. "I know," Bushrod said. "I preach too damn much. Stop me if I start any more sermons." "I'll do that all right," Ruby said, smiling into her tea. She would rise smartly once she had finished, but until then would do as she had been bade: be sociable.

Bushrod expanded under a second highball, visualizing a much more telling report than if matters had been as represented. He narrated his meeting with Aronson, imitating the accent, to the amusement of all. He began to tell Swede stories.

"It seems there were these two guys, Olie and Sven, out fishing in a rowboat. They caught so many fish that Olie said, 'By Yiminy, we ought to remember this spot on the lake, so we can come back here.' 'You right, Olie,' Sven said, 'Ay mark it.' So he takes a piece of chalk out of his pocket and makes a mark on the side of the rowboat. Wait, that's not all," Bushrod said, laying a hand on the laughing Ruby's arm. "So Olie said, 'Why, Sven, that's the dumbest thing Ay ever heard.' And Sven said, 'Why, what's dumb about it?' 'What's dumb about it? Why, you fool, what if we don't get the same rowboat next time?' "

They were all in better spirits now. Clara kept an eye on Beau's hand which crept rather more repeatedly than was wise to the plate of toll house cookies. Bushrod gave another chuckle, and took a pull of his highball.

"What's smarter than a smart Swede?" he asked. "Give up? A dumb Dutchman."

When his wife and mother left to look at the gardens, taking Beau along, Bushrod stayed behind to finish his drink. He stood up because Ruby was on her feet again, working at the sink.

"This whole business about ethnic groups, the things that get started and take hold about them and so on, is interesting," he said, leaning against the wall with one foot crossed over the other. "The Swedes actually resist assimilation as much as anyone. They're really very clannish. And as tight and sharp as others are accused of being."

"Then why aren't they a minority group?" Ruby asked with her head in the icebox.

"There aren't enough of them. You need a quorum to irritate the American people."

"How many are there in this country, would you say?"

"They total about four million, but only two million first-generation."

The subject seemed closed, or at any rate dropped. Bushrod stepped to the window to make sure the others were all outside. They were, Moo Moo and Clara strolling among the delphinium, Beaumont heading off in the other direction under the apple trees.

"Look, Ruby," he said in a lowered voice, "Beaumont is sort of a weight problem, as you can see. I'd appreciate it if you'd see that he doesn't run scot-free in the kitchen here. I mean as much as you can, and without being too obvious about it. I hate to ask this but it's important."

"Certainly, Mr. Marvel. I'll do what I can. Have to kind of watch my weight myself."

"Nonsense, you have a lovely figure." He rinsed his empty glass after dumping the ice cubes in the sink. "Well, thanks a lot. Think I'll go have a look around the old homestead myself. See you, Ruby."

There was a twist of smoke above the apple trees near where Ruby was emptying trash into the incinerator.

"Fire! The gazebo's going!"

It was what they all called the arbor, toward which people now tumbled from the kitchen with buckets and pans of water. Bushrod snatched up a garden hose, luckily connected, and yanking and snapping it around obstructions brought it toward the crackling latticework. Though dry as tinder the wood was choked with green vines, and the flames were extinguished before they had more than charred one side.

As they stood in a heavy-breathing circle watching the wood smolder and drip, Clara sensed someone was missing. She turned to the house, in time to see Beaumont's face withdrawn from an upper window.

Bushrod found matches in Beau's room, after which he and Clara took Mrs. Marvel aside and conscientiously admitted Beau had a slight history of arson. Nothing to worry about they hoped, nothing that building up his basic security wouldn't correct, since what is an arsonist but someone who has failed to set the world on fire?

"We'll move out if you like, Mother," Bushrod said in the sun room to which the three had repaired for conference. "I noticed a new motel on the highway."

"I wouldn't have it said. Just punish him good and hard so he'll *understand.*"

"But this is different," he said as patiently as possible. "This is serious."

"That's what I say. Beat the tar out of him."

Bushrod chewed a thumbnail as he paced the floor, glancing at Clara who sat with her hands clutched in her lap. "What'll we do?" she said.

After a moment of munching his nail, he paused. He said: "Give him something sweet."

"I see what you mean," Clara said. "The problem is related to the other."

"Exactly. He's deprived while others have all they want.

Here again, he's forbidden teacakes while others reach freely into the plate. No wonder he feels discriminated against. Clara, we've got to let the bars down again."

"You're right. Moo Moo, do you have a treat for him?"

Mrs. Marvel swiveled about on her chair a bit, leaning well out of it toward the others. "You mean this is what he gets for trying to burn my gazebo down?"

"Mother, your gazebo is not the issue. We'll pay for that, of course. He may not have done it on purpose, but if he did, don't you see that's all the more reason for handling it right — for not cracking down on him?" Bushrod said, trying to be patient. "We don't punish in the old-fashioned sense any more. We remove the cause."

"You remove the cause?"

"What the child is trying to compensate for, or release his hostility about."

Mrs. Marvel began to move her head slowly up and down, thinking. She was making an honest effort to be as intelligent about it as they were.

"Well, I have some homemade ice cream," she said at last. "It's in the freezer. I've been keeping it for a special occasion."

"Get it out."

They watched Beau do justice to a plate of it at the kitchen table, joining him with a spoonful themselves so as not to make it too obvious. The kitchen of this two-hundred-year-old house had been modernized in some respects but not electrically. There were no wall outlets, so the cords of all appliances met in a ganglion of plugs under the ceiling light over the table; breakfasters peered at one another, like jungle creatures, through a vinework leading to toaster, orange-juice squeezer, percolator. None of these were hooked up now of course, but an iron plied by Ruby in a corner was, and so was a softly whirling fan. Ruby showed no reaction to the countermanded order, having worked in many homes with enlightened views. Beau, serenely sucking, watched where Moo Moo hung the freezer key after putting the half-gallon container away again.

They adjourned to the living room, there to pick up magazines or admire, again, the fortune in old furniture. The piecrust table was back. Everything was authentically Colonial except for a few overstuffed chairs on the backs of which were immaculate white tidies, and on the arms, ashtrays affixed to beanbags full of buckshot, to prevent their sliding off. Bushrod sat in one, paging through a copy of the *Saturday Evening Post* and shaking his head. Mrs. Marvel gazed from another at Clara fixing herself and Bushrod highballs, using the candle snuffer for a jigger. Beaumont read a comic in a Boston rocker, holding a bottle of No Cal . . . A summer afternoon of pleasant heat, no sound in the house but the intermittent buzz of a fly stitching together the patches of summer silence . . .

"There are lots of books upstairs, Beau," Mrs. Marvel said, "old books your Daddy read when he was young. And toys — you should see what I dug out of the attic! Oh, lad, you'll find them all downstairs in the rumpus room."

"Do that, Beau," Clara said. "You shouldn't have your nose in a comic all the time."

"Oh, not that I hold with thinking comics are all bad," Mrs. Marvel said. "Sure they're junk, but so were most of the books we read when we were kids. At least they're better than this rotgut you see on television."

"Some comics are all right, of course. We got one for Beau that explains the coöperative movement, and there's a series out now that give the Gospels in comic-strip form. Bushrod feels they should have *some* religious instruction."

"Does your sister still live in LaCrosse?"

"Yes. Bob's been transferred there for what looks like good."

"Any children yet?"

"No. They believe in planned parenthood, so they don't have any children. She's always arguing with my other sister, Eunice, who's just the opposite. Sends her pamphlets and tells her what she thinks of anyone who brings six children into this world. But Eunice won't listen. No planned parenthood for her. She's got another on the way."

"She should be told a few things," Bushrod said, putting the *Post* aside. "About population crises and what's going on in the world. Or maybe Jim should be sterilized . . . By the way, where's Dad?"

Mrs. Marvel had just begun to explain that he should be home from the office any minute when a noise outside sent her to the window. A car pulling a rented U-Haul trailer the size of a doghouse drew to a stop behind Bushrod's and people began to climb out of it. They stood frowning at the house and unsticking their clothes from their persons. "The Trautwigs are here!" She ran down the stairs with open arms.

"Elsie, you look as though you came to sta-hay!" Mrs. Marvel laughed as she crossed the lawn to embrace her eldest daughter.

"We took some stuff to drop off at Art's folks on the way, and then I found a lot of Lee's summer things to take along, so with all the grips and boxes, you look fine, Mother. How's Lee?"

"Oh, great. We'll have a talk later, but she's getting

along fine and loves her work. We manage to keep her amused. Have you heard from her?"

Another voice here.

"When April last her green preamble strewed across the drooling hills we heard her April laughter, by long distance phone. Since then a missive in her hand, or an occasional scribbled card, inform us that she's yet alive, enlivening other purlieus than our own."

"Chester! He's the same as ever!"

"Worse," his stepfather murmured. Art heaved his trousers up with the sides of his hands, in one of which a cigar smoked. "I take him bowling and everything. How are you, Moo Moo?"

Bushrod and Clara came out of the house hand in hand, shepherding their Beau before them. Marvels and Trautwigs exchanged greetings in which some cheeks were pecked, then Mrs. Marvel became again supervisory.

"Take your things up to that room there" – she pointed at a dormer – "Elsie's old room, and Chester either next to it or – Wait. I just had a brainstorm. Maybe he'd like to move in with Beaumont. They've loads to talk about."

Many hands helped cart the remarkable number of bags Art extracted morosely from the U-Haul, and soon the Trautwigs too had washed up and begun to come downstairs in fresh, light clothing. Art was first, rolling up his sleeves and humming a tune as he strolled into a parlor containing otherwise only Bushrod, bent over a book. Bushrod held his eye to the page till the last as he closed and put it by.

"Well, Art," he said, reading the name on the cigar band his brother-in-law had dropped into an ashtray, "I'm surprised you'd smoke those."

"Why?" Art inquired through match flame.

"Their employees are on strike. Didn't you know that?"

"No, I didn't know that. How would I know?"

"It's been in all the liberal journals. They're asking for hardly more than a living wage. We always boycott products like that."

Art waved the match out, looking around for liquor.

"I don't know how liberal I'm supposed to be, but I gave a hundred bucks to the overseas relief last year. You gitny scores yet? How'd the Giants make out? The radio in my car's broke."

"No, I haven't heard. Whom are they playing?"

"Pirates." Art appraised Bushrod, who was drawing a horsehair from his coat lapel. "Not the ones of Penzance — your sister's been giving me that. Well, the average income of big league ball players is estimated at twenty-five thousand a year. O.K. to patronize them?"

"I guess," Bushrod said. "Don't let me preach too much. But there's one thing I do want to ask you, out of personal curiosity. How many people would you say use *Consumers' Reports* when they purchase an automobile — *the second biggest investment in their lives?*"

"I only sell secondhand cars, so I wouldn't rightly know. Those recommendations wouldn't make much sense except on new cars, would they?"

"I suppose not. Something well rated could have been beat up by the previous driver."

"I try to handle only a clean, one-owner car. Something that has my personal guarantee. No doctored speedometers or cork in the transmission to make her run smooth on my lot."

"Swell."

Bushrod looked toward the back of the house and began to sniff.

"Do you smell anything?"

Art sniffed. "No, I don't smell anything. Like what?"

"A sharp, acrid odor not unlike gunpowder."

Art inspected his cigar, surely blameless save on the score of social conscience. He held it away and breathed in from another direction. "I get it now. Silver polish. I'd know that smell anywhere. What'll you bet somebody's not polishing silver in the kitchen?"

They went to see, to find Ruby rubbing away at a mountain of flatware on the table, not in the best of spirits.

"I don't know how I'll get this done along with all the cooking. Should have been taken care of long before the big doings," she said to Bushrod.

"You're right, Ruby. But Mother's cleaning woman stood her up. Here, let me give you a hand. No, really, I haven't anything better to do."

Art wandered back to the parlor where he managed to assemble himself a Scotch highball. He stood drinking it, looking around for a radio. Footsteps in the ceiling made him wonder what was keeping Elsie. He went upstairs to their room. She was pressing his clothes with a traveling iron.

He closed the door softly behind him, with a sigh kept carefully inaudible, and advanced with his highball extended. "I've brought you a drink," he lied. She shook her head and went on with the ironing, done, with a put-upon air at which she was a master, on a small portable board laid across the dresser, so that two images reproached him, one in the mirror. A suggestion of angular weariness recalled

Picasso's painting of the laundress, for which she had once striven to generate some appreciation in him. Art was not surprised to find her toiling and had anticipated her rejection of the drink. Only after taking another prodigious pull on it himself did he sit down, and then on a stiff straight-back, not the deep chair his occupancy of which would have furthered her self-immolation.

This mood had begun to be generated midway their journey, following a dispute over his failure to repair in time their broken Cardrobe, in which their clothes might have traveled hung-up. Elsie had had to cram them all into grips, from which they had now been extracted hopelessly wrinkled. For this he was being punished not by having to iron them himself — oh-ho no — but by the far keener retribution of seeing her do so, on this supposed holiday.

"Why do you always have to act like a damn martyr?" The question had bored him for ages, but this time he put it with a glimmer of fresh curiosity. "Your brother was just at me for smoking cigars that the employees of are out on strike. I'm in the house ten minutes and that's my welcome. Does it run in the family? Is this a Puritan or New England deal or something, making a guy feel guilty?"

Since she did not answer but went on servilely creasing his overturned pants, pressing down with a force that rendered nearly superfluous the iron's heat, he quietly reviewed the labyrinthine union that had led to this moment.

He had returned from work one evening the first winter of their marriage to find her shoveling snow in a mink coat, hacking at the doorstep with a garden spade for hadn't he also neglected to get a proper shovel? It may have been the mink coat, souvenir of bygone glamorous Mercury days he could not provide, that got him. He had marched into the house and pulled from the bureau drawers all the shirts he could find without buttons and sewn them on.

Thus when she came in it was to find *him* doing *woman's* work, equally neglected if it came to that. It was how they fought, doing one another's chores. She would mount the ladder and put up storm windows he had been badgered in vain to get at; coming home to find that all shipshape, he would tramp inside and wash dishes let accumulate in the sink. Once a woman dropped in, of the neighborly sort who do so without knocking, to find them both sitting on the parlor floor, polishing one another's shoes. "Aw," she said, beaming on the scene, "how sweet. I wish Jack and I got along like that." Elsie rose but Art sat grimly buffing, putting a luster on a pump. When they were alone again she called him on not rising when a lady entered, and he threw the slipper at the wall. Why the hell didn't her friends knock first — weren't they housebroken? "If there's anything I hate it's the pleasant old custom of dropping in!"

"Was that aimed at my family? Because you're always taking sly digs at New England, where we're from. Why don't you come right out and say it?"

"All right I will. I'll come right out and say why don't *you* come right out and say you're ashamed of my background. If Illinois is so beneath you why did you marry somebody from it? Your attitude is getting to be a pain in the ass to me. A pain-in-the-ass."

"I've married beneath me."

"So have I. So we're even."

Art assigned himself the task of keeping his trap shut during Old Home Week. That did not rule out countermeasures, however. He picked up some stockings of Elsie's and took them to the bathroom across the hall. He was washing them out in warm suds with the door open when Moo Moo happened by, and doted on the double scene: Elsie pressing Art's suit, Art Luxing Elsie's things. She took this as the absolute epitome of Doing For One Another, the key to marital cohesion, but did not say anything, which was just as well because Elsie was bursting with complaints to air while Art was busy drafting his defense in an imaginary interview with Moo Moo.

"One day it's all that fine-heritage deal and the next it's this accent-on-living crap. So that I never know when I come home whether it's a book I'm going to have shoved at me or a brush to paint something gay, with hex signs like on Pennsylvania barns. Or I wake up at night and she's not in bed but in the basement wiping mildew off my fishing boots. Then it's up to me to guess what I've done now. I arrive home to find her sewing up a turkey in her lap, with the Grand Opening orchid from the new supermarket pinned to her baggy old housedress — to show that We Never Go Out. She won't speak to me for days, in between hollering at me. God only knows what she tells Patchkiss."

"Does she still go to him?" Moo Moo would say in fancy. "That must be expensive for you, Art."

"I don't mind. If it helps . . ."

Moo Moo was inside the bedroom saying something actual to Elsie. He didn't catch it, having drawn the basin plug and started fresh water for rinsing. He hung the stockings over the tub curtain rod and joined them.

"It's so nice to have the nursery full again," Mrs. Marvel was saying, turning to include Art in that. "Like old times. Art, why don't you go down and have another drink? Some of the others may be there. And Ben will be right home. Elsie and I have a few things to talk about."

Let them talk, he thought as he descended the stairs with his glass. Through a parlor window he could see Chester and Beaumont playing catch. He poured himself another drink and stiff-armed the swinging door to the kitchen, where Bushrod was helping Ruby polish the silver for the benefit of the politically naive, now entering.

"How about introducing me to the lady?" said Art. The parody was lost on Bushrod, but Ruby grinned a little among the heirlooms.

"Oh, don't you know Ruby? Sorry. Ruby Crawford. Mr. Trautwig."

"Pleased to meet you. Can I fix you a drink?"

Ruby looked up with the expression of one for whom things are getting a bit thick. "No, thanks. Thanks just the same."

Elsie's troubles began when on her wedding night she had been forced to commit an unnatural act: sexual intercourse. Initiation had been the work of Louis Squalante, the first of her, so far, three husbands. Louis trusted the principle that ice conceals natures all the warmer underneath, but did not, fishing through this ice, catch any tropical fish, which was what he expected and what his own nature needed. After eight patient months which yielded no sign of a thaw he took a little Flemish girl home from an office party one night and . . . That proved to Elsie that men were what she had all along resisted them for being — all alike. Instead of keeping her fingers crossed, against pregnancy, she kept something else crossed. "It takes two people to make one frigid woman," it said in a book recommended by Patchkiss, the marriage counselor she had seen on a trip to New York. It was shown, underscored, to poor Louis, who agreed to a divorce and went his separate way. None of the Marvels had heard of him since. Elsie was still only nineteen.

She fled to New York and a job as a receptionist in a broadcasting network. Harry Mercury came in for rehearsal, one winter morning, and noticed the girl huddled over her typewriter. The nape of the neck often conveys to men the idea of feminine fragility. The same vibration was set up in him by the poor little snapdragon mouth that, half open, smiled at his quips.

"Free for lunch?"

"Yes."

"Well, I'm not. We'll have to make it dinner. And fix roast beef and Yorkshire pudding. I love it."

The emotional warmth he radiated (as distinguished, she said, from mere sexual heat), his bluff schmaltz, combined with an underdog note of his own, managed to sweep her off her feet. She married him.

Then came the Bridal Night.

The same crime was enacted, the malefactor rounding the hotel table on which the same champagne bottle stood cocked and ready as the lights went out, the same knuckled limbs overpowering her in the groaning bed. Could no one wait, while she was prepared in techniques of tenderness? Did none of them read books? Let it take weeks, first the gathering of tinder, wisp by delicate wisp till she was ready for heavier kindling, and a spark discreetly struck when she was in the right mood . . . Harry had promised to be gradual, but once between the sheets forgot the arts of love and simply claimed his mate. He too tried to light a fire with a poker.

"Well, it also takes two to cure a frigid woman," he said when shown the underlined adage. He was always attentive, and detailed in his appreciation. That was part of it. Must he love *all* of her? The portions of her body on which he was prepared to rain homage took her unawares and, at length, shocked her. He worshiped with all his five senses, a contingency for which she was also unprepared. "You smell like fresh bread," he said, nuzzling the hollows of her arms and flesh of her shoulders. He rolled the tips of her breasts in his teeth. "Jujubes." He worked his way steadily southward into more tropical zones. "Wet catalpa blossoms! Pine needles in the sun! Tomato vines! My absolute and all-around flower!"

She was disgusted. She bore him two children, and a good deal of resentment. The passing years confirmed her opinion, bolstered by additional reading matter, that Woman is the victim of a culture which requires educated attainment of her while obstructing its fulfillment and keeping her at best an economic asset and at worst a physical entity, or what's-on-the-menu as Harry called her body, the frenzied consumption of which seemed at times an extension of his life as a gourmet. Mercury never quarreled with this thesis — he thought women got a rotten deal — and went to any lengths to give her the freedom and creative elbowroom she wished. Those were the days when he came home to find figurines in the oven instead of roast beef, as Moo Moo said. When their relationship declined to a point where it seemed irretrievable, they decided to "stick it out till the children were older." When they were, they got divorced.

Impossible as it seemed to have a satisfactory union with a man, living alone was worse. On a trip to Trenton for an advertising firm for which she briefly did "market research" in various supposedly typical American cities, she met Art Trautwig. The widower owned a prospering used car lot, seemed "a nice clean fellow," in her mother's eternal phrase, and possessed a patient irony. He had also the virtue of lacking ardor. After the bustling unsettledness of life in radioland with the mercurial Harry, he seemed the solid rock she had been looking for. Elsie left New York and moved under his roof with her half of the family, Chester, then not yet in his iambic pentameter phase.

Again we have the ritual of the Nuptial Night, with the malefactor (male factor?) breaking and entering in the same old way despite all the expectations aroused by a desultory courtship. However, they managed in time to settle down to a placid sort of existence, going to the movies very often when not performing tight-lipped services for one another. Elsie was rounding that equinox no woman can be blamed for hating. Regret for her womanhood was then compounded by the knowledge that she had never really wanted it, stirring contritions that had to be worked out on Art, the handy vent for her resentment of all men. In that case he might better have quietly borne the role, till the crisis passed. But he was not a psychiatrist, or even a patient, he was just a guy trying to get along on the normal supply of human instincts. Thus it was that Moo Moo, too, came upon them tending one another's things in cold hate, and beamed with pleasure on the scene.

Mrs. Marvel closed the bedroom door for her first good talk with Elsie in years, as Art was heard picking his way down the stairs. She sank into the armchair and lit a cigarette, watching Elsie pluck hairs off the suit before hanging it up.

"Lee will be over the minute they break for dinner. Of course if things get gummed up — that's show business — we can pop over and see her."

"She wouldn't like it," said Elsie from inside the closet. She might have been about to close the door on herself in a supreme act of immolation, continuing her part of the conversation in total darkness.

"She's always glad to see *me*."

"I know her better than you do." Elsie came out of the closet, exhaling in a harried way. "Could I have a cigarette? . . . You say Lee seems happy and getting along fine with the group. That's one thing about theater and entertainment people — this wonderful *esprit de corps*." She bent to take a light from the match Moo Moo held out. "I always seemed to be shut out of it. I hope Lee enjoys being part of it. But the thing I hate is her being up here all alone."

"Harry's here, Elsie," Mrs. Marvel said, finding a place for the match in an ashtray.

"Oh, God."

"Now, don't panic. You just said you hated her being up here alone. So now you've learned she isn't. Harry's working on material for fall. He has this Goddamerung Beer sponsor, you know. He's got his writers with him. But about Lee, she was dating a boy I didn't approve of for one single solitary minute. I say was because I have reason to hope it's been broken off, by a practical no-nonsense chap *I* introduced her to. He found out something very shady about this operator, never mind where, and sent him packing. Really scared him out of town. So maybe our entry is back in the running. I don't know whether you've ever heard me speak of Malcolm Johnsprang. He moved to Hickory when? Fifty-seven. Long after your time here. Malcolm is what? Twenty-five. I'm not sure but I don't believe you've ever there's the telephone."

Mrs. Marvel heaved herself to her feet and ran for the nearest extension, which was in Cotton's room across the hall. It was Lee.

"Moo Moo, are they there? . . . Sure I want to talk to Mother, but first wait. Moo Moo, I can't get away for dinner tonight. We're breaking in a replacement for that boy who got sick, and I'm on props. I'm awfully sorry, because this is your big weekend, so look. It's tomorrow that's really the big thing, isn't it, so, Moo Moo, I want very much to take somebody to the dinner if I may."

"Of course, darling." Untwisting, as if in a dream, a kink in the telephone cord, she asked, "Who?"

"That divine boy I met at your house."

"Malcolm."

"No, the other one. Neil Sligh."

"Hasn't he gone back to Boston?" Mrs. Marvel felt around her for a chair. "Because I know he moved out of the Inn . . ."

"To a place on the Cove nearer the theater. Also because I'm at the Inn and he wants everything to look right. That's how serious he is. Staying in the dump on the Cove for little old me! He sort of commutes to Boston. So tomorrow's your anniversary, I know, but that's just the whole point. Moo Moo, Neil wants to meet my family."

eleven

MARVEL had had lunch with Cotton that afternoon. Cotton had offered to leave the house freely at the first sign of relatives needing quarters and was now staying with some theater friends in a garage apartment at Smugglers Cove. He was at work on his play. Lee had read the first act at the Marvels' while waiting for Moo Moo to iron some shirts of Franchot Tone's and been ill. The purpose of the luncheon was to discuss final plans for Marvel's gift to Alma, lights for the garden. One of Cotton's friends was a stage technician who had the thing in hand. Judkins, the friend, who was a skilled electrician, had drawn a sketch which Marvel had approved, but the tricky part was the installation if it was to be the surprise Marvel intended. The plan was for Judkins to set out the floodlights and spotlights roughly according to the landscape design on the following afternoon while Alma went to the railroad station to meet the last of the arrivals, the Glimmergardens, who would take the train to Hickory from Boston after flying to Boston from Chicago. Everything would be rigged up temporarily for Alma to make any changes in later, but in such a way that a single flip of the switch would turn her beloved bowers into the glowing wonderland she had often dreamt of their becoming. The risk was that she would see or even possibly trip over the wiring, left above ground for the time being, but it would have to be taken; everyone would be in on the secret and the conspiracy to keep her from going into the back yard between the time of her return from the station and the surprise dinner ceremony. The Clan dinner was to follow a day of Open House, all outside as it now seemed likely the weather would permit.

All this settled, Marvel got his son on the subject of his future other than professional. Did he think he might marry again? Cotton thought not; why perpetuate this botch anyway?

"How could a species get started, of which all you say is true?" Marvel asked. "Why would it go on perpetuating itself?"

"That's easy. Nature's old safeguard. Every man reaches the point when he realizes he were better off unborn. By that time he has reproduced himself."

"How well I know that feeling."

"I hear Marjorie has turned to the church."

"Perhaps you should have stuck. She needed you."

"We were incompatible."

"Oh, rubbish. You young people stand on your rights too much. Do your mother and I strike you as precisely similar?"

"An atheist can't live with somebody who believes in Santa Claus. What beats me is what comfort people can find in the idea that somebody dealt this mess. There can't be any god. Can there?"

"I'm not the Answer Man, Cotton."

"There is no Christ."

"That is our cross."

"Did you read about that plane crash in Minnesota? The victims found in the trees. *In the trees.* Who is the Great Artist now, Salvador Dali?" When Marvel did not rise to this bait Cotton said: "When will people realize that we have only our own two feet to stand on, our own human courage and grace to see us through?"

"That's what I was wondering."

"There is Nothing. The universe is cooling off."

"So is your chop. Eat."

Riding home in the car Marvel indulged in a game he often played with himself. He imagined what his four children might be doing at a given moment, guessing something for each. Cotton was trudging back to the garage apartment. Evelyn he now clearly saw as flopped on a bed for a cigarette among unskillfully crammed suitcases and strewn clothes in her Chicago apartment. He smiled fondly, shifting gears with complete oblivion to the traffic light he was obeying. Evelyn was his favorite, whose slim body he had watched blossom from the days when bathing her as a child he had called her a little coin bank — a joke to which she gave blushing appreciation and her mother clucking disapproval. Something was preserved like a cameo in his mind: Alma toiling upstairs with Marvel behind her, on his way to Evelyn's room to speak to her about a new dress she wanted when she was twelve. Alma pulled herself along by the railing as she said, "Knock before you go in. She's developing." She added, puffing, "And no more coin banks and such." He remembered it clearly . . . Well, back to the game.

Evelyn was in bright shorts and halter in the Chicago

summer heat, among a bedroom chaos of which the luggage was but the half. There were heaped ashtrays, nail-grooming gear, overdue library books . . . Johnny Glimmergarden couldn't afford every novel she might want, much less every dress. What he had certainly given her was a name that fitted her as it might have few women. Glimmergarden. Flickering across a room or down the street like a golden feminine flame, her hair dancing on her shoulders, her heels tapping a rhythm for the music in every limb, she lived up to that almost impossibly euphonious proper noun.

Elsie was something else again, Marvel thought as he guiltily gave her some of his attention. She would be at the moment scowling at — Oh, no, please. Let's forget that. He must give Elsie the more tenderness for every memory of how little she had ever inspired it. *She* hadn't wanted you to put your arms around her as a tot, or fondle her ringlets, and as for jokes about coin banks . . . Marvel noted a reflex of his hand to his head, and realized he had left his Panama hat in the office. He hated hats. His palm lingered over his silver thatch, still abundant for his years. And the grayness did lend distinction, didn't it, if one could call so permanent a gift a loan . . . Had he enough life insurance? Well, many a demise was hastened by carrying too much of that, wasn't it. When he would be really old, an old man with more than enough dents in his hat . . .

What about Elsie? Let's see, what could she be doing besides scowling?

She was scowling at the ironing board. Not that she really saw what was on it. It wasn't because of that the frown had come to her face. She was thinking of something brought to mind by Moo Moo's news that Harry was here with his writers. It meant that Chaucer was in town.

Chaucer had seen Elsie often when she was married to Harry. She brought the two men coffee as they paced the Mercury apartment hammering out material, she let them try things out on her (not her best role). Chaucer ran into her at the studio and at radio-crowd parties. He quit Mercury at one point to write a daytime serial. Mercury never gave off trying to lure him back. He told Harry he was happy with *Young Mother Mary*, but off in a corner with Elsie he would air his dissatisfaction with soap opera as an art form. Chief among many headaches was the sponsor's insistence that he get "realism" into a medium he knew tolerated only falsely melodramatic realism — Elm Street widows entangled with international spies, brides-elect seized with functional blindness on the eves of their weddings. Once, preparatory to leaving for a Mexico vacation, Chaucer batted out a two-weeks' advance supply of scripts built around a milk strike. The second day of his stay in Tijuana he was routed out of bed by a phone call from the agency handling the account, demanding that he return instantly — there *was* a milk strike. "You wanted realism," Chaucer protested. "What could be more true to life?" "Did you hear what I said? There *is a milk strike*. Do you want us taking sides in labor disputes or something? Get back here on the next plane and write it out of the script."

He had done so, but dropped radio drama and returned to Mercury, who was grateful to have him back after eight months with writers he couldn't stand.

In Elsie's response to his troubles, he sensed more and more her own cheerless misery. He had little capacity for either friendship or romance, but he had an unfailing antenna for frustrated women. It was those he went after. Neither especially attractive nor interesting himself, certainly not rich, he wasted no time pursuing the unavailable flesh of glamour girls or those otherwise out of his reach, confining his sexual forays to those as lackluster as himself, the sad breed who are grateful for any attention. He could spot them at a glance, and the rewards were often great. He made no overtures to the wives of friends or employers, but soon after her return from a Reno divorce he called Elsie and asked her to dinner.

Elsie's response to Chaucer grew out of her loneliness, her fear of loneliness, and her puzzled wretchedness over her failure as a woman to yield to pleasure. Perhaps another try with another man would help, in some way not anticipated. Wasting no time on preliminaries once a target had been elected, Chaucer came to the point well before coffee. She resisted at first, but when sheer repetition acquired the quality of ardor, she agreed to come to his hotel apartment the next afternoon.

She was firmer than ever in the tolls exacted: an affair had more even than a marriage to be "beautiful." Chaucer was duly gallant: flowers to her place, flowers in his when she arrived, champagne. He waited in the sitting room while she got into the silk nightgown she had brought (in a Manila envelope to encourage assurances at the desk that she came bearing finished stenographic work for Mr. Chaucer).

"Do you know any poetry?" she asked, in the bed.

Chaucer lifted his head from her stomach, as though some abnormality had been proposed. "Whah?"

"Poetry. I'd like you to recite some."

This was an area with which Chaucer had but scant familiarity. He could recall very little verse, and no love verse at all, at least in the heat of passion. Yet he sensed her need to hear some; she needed a ceremony of grace, some evidence that they were not just animals wallowing in clean sheets.

"Anything," she said desperately, seeing his stalled profile against the window shade as he sat beside her now, one arm across her, braced on his hand. He could think of only one or two poems from high-school English, and they ran together in his mind. He seized her and said into her bosom:

> "You know, we French stormed Ratisbon:
> A mile or so away,
> On a little mound, Napoleon
> Stood on our storming-day;
> The something something bubbling groan,
> Unknelled, uncoffined, and unknown."

"Call that romantic?"

Elsie lay with her head turned away on the pillow, examined by Chaucer with interest from a sitting position. The effort to evoke something more suited to the occasion brought results that surprised him. He suddenly remembered a recitation contest in Friday Assembly in which he had participated, representing his English Literature class. He intoned his entry now with feeling:

> "Build thee more stately mansions, O my soul,
> As the swift seasons roll!"

he began. The act of recollection revived another memory — the disappointment he had experienced when in face of all assurances from friends that he had been better than anybody he had been awarded only the third prize. Stirred to vindicate himself, as if before an audience giving him another chance, he declaimed with mounting expression sitting in the bed, executing the gestures with which he had swept through the lines on the assembly platform and enunciating with dramatic diction:

"Leave thy low-vaulted past!
Let each new temple, nobler than the last,
Shut thee from heaven with a dome more vast,
Till thou at length art free,
Leaving thine outgrown shell by life's unresting sea!"

She was genuinely moved. Pulling the covers over drawn-up knees, as she sat apart to have a cigarette, she said:

"People had values then. Why don't we? We live without them, on an utterly materialistic level."

An interesting discussion ensued, over the remainder of champagne, on the evils of culture without standards. Not in the best of moods over this turn of events Chaucer spoke crisply, sometimes caustically, proving to Elsie again that men were "hostile."

He was curt when he ran into her on the street some time later, after an interval in which Elsie had tried again with another man, this one an investment broker of middle years who didn't get along with his wife. She hoped that a companionate unhappiness might lead to a fruitful rapport between them, and an ability on her part to feel something and thus overcome the block which a psychiatrist was also trying to help her analyze her way out of. Chaucer did not hesitate to give her the benefit of some other advice. "With all this sleeping around," he said, "you're getting to be known as a nymphomaniac."

"Well, Lee's not getting off for dinner," Moo Moo said, returning from the phone call. "But she's coming tomorrow night, and guess what. She's bringing her young man. Now everybody'll have a chance to meet him."

She directed her last words through the curtains of the window, to which she had gone on hearing another car below.

"Here's your father, thank God. About time!"

She hurried down to intercept Marvel on the porch.

"They're beginning to arrive," she whispered, smiling for the benefit of any who might be watching them, "but the minute you've said hello to everyone, meet me upstairs. There's something I've got to tell you."

twelve

"HOW COULD YOU get yourself into such a damn fool mess?"

Marvel lay on the bed braced on his elbows, like the man in the foreground of Seurat's picture of the Grande Jatte. Any secret amusement with the now fully told story was dissipated, and his face bore a look of brooding distaste for what must be shouldered. "What on earth do you *care* about your ancestors?"

"Don't you?"

"Of course I do, but not in that way. My grandfather —"

"The Civil War means nothing here. We've been through all that." She moved in and out of his fixed gaze across the foot of the bed, like a sentry.

"The trouble we go to to come up to scratch with fools."

"Intelligent people we don't have to impress. They take us for what we are. We've been through all that too. You still don't seem to understand women. I'll explain it once more: *the sillier they are the more you have to beat them at their own game*. And it's not your ancestors you do it for, it's your children. I thought this would be such a nice present to give them for the Anniversary. Make them all buck up and take some pride in their family. And for your grandchildren. Think how nice it would be for Lee if he'd stayed on that ship. Rat! Social status means everything, whether you like it or no. Think what being a D.A.R. did for Susie Wetwilliam. The best circles, doors opened, presented at Buckingham Palace."

Here Marvel sat up and a gleam of interest kindled in his eye.

"Let me get this straight. You want your ancestors to have fought King George so your daughters can meet Queen Elizabeth?"

"Yes. What's wrong with that?"

Marvel fell back, this time flat. "When is this young man coming did you say?"

"Tomorrow for dinner. He wants to meet all of us."

"I shouldn't wonder."

"The insolence. The utter cheek. I wouldn't trust him with a ten-foot pole."

"I'm rather looking forward to meeting him too. Of course he'll put his best foot forward. We won't meet his character, just his personality. You're absolutely sure now—"

"Oh yes!" Alma screamed in a whisper, clasping her head. "Don't *you* try to mix me up now. So the Anniversary isn't to be fun any more, it's to catch a greased pig."

"That's supposed to be fun."

"It's all right for you to joke. I've got to be ready to stand up to him, and to the whole town." Though his gaze was elsewhere, on its border Marvel could see her hands at their eternal work of tucking in blouse-ends. He had a vision of them as shirttails being stuffed into jeans, after which she would buckle on shooting irons to go out and show them. These fancies that demote the loved one, and confiscate dignity, O Lord forgive!

"Anyway now you're up to date on everything," said Alma who had also told him about Beaumont and about the Aronson business. She opened the door. "Let's go downstairs. People will think there's something wrong . . . Well, Chester. All settled?"

"Such was my supposition, and in principle 'tis true. But on the bed assigned to me, me thought, me finds the counterpane disturbed, as though my roommate had rested on't. Developments more curious than this vex my mind, so doubts are breeding in't. Beneath the spread I find these crumpled husks that various sweets did once invest—Oh Henry, Milky Way, and Charleston Chew. So I must ask the question once again to set the matter straight: which is my side of the room?"

"Either one." Mrs. Marvel snatched the wrappers and thrust them into a skirt pocket for later disposal. "Come downstairs now, Chester. The grownups will be wanting cocktails, and there's plenty of Cokes and things for you youngsters."

They were passing a closed door, behind which Elsie could be heard. ". . . and for God's sake don't smell everything before you eat it. How do you think I like it, married to a *thin* slob . . ."

"I thought you and Beaumont were playing catch."

"We lost the ball in the raspberry patch."

"I want to see somebody on the teeter-totter," Marvel said, steering Chester down the stairs. "Those playground things have been left there all these years, waiting for grandchildren."

"Beaumont's not the best company on the other end of a seesaw," Chester said, in plain English. "He gets you up there and won't let you down, like a coon up a tree. He has the advantage."

"He can't help that. It's important for you to be nice to him. O.K.?"

"O.K."

"Well, Bushrod, fix your old man one while you're at it. And sherry for Mother. Then let's all go outside. It's going to be a beautiful evening. No soda for me — water. So Aronson's a Swede and Beau set fire to the summerhouse. Sorry to hear it," Marvel said, sweeping the disagreeable out of the way with characteristic haste, "but let's try to forget everything and have some fun. Elsie! Art! Come on down!" A doorclap followed the summons, and Art shuffled down with his empty glass. Marvel thought it inexcusable of Bushrod to splash Bourbon into glasses without using his mother's candle snuffer. He covered his irritation by moving to Alma's side and putting his arm around her. She sensed the sudden current of his tenderness, and put hers around him.

Outside, Chester found a chance to ask Moo Moo: "Where's my father? I know he's here."

"Shh! He's lecturing tonight. I'm not supposed to tell because he doesn't want any of us to come. He'll be here tomorrow. I know he's anxious to see you. Don't say what I told you, here comes your mother. Well, now we're complete as far as today is concerned. It's such a lovely evening why don't we have dinner out here on the terrace too. Ben? Where is your grandfather?"

"Down cellar to get the wine."

Marvel stood a moment contemplating his modest collection. He took the same pleasure in merely handling his bottles that he did in fingering the volumes in his library. He drew several fondly from the honeycombs, read the labels, thrust them back, or held them momentarily up to the light. On the floor two cases of champagne stood ready for the big dinner tomorrow night, as well as a case of white wine for the punch to be served during the day's Open House.

At last he pulled out two bottles of Pommard and blew a cloud of dust from each. Wiping them with a cloth, he smiled. His words with Cotton at lunch about compatibility met a memory of the first glass of Burgundy he had poured his own bride of a year. Tired of the sweet sauternes to which her taste ran, he came home one night with a Chablis. One sip had made her pull a face and reach, to his horror, for the sugar bowl, as though she were drinking coffee. A slight and silly incident, but enough to start building a case of incompatibility on if you were so minded. Nor had that been all! Her famous remark at a party, "I can't say I like your Proust, Ben, but, my, he certainly has a wonderful command of the English language," was another inkling of what had to be shouldered. As for Bordeaux and Burgundies, she had continued to sweeten to taste, setting the spoon down quickly after stirring, and sipping before the undissolved sugar settled to the bottom, for these wines must be drunk turbulent. On an early anniversary she had insisted they have a jeremiad of champagne. The less said about the Erotica Symphony the better.

They did dine on the terrace, Bushrod simplifying the disruption for Ruby by personally setting up two card tables together outside. Chester and Beaumont were seated at the picnic table on the grass, to get better acquainted. Bushrod loved to carve so the roast of beef was set before him and he did the honors happily. When Ruby had settled down in the kitchen with a plate of dinner for herself he carried her a glass of the Pommard, which she took without looking up from the magazine she was reading. Bushrod hurried back to the table to continue a discussion he had going with Art Trautwig.

"No, the housing bill was one of the most important pieces of legislation in years and your congressman voted wrong on it as I remember. What's his name again, from your district there?"

"I don't know."

Bushrod lifted his head from an unbitten ear of corn, his mouth open. "You mean you don't know the name of your congressman?"

"We were out of the country when he was elected."

"Where?"

"Spain."

This time Bushrod set the corn down.

"*Spain.* You mean you could go to a fascist country like that?" He looked around at the others, inviting them to share his incredulity. "Don't you know with every dollar you spend there you support that rotten dictatorship?"

"We didn't have many to spend. We saved up two years for that vacation. Anyhow, it's a beautiful country. Didn't we find it so, Els?"

"Lovely. Truly lovely. You're in another world there, all right."

"Well, Clara and I feel differently about that question. We think you should boycott what's bad and support what's good. Matter of fact we picketed a travel agency down home for exhibiting Spain posters in the window. I mean, Sis," Bushrod went on, turning to Elsie, "with the state of the world —"

"With the state of the world what it is let's at least forget the damn place while we're at dinner," Art said. "Moo Moo, this is wonderful corn for the first of the summer. Where does it come from?"

"Virginia I believe."

"How about that regime!"

There was general laughter at Art's joke, but it wasn't enough to dissolve the tension between the two men. They ate their corn as though in a race to finish first. Each nibbled a row of kernels then twitched without interruption to the next row in a way that reminded more than one there of the animated cartoon in which the consumption of an ear of corn was pictured in terms of a typewriter carriage moved furiously from right to left with a bell rung at each reversal. Husks flew from Bushrod's lips like shells from a clip of machine-gun bullets. Mrs. Marvel's mind was working swiftly. Changing the subject might leave their hostility undischarged, maybe for the rest of the visit, while a discreet pursuit of the argument could lead to its friendly resolution. She therefore remarked as neutrally as she could: "Our Secretary of State visited Spain recently, didn't he? Doesn't that mean we're on good terms with them officially?"

Bushrod wiped his mouth quickly with his napkin. "The present Secretary of State is not a diplomat, he's an exchange student."

"Do you agree with that, Art?"

"Nope. I think this administration is doing all it can."

"He can say that again!"

"Cotton? What's your opinion? Is our plan for winning the uncommitted nations a good one?"

The trouble was that Cotton was deep in a dream of this as a faculty dinner on a conservative Eastern campus and in his response chose to impersonate a college president of great asininity: "Woe betide, you see, any attempt to buy off foreign hate with a sackful of toys called Foreign Aid. The more you give them the more they'll hate you. The battle for men's minds, you see, must be waged with ideas, not a materialistic playing of Santa Claus."

"Hear, hear!" from Bushrod. But before he could swallow something in time to develop this his wife spoke up. She was on Cotton's right. Gazing at a point midway between their plates, and smiling her apologetic smile, she said, "Cotton, I gather from this and something else you said a while ago about matter being an illusion, that you're a Zen Buddhist?"

Cotton's lips twitched forward once. "I meant that in another, you see, connection. I was making the point that the more we analyze matter the less it resembles anything we know of it with our five senses. This table is a dance of atoms, this cloth anything *but* the blue it seems, blue being the color it reflects rather than is. So I merely made the point, you see, that no mystic can hold matter to be more illusory than our scientists show it to be with their instruments, which are themselves illusory, et cetera, et cetera, et cetera."

Mrs. Marvel returned from the kitchen with a steaming bowl of fresh corn.

"Now *you*, Cotton, believe all matter is illusion, while you, Art, think this administration is just ducky. Perhaps the truth lies somewhere in between the two."

The bowl was passed around while hands helped themselves to it.

"That's a very interesting idea, Cotton," Marvel said the length of the table to his son. "I've just been reading a book on contemporary philosophy, and I must say there's nothing as neat as that in it. Are you maybe moving in that direction? Zen Buddhism?"

Cotton was so deliberate in his response that the benefit of it was never given. Elsie chimed in first, "That Oriental philosophy throws me. You have to be a genius to understand it."

"And a fool to believe it," Art muttered.

"Well, I've been rereading some of the German philosophers," Cotton said, "particularly the idealists, in the light of what we were just saying about matter. I must say Leibnitz still makes stimulating speculation. You remember his philosophy of the windowless monads. Very stimulating."

"So, Cotton, you're still interested in monads," Elsie joshed.

"Well, intellectual often goes with high-sexed," said Mrs. Marvel, smiling tolerantly into her plate.

"No, Mother, *mo*nads. Units of reality."

"Oh, yes. Those." Moo Moo clapped her hands. New subject. "Who's read any good novels lately?"

"I can't," said Bushrod. "It seems to me writers no longer have any more class consciousness these days."

"Oh, I don't agree with you there. John O'Hara for one is full of it. He never *fails* to tell you not only what class every character was in, in what college or university, but all his clubs and fraternities and prep school as well. No, I'd say he has plenty of it. Too much."

Most of them ate rather busily in the silence that followed this. Marvel was the first to recover, perhaps from long experience in handling such conversational turns. "Well, if you look at it that way, my dear, you might say the same of Marquand."

She nodded. "Yes, Marquand too. Yes, I agree with that."

Mrs. Marvel had it thoroughly planned that the food would consist wholly of their remembered favorites or her known specialties, and the dessert was to be a chocolate soufflé, her knockout. It was not to be entrusted to Ruby or have its ingredients mixed beforehand, so they were all ordered to relax outside and let their dinners settle while she went in to bake it. "Give Beau an extra helping," Bushrod whispered with a glance at the charred gazebo.

The men strolled under the trees and among the flowerbeds smoking cigars. Elsie helped Ruby carry the dishes in, mostly to have a private moment with Moo Moo.

"Where is he?" she said. "I don't see why you can't tell me."

Mrs. Marvel sighed and consulted the kitchen clock. "Well, it's too late for anybody to go hear him now so I've kept my promise. Harry's lecturing tonight at Winooski College. That summer conference?"

"*Lec*turing." Elsie sat on a stool, huddled over herself as though frozen stiff — her eternal posture in all weathers. How often hadn't Elsie sat on that stool, airing her grievances and unburdening her soul. Tonight she looked more wretched than ever. "What on earth on?"

"Why We Laugh," said Moo Moo, reaching under the sink for a mixing bowl.

thirteen

HARRY stepped up to the lectern in a mood of black misery. He was gut-sick. The same pains that flashed through his middle when the mike went hot in a broadcasting studio harried him now, to be ignored, to be risen above. He wet his whistle from the tumbler of water. This audience would be worse than a studio audience, from whom the first laugh cleared the air and set him at his ease; they would just sit here tonight with no sign that he was making anything but a damn fool of himself with his dissertation. How had he let himself in for such a thing! Gazing out over the slouched forms sprinkled through the auditorium he picked out Prufrock's in the last row. There was the sadist.

While he drew his manuscript like a tin sword from his bosom, he appraised the house further. It was hard to know whether sixty people in four hundred chairs made it better or worse. They ranged from very young to very old. A rooster of a man with pince-nez on his beak sat with pencil and notepad ready. Mercury almost laughed. Behind him sat a woman stiff as a stick in a violet dress. In the haze of introductions beforehand they had been presented as faculty members, but of what? The college or just the summer conference? Out there must be some well-known artists and writers — who were they? What did they want? They wanted to know why they laughed, yet they all looked as though they had spent the last twenty years sucking on lemons. As he flattened down his manuscript he remembered an accomplished lecturer once saying that success lay in singling out one member of the audience and speaking directly to him or her, thus reducing the assembly to one and the auditorium to a living room. Mercury's eye fell on a grubby girl in black who looked as though she would believe anything, slumped in a front seat beside a bearded youth also in black. On a book in her lap he could make out the name "Sartre."

"Comedy is the cloak of tragedy turned inside out."

Mercury cleared his throat suggestively and waited for the laugh, till he remembered this wasn't a gag but an epigram, besides being utter twaddle. He returned to his typescript like a dog to a plate of something it had never eaten before.

"Why do we laugh? That question has been answered in different ways by different men, and I propose this evening to give you some of those interpretations, and then in conclusion to see, between us, what if anything they have in common.

"Now, basic to most amusement is the element of surprise, a chair pulled out from under someone, a word or thought given an unexpected twist. But why *laugh* at that? Why not make a baying sound, or growl, or lift one foot? It is interesting to note that when a baby is suddenly surprised, it laughs. If it is swung in the air toward its mother, then at the last second swung in another direction, toward its father say, it will laugh. It finds a nervous resolution of its fear in the safe harbor of its father's arms. This and a professor on a sofa with a broken leg," he said, turning two pages at once.

It was certainly a new experience, knowing from the fact that you could hear a pin drop that they were with you.

"Bergson's theory of humor goes as follows . . ."

The faces swam into one face, sorted themselves out again in a stir, a cough, a smile.

"Let us examine another of these 'safe harbors.' What is the Freudian interpretation of laughter?"

He found the tumbler of water and took another gulp. His air of brooding intensity rose mainly from a stone in his shoe, acquired on the academic gravel.

"When Freud first began offering his interpretation of dreams," he resumed, trying to work the pebble under a more comfortable part of his arch, "he noticed that people laughed. This indicated to him that dreams and laughter must have something in common. What was it? According to him, the release of hostility *in a socially acceptable fashion.*" (Deadhead bastards) "Animosities and anxieties get by the censor in both cases by wearing disguises. We all know the sadism of the wit, the sadness of the clown . . ."

He got through it somehow. At least nobody walked out. As he reached the last page a flood of relief came over him. He sat down to a round of applause. Waiting on the platform for the chairman to conclude his expressions of gratitude and dismiss the meeting, he thought of the steak he had promised himself, after the long day of indigestion. But what was this the chairman was saying?

"— has brilliantly covered the subject, nevertheless you are all looking forward to the question period. I'm sure your minds are all popping with things to ask him. Please rise, state your name, and the question."

Mercury cast a stricken look at the rotten Indian, who rose and glided out the back door into the corridor, like a snake vanishing behind a rock. After a thirty-second silence, the kind that always precedes a rain of queries from the floor, Mercury rose and, shrugging modestly at the chairman, started for the platform steps. He was stopped in his tracks by a figure rising from the front row.

It was the beatnik girl in black, who proved to be five feet tall and round as a cheese.

"My name is Feluka Dobbs. I would like to ask Mr. Mercury this. His various interpretations are oal very well, but what of the controlling somatic agent in the phenomenon we call laughter? Is it not the phrenic nerve, which leads to the diaphragm — and incidentally asthmatics like to laugh — it gives them relief — Well, in view of oal this, to what extent would Mr. Mercury say that, by thus bringing the diaphragm into play, laughter serves to combine in a single nervous discharge the affection-hostility syndrome at work in oal our make-ups?"

The chairman moved away from the lectern with an invitational smile at Mercury, who had nowhere to go but toward it. What was the girl talking about? What the hell was the phrenic nerve? If it led to the diaphragm maybe it was his own that was acting up. He really ought to go see a doctor, maybe this time it wasn't psychosomatic. The pains were again flickering in his weary and long-suffering gut. He gulped. "Uh . . ." He swallowed another mouthful of water, rolling an eye at the door through which his writer had escaped. He wiped his mouth with the back of his hand, having dribbled somewhat down his chin. "I would say that, basically and fundamentally, yes, that is right, Miss. For we all have that within us."

"We oal have what within us?"

"What you said."

Madly there came to mind: "Yassuh, Kingfish, we sho' has dat affection-hostility stuff, we sho' is chockful o' dat, yas*suh!* Splain dat to de peoples so dey understands it better. Splain dat to 'em." Jerking himself smartly back to reality he thought of something else. He remembered a word: "dichotomy." It was his impression that in all intellectual discussions these days the first person to use that word won the argument. Twenty-five years ago this would not have been the case. "Orientation" would have picked up the marbles then. But today it was indubitably "dichotomy."

"The thing we must remember," he said, striking out wildly along those lines, "is that we all have this dichotomy in our natures. It is perhaps fundamentally the love-hate dichotomy. I would add that it is furthermore to a large extent, an extent perhaps undreamed of by the analysts, and I don't mean just psychoanalysts, because I have presented the opinions of several whose approach is not psychiatric at all—and we must remember in this connection . . ." The thread of his syntax was now so hopelessly tangled that the audience could not have been expected to follow it either, so when he finished with "that what I say is essentially sound," nobody knew *what* he had said, hence no issue could reasonably have been taken with the answer. So the girl nodded and sat down. She leaned her head toward her friend and they whispered together.

By now he had learned the technique of handling questions, and after a few more he looked at the clock on the wall, shook hands with the chairman and a blur of additional functionaries, and fled through a side door. He found Prufrock waiting for him with a taxi with the motor running.

"You were great."

Mercury spent the eight-mile ride to Hickory staring chin-in-hand out the cab window, after emptying his shoe. The mixture of relief and rage inside him was by no means resolved, nor the question of how much of either of it was Bill's responsibility. To say nothing of whether Bill's exact reproduction of his posture at his own window expressed sympathy or concealed mirth. Another puzzle – to what extent the revived pangs in his middle were those of hunger. He was starved, and didn't feel like eating. A final turmoil lay in the war between his wish to go to the Marvels' and his doubt that he should, at least at this hour without having first dined. The bad Indian wore moccasins.

"You eat yet?"

"Of course not, Harry. You know that."

"Why didn't you tell me there was a question period?"

"I didn't know. And isn't there always?"

"What the hell is the phrenic nerve?"

"How should I know? But you did all right."

"Then you were listening at the door out there."

He took Bill along for a steak dinner at a restaurant they had all been recently discovering, where you got what Harry called same-day service. They grabbed the only available table in the place. The waiter hurried up and drew some silver from his pockets which he laid out with casual precision. Mercury's humor continued foul. He drank three Bourbons-on-the-rocks before their steaks were in sight. Bill stopped at one, having guessed that Mercury had committed himself to one of his rare, but roaring, drunks, apparently necessary to the periodic ventilation of his spirits, and that he might have to stay along and put him to bed. It was a ministration he was used to, and that had a certain value to him; it both exercised some unused biceps of humanity, and enabled him to witness a person's deterioration, which intoxicated him in another way.

Mercury leaned back and got him into focus.

"I had a chance to look at that new material. I see I'm taking a sick parrot to the polyclinic. That that intellectual type humor you were hired to write?"

"Me cerebral. But always get clunked on head when make with the nuances, so me get discouraged and go back to meat-and-potatoes stuff. Boss no like tenuous kind of thing." With Harry half stewed *he* could let down the bars as though he himself were, and besides Harry had always been amused when he did this character, grunting subtleties. "Me think offbeat symptomatic of our culture. Human nature heap decadent. Me go back, seek what Henry Seidel Canby call seminal values. Me from old tribe of seminal Indians. Many moons ago —"

"Wasn't your father a Cherokee?"

"You're thinking of Will Rogers. Me son of Chippewa, but only illegitimately. So that O.K. You see, Mother have more self-respect than to marry man who seduce her. Ugh!

Very fine point. Not for nothing she known as Sweet Sioux. Speaking of fine points, the jokes in that sketch about —"

"I don't want to talk about it now. And where's Chaucer?"

With a load on, Mercury ceased rapidly to resemble himself, which was perhaps after all the purpose of a bat — a night's self-exorcism. From ragging Prufrock he went on to ragging the waiter, unheard-of behavior for him. From dreading to see Elsie he insisted on seeing her, thumping the table as though she ought to be fetched bodily to the Sizzling Platter. The rabbit running from physical violence became an old dog spoiling for a fight. He demanded to see Pentecost, now far away in the White Mountains of New Hampshire. By the end of the dinner he had polished off three more whiskeys. Prufrock led him from the restaurant protesting a grasp of Godot possessed by no known exponent of that role.

An hour ago Mercury would have thought anyone crazy who told him that shortly he would take a poke at a brother-in-law whom he had never met.

He had decided by now that he would look in on the Marvels. So when Bill ruled that out of the question in his condition he knew he must first shake his keeper. He did so by proceeding docilely to his room at the Inn when led there, sneaking out again when the other had gone to his. He walked five blocks to the Marvel place.

When he got there, it was dark except for a light burning in an upstairs bedroom or two. It was nearly midnight. In anticipation of the big day ahead tomorrow everyone had gone to bed except for Bushrod and Art Trautwig, who, having indeed talked out their differences amicably since dinner, were having a quiet nightcap on the terrace. Art had a stabler version of Prufrock's pleasure in watching a mind tick. Bushrod had plunged into a long, historical analysis of the entire problem of anti-Semitism. "This is the case against the Jew," he said, warming to the subject. "I'll list all the arguments, one by one, and then show how each is fallacious and ridiculous in the face of reason and facts." When Bushrod marshaled arguments, he clutched in his fist, rather than simply touched, each finger as he ticked the points off in turn.

"One, Jews are egotistical," he began, grasping a thumb for the first point. "Two, they never create wealth. They only use it. They use it or they loan it . . ."

It was at this moment that Harry Mercury, weaving unsteadily across the dark lawn in pursuit of the voices he could hear back there, walked up and stood listening. Bushrod grasped his middle finger. "Jews are never farmers —"

"Heil Hitler!"

The two rose from their chairs and turned.

"Bravo!" Harry said, clapping. "Less go out'n burn coupla swastikas, eh? Good going."

"I don't believe . . ." Bushrod said uncertainly, coming forward a step. Then he recognized the figure. "Harry Mercury! As I live and breathe! I'm sorry we've never met before, but then that's my . . . I'm Bushrod, Elsie's brother. This is Art Trautwig, her present —" Having by this time taken in Harry's condition Bushrod thought better of identifying Art more specifically. Mercury was in fact dancing slowly about the terrace with his fists up, in the manner of old-time prizefighters.

"Put 'em up."

"What? I . . . don't believe I quite . . ."

"Put 'em up!" He shuffled rhythmically about on the flagstones. "Don't have to say care to step outside — we are outside. Care repeat some those charges? Ready defend 'em physically, are we, well as shoot off mouth?"

"Now look. You misunderstand." Bushrod backed slowly off into the grass, his palm on Mercury's chest to keep him at arm's length. The gesture inflamed Mercury further.

"I understand perfectly. Some of my best friends and all that. My hearing isn't that bad, pal. I heard you the first time. And this is what I've got to say!"

Bushrod had been signing to Art to steal up around Mercury and help subdue him discreetly from behind. Therefore when Mercury's fist shot out and clipped him on the chin, it caught him completely by surprise, or at least off balance. He stumbled against a chair left out on the lawn, and before he knew what else had happened he was lying flat on his back on the grass with Harry astride him. Rather than offer further resistance, he thought it best to continue reasoning from this position.

"Permit me to clarify the situation. I was putting the case against the Jew *as it exists in popular fallacy*. I was coming to the rebuttal next."

"You were?"

"Yes." He rolled his eyes up into his head. "Ask him."

Art nodded, hanging over them both with a drink in his hand. He seemed not too perturbed at the sight of Bushrod getting his lumps, but he did what he could to set the matter straight.

"That's right. He was just airing the whole thing. He's up here trouble-shooting for some civil liberties outfit. He's O.K."

Bushrod smiled up at the assailant seated on his chest,

with an effect of almost coy communication. "I'm the liberal one."

Harry dismounted and got to his feet, somewhat sobered. They both stood breathing heavily, brushing down their clothes. Harry picked some grass from the other's back for him.

"Sorry . . . Ought to have some coffee. No, hell, I had some coffee. I mean I wish I hadn't . . . Sorry."

"It's quite all right, old man. Sit down and let's go on with the discussion like two intelligent people. Three," Bushrod amended, politely including Art. "Now, I was going to state the argument next that the Jews own Hollywood. The Jews *don't* own Hollywood."

"Ever been there?"

"The banks own Hollywood. And very few Jews are bankers, popular superstition to the contrary notwithstanding. I don't know if you have ever read the list of directors of an average bank —"

Harry was bored with the subject. He gazed at the dark house. "Is everybody in bed?"

"Yes. Getting ready for the big day tomorrow. When we all hope you'll be with us. Look, if you're not feeling so hot, maybe . . ."

"Yeah. Maybe better go back to the Inn. Stomach not so good again . . ."

"You need a good night's sleep too. Come on, I'll take you in my car."

Art began an offer to accompany them, but Bushrod cut him off with a shake of his head, apparently thinking it best for some reason that he take Mercury alone. So Art went into the house through the kitchen while Bushrod piloted Harry toward the sidewalk. There Mercury decided the walk home would do him good, so they started up the street arm in arm, their murmurs drifting back on the quiet night.

Mrs. Marvel thought she'd heard some commotion outside but did not get out of bed to investigate, being glued to the book she was reading.

It was a collection of "cases" from the files of Charles Patchkiss, the marriage counselor Elsie went to, which she'd found in the Trautwigs' room. She had just finished "Case Number Three — Problems of Ethical Difference and Money Matters" when she heard Art come up. She was riffling through the book looking for another chapter to read when her eye was caught by the title "Case Number Nineteen — The Problem of Sex and the New England Heritage."

She had been reading for about five minutes in this when she nudged the sleeping Marvel and said, "Do you smell smoke?"

"Oh, God, you're always smelling smoke," Ben said, rolling over. "Women are always smelling smoke. Put the light out and go to sleep. We've a big day tomorrow."

She knew she ought. But before doing so she slipped out of bed to investigate. The odor was unmistakable in the hall. She seemed to trace it to the Trautwigs' bedroom. She stood beside the closed door, sniffing cautiously. No mistake about it. She rapped quietly with one knuckle.

Art came to the door barefoot and in shirtsleeves. "Yes?"

A checked skirt of Elsie's lay across the ironing board, which he was obviously pressing. "Nothing. Good night, Art."

After closing the door again, she stood a moment in the

hallway, smiling. She heaved a sudden pleasurable sigh. It was so good to have them all back in the nursery again. So good. It was as if they had never left it. It was as if they belonged there.

fourteen

THOUGH THE LAST asleep, Mrs. Marvel was the first one up. Ben had honored the day by beginning it with an embrace, giving proof of his love as he wished. She had been glad to see him roll, porpoise-like, away and go back to sleep, stealing, herself, down to the kitchen to fix the buttermilk pancakes for which she was celebrated. She wanted the Day begun that way, as so many days had begun in years past.

Elsie slipped in as she was getting her utensils together and, having wished her a happy anniversary, took her place on the stool and began.

"Have you any idea what men are like?"

"Vaguely. I've been married forty years, and what God sees fit to create . . ."

"You used to take us out to Uncle George's farm in the summer and all."

"I know. Being realistic about sex and manure and so on. I can't see that you are."

"You aren't." Mrs. Marvel wheeled about with a huge wooden spoon in her hand which she appeared about to wield like a gavel, rapping for order once and for all. "Look. I've been married like I say forty years. After all that time I don't want to learn about sex from the issue of that union."

Nevertheless she was. Elsie reopened certain considerations relative to her husbands, and since she had a history of failure Mrs. Marvel felt she owed her a chance to state her case. But she also reserved the right to spare herself the needlessly graphic detail into which Elsie went, and for this she had developed a technique of censorship. It consisted in deleting, by noises judiciously distributed, pans rattled and water spigots opened at the right moment, particulars too intimate for Mrs. Marvel's taste. She did not want too much information. She knew by instinct born of experience just what the crucial words would be and where they were likely to fall, and how by split-second timing to excise them from the narrative. If she hadn't an egg beater in her hands to set whirring just then, or a ladle to clatter in a crock, why, she would clear her throat loudly or cough. She had already missed the name of the husband Elsie had launched the first bill of particulars about, so it was a triune, composite masculine more or less anthropoid form she had a sort of phantasmagoric vision of climbing omnivorously all over her daughter in the bestial dark, in a recital that reached her something like this:

"—isfied till he's drawn blood. He wants to *rattle* my *bang* and *clatter* my *smack* and tickle my little *kerplush*." Here Mrs. Marvel found herself momentarily in the no man's land between the sink and the icebox with no defense, and she got more information than she wanted. "Think of passing a lozenge back and forth in your teeth, as though we're pigeons or something."

"He never worked from Thursday on, and that gave you a long week-eh-heh-hend," Mrs. Marvel said, thinking she knew who this was.

"Never a smidgeon of beauty to it. Never a suggestion that a woman is a delicate instrument to be played on, to draw exquisite music from. Do you know what he likes to bite?"

"Wait a minute." Mrs. Marvel grabbed a frying pan by the handle and ran across the floor to the range, planning to clap it down on a burner – too late. She heard what he liked to bite.

She looked around with absolute nonchalance. Wiping her face with her apron, she said blandly, "You've got sex on the brain."

"And when not a mistress, a mother. Stomachaches, headaches, sinus. Oh, those sinus years."

"You're what. Thirty-nine."

"From nineteen forty-four to nineteen forty-eight, every time I looked at him he had two sticks coming out of his nose, like a walrus."

"Couldn't you think that was when he may have needed you most? When he was plugged up with cotton?"

"He didn't need me, then or ever, except for one thing. If I felt more that I was wanted, for myself, I might have stuck. Sometimes he stood up in the cedar closet to clear his head. Nobody is that important. Then the lashing out at one another. Once we were playing badminton at the Everlys'. The shuttlecock went way up in the air and down straight for the net, and both thinking it would come down on his side, we both slashed at it with all our might – coming down with the racquets on one another. I hit his shoulder and he grazed my head. Showing that sub –"

"Yes. Then what? The scenes, the recriminations," Mrs. Marvel said, cueing her along less erotic lines in a recitative she had been through before. "Till he would say something mean and you would forgive him."

"Getting him mad. 'I don't want to be forgiven, I want the indictment quashed!' And so on, into the night. One night he was really cutting. I'll spare you the details. But at the height of the argument, in a burst of self-hate —"

"Yes?"

"— he struck me."

Mrs. Marvel sank onto a chair. She thought she had mastered the current jargon where everything was the opposite of what it seemed — a man is arrogant out of insecurity, etc. — but this was one too many. She wiped her face again and said: "Have you joined any clubs?"

"Oh, clubs. And now take Art. He smells everything before he eats it. Would you take him to a church supper?"

"Well, they say the Unitarians are very broad —"

"When he drinks his coffee he says 'Ah!' after each sip."

"He's a Yea-sayer. He hits out at life."

"He's a beast."

"I will not have you talk that way about my son-in-law."

"Well, he is. All men are."

"That's better. But don't single him out. Why did you marry him then?"

"You don't notice those things beforehand — habits and all. I had eyes only for him. Have I ever told you his specialty?"

Mrs. Marvel rose and began to beat the batter, which she had all this time managed to assemble, plying the spoon briskly about in her vast yellow crock.

"He likes limericks. He knows more 'love poems,' as he

calls them, than any man I ever met. Whispering them to me has become part of the ritual. Outraging me seems to give him pleasure. I suppose it's his way of getting a defloration every time. As he recites one in my ear, he'll gently lift my *clatter* and *clack* and *rattle* and *bzzzz*" — for Mrs. Marvel had the electric mixer going in the batter now, and she stood there watching it churn till she sensed Elsie had finished, serene in her safety from this confidence. She had had a purpose in giving her her head. After a moment she shut the blender off and turned around.

"All right. I've let you have your say. Now I'll have mine. So now then — if it's men who are all at fault, *why blame me?*"

"What?"

"Case Number Nineteen. That book you brought along, by your precious Patchkiss. Oh, I read it last night. It's you, isn't it? Names anonymous to protect the innocent — huh! Not very innocent you think your mother, is it? She's the villain. Responsible for all your blocks and inhibitions, or whatever, because she taught you sex was dirty."

Elsie was stunned. She sat weakly on the stool, watching her mother. After a moment she said, "Well, your insistence all the time on cleanliness. Find some nice *clean* young man. Is he a good *clean* boy. Keep your vessels *clean* . . ."

"What's wrong with that?"

"It's dirty. By continually emphasizing cleanliness you imply sex isn't —"

Mrs. Marvel revolved once, flinging her arms into the air. "Oh, my God! Will somebody please explain all that to me? Are we to have no peace? I'm old and tired, will somebody please explain it all to me?"

Elsie sat staring at the floor, her knees together, her mule-shod feet on a rung of the stool. "Well, Patchkiss seemed to want to go into my background and I . . . . That was all I could think of to tell him."

"Well, *I* can think of something else to tell him — as I goldarn well am as soon as this jollification is over."

"Mother, no."

"I am going personally to New York," warming to the notion, "beard him in his fancy office and tell him exactly what I think."

"Of what?"

"Of all this. Blaming your parents and your family for everything." Mrs. Marvel became explosive, keeping her voice down with difficulty. "It's all too easy! Because if your generation wants to blame us for everything, we can blame our parents, and they can blame theirs, and nobody will ever take any responsibility for anything."

"What about the natural hostility between the generations?"

"Blllach. And another thing —"

The swinging door opened and someone entered from the dining room.

"Good morning. Scarce had Apollo with his golden car clomb heaven to that point where't cleared the trees on yonder hill, than the first glimmer from its fiery wheels mine eyes pricked ope, mine ears likewise awakening to the sounds which issued here below, where now matutinal odors greet my nose. Such clatterings prosaic ought not to be thy matins on this festive day. For which my heartiest felicitations, Moo Moo."

"Oh, Chester." She caught his head, holding it a moment. "You're the sweetest thing that ever lived." As she clutched him she noted he held a white scroll tied with a red ribbon.

"The prothalamium. When can I read it?"

"Well, Chester," she said, worriedly, "remember we dropped all that special occasion stuff, entertainment and all. But we'll find some time for you to read it. Otherwise just let Grandfather and me — May I glance at it now?"

"Sure."

She unrolled it warily and read: "My twi-bulbed source —" She thrust it into an upper cabinet for later perusal. Others were coming down now, and when she had the first batch of buttermilk cakes on the griddle she saw by the clock that it was time to fetch Ruby from the bus stop. Bushrod offered to perform this errand, and was off on it before anyone knew he had gone.

They all loitered so long over the pancakes, which the children said were as good as ever and the grandchildren better than anything they had ever tasted, chattering and planting cigarette stubs in the syrup, wandering out to the sunny terrace with second and third cups of coffee, that before they realized it guests had begun to arrive.

The first of these was a contingent from the *Blade* at whose head marched Matt Shaw, their editor and publisher. That was five minutes after eleven, between which hour and six P.M. Open House would be held, according to an announcement on the social page. Now the photographer wanted informal shots and reporters statements on the secret of a happy marriage.

"Oh, it's just not to have any secrets," Alma said, laughing under a picture hat as she threw her arms around Ben. "Then we can say with Julia Ward Howe when she was what. Ninety. All the sugar was in the bottom of the cup."

Cameras clicked in the summer sunshine. Art moved back, getting movies. There was some bantering about give-and-take and who's boss. Someone tried to edge in from the rear of the group, clearing his throat. It was Reverend Korn. Cheated of a moment in the limelight by the elimination of after-dinner speeches, he was wistful to get in a few words anyway, for possible quotation in the *Blade*.

"Marriage you know," he said when he had their attention, "is like this modern furniture. A lot easier to get into than get out of."

This was a stock mot of some years' standing which for the first time fell flat. The blank faces of the younger generation told him why. It was no longer true. His whole little gem of a speech fell apart inside him. He grinned and said, "Well, anyway it used to be."

"What have you got to say about it, Ben?" Matt Shaw asked. "Can't let my boys go without a statement from you."

Marvel had of course armed himself with a little something. Pinching his nose he smiled at the grass and said, "Well, I think the difference Reverend Korn so beautifully put his finger on is this. We used to go to the likes of him to tie the knot. Nowadays they don't tie knots any longer. They just tie bows. Easier to loosen."

A shout went up out of proportion to the pleasantry. When he looked up it was to see everyone running alongside the house to the street. The last of the clan, Johnny and Evelyn Glimmergarden and little Roy and Jenny, were stepping out of a small red Renault Dauphine. "Surprise!" It had been a hoax that they were to be met at the station this afternoon; they had flown in from Chicago on a night plane, in order to drive, from Boston, the present on which they had all chipped in and which Johnny had got at a handsome discount through a business connection there.

"I don't know the shi-hi-hift," Mrs. Marvel screamed, beside herself with joy. Their old Buick's readiness for the Smithsonian had been a family joke for years.

"Hop in," said Johnny through a growth of stubble. "We'll show you."

A gay parade formed, with the Renault driven erratically by Moo Moo at the head of a honking cortege, of which the rear was drawn up by Matt Shaw's Cadillac. He sat proudly with his two grandchildren, snatched from their mother in the reunion. Jenny was nine, Roy seven.

"How are you getting along?" he asked them. "We haven't much time. How are you getting along with your stepfather?"

"He punishes us," said Roy.

Matt slowed, stiffening at the wheel. "What do you mean? How does he punish you?"

"He hits us."

"That true, Jenny? Because by George . . ."

"Yes but not very. He doesn't hit me. Just Roy. He hit him the other day."

"Where?"

"In Marshall Field's."

"Of course I don't mean it that way. I mean what part of you."

"He spanked me. Where would you spank?" He twisted a fist in a dry eye, hoping to extract some funds from his grandfather. "He spanked him for trying to—" Jenny's words were stifled back by Roy's hand, but Matt Shaw had heard enough.

To get this Glimmergarden aside was his great aim when he regained the procession, which was not till it had returned to the Marvel house and people were streaming again across the lawn to the back. Cold punch awaited you there, in an ancestral cut-glass bowl.

Weeks of planning and days of work had been essential to Mrs. Marvel's determination to do this as she was honor-bent on doing it — herself. It was going to be *their* Open House, not a catered affair with white-jacketed waiters equaling in number the guests. *She* was going to have her townfolk in, personally. Dinner (for just the Clan) was ready inside, two casseroles of turkey Tetrazzini having but to be heated. Ben had mixed the punch, red and white wines and liqueurs in which floated a dozen brandied peaches. A few concessions to commercialism were unavoidable, one being the rented chairs already strewn about the warm lawn, the other the cake squares just delivered by Thompson's bakery. An alternative drink was coffee, which Ruby darted back into the house to get, the humanitarian Bushrod at her heels.

Moo Moo was squeezing that Johnny Glimmergarden till he emitted involuntary musical notes, like a bagpipe. "I just love that car. After that old Buick it'll be so, whose idea was it?"

"Now, now." From his six-feet-three, of which the three inches were negated by a slouch, he grinned down at her, his famous snarling grin which bared one side of his white teeth. "Everybody's idea. Nothing too good for the lady I love second-best. But look, Moo Moo, do you mind if I catch a shave? And maybe even forty winks while I'm at it?"

Matt Shaw had been watching. When Johnny started toward the house, picking up a Gladstone bag on the way, he overtook him and tapped him on the shoulder.

"I'm Matt Shaw. The children's grandfather."

"Oh, sure." Johnny shook hands after shifting the grip.

"I'd like a word with you. Reports have come to my ears . . . You might say it's none of my business, but if you'll excuse me, it's the kids. I hear you punish them. Is that true?"

Johnny shifted the bag back to his right hand, grinning down. "What do you mean by punishment?"

"Only physical. All other types of discipline are your province and your right." In the concessionary part of his statement Shaw cut the air with his palm, as though to sweep the qualifications clearly into an agreed category. Johnny continued to shift the bag and to flex his hands, as though he were about to hurl it over the assembled heads in some little-practiced form of weight throwing. "But the physical I think I might take exception to, in my son's name, since they're his children. 'Cha think?"

"Where is he?"

"He's not here. Do you strike the children?"

Johnny hung over him a moment longer, like a sagging tower. "Let's just say I'm like a father to them."

Matt Shaw watched him turn and walk up the stairs and through the screen door into the house.

Mrs. Marvel studied another back. Mrs. Wetwilliam sat on a folding chair, talking to Cotton. Drinking liberally from her second cup of punch, she moved a step closer to eavesdrop. Cotton was still in his windbag phase, imagining himself to be talking Mrs. Wetwilliam out of ten thousand dollars for the college *without once mentioning money*. "We shall ill deserve our material power," he said as she bobbed assent, "if having that as a nation we have naught else . . ." He would show them all yet, cutting some ice in the high councils of the Seaboard. Overhearing his conversation even his mother felt momentarily lifted. But the dream collapsed and he walked "funny" to the punch table, like a victim of classic syphilis. Cup at lip he viewed the crowd with a smile of natural superiority, visualizing his end among the ateliers and brothels of old Europe . . .

Mrs. Wetwilliam adjusted a shawl over her shoulders. Mrs. Marvel took pleasure in the increasing size of those shoulders, with their galactic freckles. The woman overflowed the chair nicely, the flanks of her dress tight as plumskins, over flesh of that kind which, however, when you poke it, it stays poked? Know what Mrs. Marvel means? She took another gulp of punch and went over.

"I have always liked that dress," she said in Cotton's vacated seat. The smiles the two women exchanged might have given an onlooker the idea that they were baring their teeth in a comparison of dentrifices to which they were individually loyal. Mrs. Marvel noted that each of Mrs. Wetwilliam's teeth was a true square, each separated from its neighbor by a space infinitesimal but sufficient to establish beyond dispute its quadrilateral identity.

"So you've been married forty years."

"How about you?"

"Thirty-three. Want to give something like this on our thirty-fifth. That'll be two years from Tuesday. I hope you can come."

"I'll put it down."

"Charles had to go to Waltham on business, he was sorry he couldn't look in on you. A thing like this," Mrs. Wetwilliam said with a wave at the grounds across which the townfolk were now streaming (at a rate which made Mrs. Marvel glad Ruby had brought her sister), "is good. It shows them the value of tradition."

This was a principle Mrs. Marvel held in high esteem, was, indeed, the point of the occasion, but coming from the other woman she tended to resist it. The "them" might moreover be construed as meaning particularly her own children, to whose defense she now came.

"Oh, I don't know. The fact that people have other standards doesn't mean they don't have any. It's so easy for us to become stuffy about our so-called heritage."

"Why, what do you mean?" Mrs. Wetwilliam's voice had always had a finely disagreeable edge, like a violin bowed on the wrong side of the bridge.

"I mean that the Puritans," Mrs. Marvel said, taking a huge leap, "flee restrictions in one part of the world and then when they get over here set up a bigotry twice as bad as the one they run away from." She leaned over and poked the fat knee, which it pleased her to think retained its indentation, like pork sausage. "That is our heritage."

"I beg to differ with you. And what do you mean 'flee' and 'ran away from'?"

"On the *Mayflower*."

"The passengers on the *Mayflower* weren't really Puritans. They were Pilgrims — Separatists. The Puritans came later and were opposed by the Separatists."

"I know. But it's the same tradition. What we call the New England heritage." Her eyes were drawn to her punch cup by the other's glance at it. She drank it off and observed, "Who knows that the sense of guilt that ravages modern man, mucking our attitude toward sex and what not, isn't directly traceable to it."

"I beg to differ with you about that. I think the New England tradition has given the country what substance it has."

"Maybe. But what I say is still ridiculous, that they became more narrow-minded than what they ran away from."

"I don't know why you keep saying ran away —"

"And then worshiping the date 1620. That becomes rather amusing, don't you think, when you realize that the Catholics had been here since 1608. I mean it's the sort of thing that brings a smile to your lips."

"You seem to know your American history, Mrs. Marvel."

"I've been reading a good deal of it lately. Lots of eye openers for all of us. Did I ever tell you about the ancestor of mine on the *Mayflower?*"

"Why, no." Mrs. Wetwilliam's eyes expanded. "I didn't realize you had an ancestor on the *Mayflower*. Does the Society know about this?"

"Oh, think nothing of it. He got off when they put back into Plymouth, you know. He got cold feet. It's always rather amused the family."

Mrs. Marvel had a bottled-up scream somewhere inside her. She felt as though her nerves were being extracted through her extremities with fine pincers. Yet she gave Mrs.

Wetwilliam an impression of offhand and even raffish relaxation — the legs casually crossed, an arm dangling from the back of the folding chair. The contents of her existence to date, all the years days dreams and suppositions, including the houses in this city from which friends and enemies were pouring to call at hers, this living pulsating personal past was being consumed in her vitals as in a crucible, to be smelted over into something altogether different. She would never be the same again. She was already somebody other than the person she had been three seconds ago. Whoever rose from this chair, it would be another than the woman who had sat down in it. She would have to lose no time in making her acquaintance.

"I mustn't monopolize you." Mrs. Wetwilliam emptied her own cup, which Mrs. Marvel took from her, and rose. "You have other guests. So nice to see you, and many, many happy returns."

"Don't you want to meet some of the others? My son-in-law Harry Mercury will be along any minute. He's the television comedian."

"I'm afraid not," Mrs. Wetwilliam said, opening an unexpected parasol. "I've got to run along."

Holding the cups, Alma watched her run along like Pigling Bland, twirling her parasol in the maples' checkered shade. No, not like Pigling Bland. A great bee, carrying on her sturdy surfaces the pollen of gossip.

Having caught up with the new arrivals in a concentrated round of handshaking, Moo Moo flew around to the back to settle the children for early luncheon snacks at the picnic table. There were mounds of sandwiches prepared in advance and taken from the freezer an hour ago: not quite long enough, the bread was still a little like nougat. But there were cookies and ice cream and cans of cold Hawaiian Punch.

"I ought to have two of these cookies," Roy complained.

"Why?"

"Because I don't like them very well."

"He pulls that on school lunches and everything," said his sister Jenny. "Because he doesn't like something, he should have twice as much."

"Oh, *I* see, to get the same pleasure the other kids do out of one," said Moo Moo, adjusting smoothly to the childhood logic from which she had been so many years removed. It was good to be back! "Well, you can have all you want, and so can everyone else!" She circled the table benignly disbursing cookies. "Jenny, you haven't eaten your sandwich."

Jenny was watching the street for the postman. She expected a letter from a dear chum from whom she was separated for the summer, and with whom she had exchanged a trail of future forwarding addresses. She languished over the soiled table, vigilant.

"I wish I was twenty-one."

"So do I. Eat!" said Moo Moo.

Jenny drew from a dress pocket the playmate's last letter. It was in dim pencil and frayed from handling, but memory aided its decipherment:

Dear Jenny:

Thank you very much for your letter. I miss you teribly. I'm out on our upstairs porch writing because there are men working to loud. You see we have a sleeping porch its real nice and quiet when their not working.

Last night a mentely retarded child tried to blow out the things they warn you with. This was in town on the street and sidewalks. He put dirt on them he blowed at them he picked up twigs with leaves on them and tried to hid the fire out. He even tried to start a fire but some people stamped it out.

Wen are you going to your grandmother. Its terible just being all the time with groanups. I cant wait for the summer to be over tho who wants to go back to school.

Hoping you are O.K.

Your friend

Prue

Marvel stood at a distance, watching the scene at the table. Behind him he could hear fragments of conversation between two women whose names he had not caught but whom he vaguely identified as the personable sort who were filling the town with cunning shops. They wore slanted sunglasses edged with rhinestones and one said "Is it Menuhin or Milstein who practices in his underwear? I always forget," while the other answered "I'll ask Brent. He has connections in the musical world." Through the long handshaking, punch-toting, cigar-offering afternoon he must worry about getting Alma out of sight for the landscape wiring. Since the Glimmergardens had now not to be fetched from the station, some other ruse must be found for bundling her off the premises for the half-hour Judkins said would suffice for the temporary rig-up. Toward six o'clock, when Cotton had the electrician smuggled into the doings as a well-wisher, another worry cropped up which solved the first. They ran out of ice. Marvel convinced

Alma that she must drive over instantly to the new cube-vending machine behind the railroad station and get two or three bagfuls for the tubs in which the champagne must now be set to chill, and she alone because the machine was off on a tricky back street no one else would know where to find. When she returned, the job was done and Judkins on his way home. Having set a case of champagne cooling, Marvel mopped his brow and surveyed the scene as it stood now, at half-past six P.M.

The children were all in the playground. Art was wandering around with his movie camera — Marvel threw another smiling wave at the muzzle swinging in his direction. Elsie was martyring herself in the kitchen, where Alma was beginning to think about dinner. Cotton was being a great help. "It depends what you mean by home," he was saying to Matt Shaw, who had stuck around the livelong day and who was nervously pushing his teeth up into his gums with the ball of his thumb. Marvel counted seventeen nonfamily still left, half an hour after Open House was officially over. This included the two women with dark glasses, one of whom wore toreador pants and was saying, "She needn't think just because she's complicated she isn't shallow." However, they seemed to be drifting away. Half of the hangers-on might still be around at dinner time and have to be invited, which was all right, since it was buffet anyway. Matt, a widower with no dinner awaiting him at home, obviously had an invitation in mind. Cotton smiled and yawned simultaneously at a point Matt was making. Nearby Johnny Glimmergarden shook his head at something Evelyn was saying up very close into his face, and walked away. Cotton snatched his coattails.

"Johnny, Mr. Shaw and I were having an interesting discussion about marriage. Why is it on the skids? What do you think?"

"It's *people* who aren't what they used to be," Matt said. "Something is going out of people."

Johnny sat down in Cotton's deserted chair. "The male," he said, "has become too domesticated," and recognized the grandfather of the children who were no kin of his.

"That makes no sense," said Shaw, bridling at the note of subtlety, which seemed to him deliberately perverse. "Isn't domestication the idea of marriage?"

Johnny wagged a finger in his face and said with a rather slipshod grin, "Law of diminishing returns." He drank what was certainly not punch and set the glass on the uneven ground. "Hence the hostility between the sexes, *both* of whom are stir-crazy. The ego is getting it in the neck, in our time, though the balance tends to be somewhat restored by adultery. Infidelity has no doubt stabilized more unions than it has undermined."

Shaw made an angry fidget on the chair. "You're crazy. It's the basic lack of *order* in our time that's making for disintegration — all along the line. Moral as well as intellectual" — he put a forefinger to the other's sternum — "*and* aesthetic. Take Picasso. Take Braque . . ."

Johnny wanted to suggest he take Miro whose influence was conspicuous in the shirt Shaw had on, a random distribution of color blobs under an open sports collar. Matt's coat lay over his lap, from where it presently slipped to the grass.

"What we need is discipline."

"Right," said Johnny, grinning wickedly in the direction of the playground, where a dispute had broken out. Instead of going over to quell it, he hitched his chair closer to Shaw's, so that their knees touched like those of passengers in a railway coach. He helped himself to another pull on his glass and lit a cigarette. "I'll explain what being a human being is like to you as well as I can." He exhaled smoke with his eyes closed, like a medium of ideas who had to lure them in a trance as a clairvoyant does spirits. "What makes a man human is his identity. Part of that is sexual. That goes for women too. That is the most important thing in marriage — one's identity. The trouble comes when the parties to it, in order to secure their own, tread on the other's. The result is a sex war which you know is in our time out of hand. What we forget in trying to analyze this war is something essential to every war."

"Combatants."

"No." Johnny wagged a finger again, pleased to hear what he had expected. "Prisoners. Woman's imprisonment we know. It is of old. Childbearing. Shaw reminds us that she resents the burden of creation being so unequally divided. Hence the Nag, the Battleax, etc. She is fighting back today by, among other things, incarcerating man in the kitchen."

Shaw nodded thoughtfully, following this, weighing it. "Where are the children? Where do they come in, in this picture?"

"More and more she wants her cultural life, and to get it, more and more must man assume the abandoned chores — the era of the cheap servant being gone." Johnny drew on his cigarette again and sat another moment in a trance, smoke streaming from his nostrils. "Eighty years ago Nora walked out of the Doll's House — where to? Nobody knows, least of all Ibsen. It is one of the puzzles of our time, which he ducked. But there is now a strong body of evidence that she is at a club meeting, or the PTA, or the board of the Friends of the Library while her husband tidies up the Doll's House. And now let us stop and consider what Ibsen would think of the male tyrant Nora fled, standing at the kitchen sink with his arms to his elbows in suds, or, an apron over his trousers, giving the children their evening baths. Oh, Jesus, spare us yet. Deliver us we pray."

Shaw sat deeply respectful, even a little cowed. Without exactly knowing what was being said he found himself stirred, as though by strains of band music. Johnny drew another long breath which contracted his nostrils. His eyes remained closed, so that he did not see that a larger audience than Shaw had begun to collect around him. Johnny was shot through with fantasies, some of them suicidal. He had worked out one method of doing himself in. Thrusting the vacuum cleaner nozzle down his throat, he would switch on the mechanism, drawing out his vital organs. She would have a bag of giblets to throw out. He also conducted imaginary conversations with Ibsen:

IBSEN: Where is she?

JOHNNY: Out.

IBSEN: What is she doing?

JOHNNY: At a hobby show. Officer in a club that puts them on, Henrik.

IBSEN: What is her hobby? What does she collect?

JOHNNY: Dolls.

While that slew Ibsen, he gathered his thoughts for a fresh assault on Shaw. Ibsen and Shaw, what a combination. What more could anybody want?

"There has always been a tyrant," he said, very carefully now, with the meticulousness of early inebriation. "Every generation has its ogre. With the Victorians it was the father. The following generation it was the mother. Today it is the wife."

Johnny felt a weight on the arm of his chair. Whose sweet rump it was he knew without opening his eyes, smelling the perfume. Evelyn had a glass in her hand too, and her other arm dropped around his neck.

"Holding forth, darling?"

"Sure."

"Am I a castrating woman?" She tickled his ear. He looked up with his snarling smile, resting an arm along her thigh. Her glass was empty. He poured half of his drink into it, including a clunking ice cube.

"Does the negative get a chance at rebuttal?"

"Absolutely," Matt Shaw said with a nervous giggle. He saw uneasily how many had crowded around, and he knew his son's ex-wife's temper.

"Well, then let's begin with that paperback I read on the plane coming over. Mrs. Lindbergh's A *Gift From the Sea.* I hadn't had a chance to read it before, so I was interested in the seashells she played with on her holiday. I can tell her something. A housewife doesn't *have* to go to the seaside for seashells. She just fishes them out of her boy's pants pockets before she throws them into the wash machine."

"You'll admit that book was well written though," Shaw said. "She has a way with words, that woman."

"As for sand," Evelyn said, ignoring her erstwhile father-in-law, "that's in the cuffs. Just turn them down and there it is." She raised her glass and drank in a very composed fashion.

Matt Shaw while interested in tirades did not like quarrels, and fearing one to be brewing, with himself possibly more than onlooker, he mumbled some excuse and made off. But he stood nearby and from there watched what followed.

"You're tired," Johnny said, as other bystanders drifted away. "You ought to go upstairs for a little nap before dinner."

"You mean come upstairs, don't you?"

"Oh, sure."

"Not now."

They were never altogether unaware, the Glimmergardens, of the figure they cut, not just as a handsome couple but as a pair about whom there was something special. Both of the "lean, clean breed," they made a glittering unity. Each had in him more than a dash of the other, a straightforward flashing emotional voltage that made their hostilities head-on but at least ephemeral, not brooding and devious like the Trautwigs'. Both had been known in school as "talented." But if an admirer recalling them were asked "Talented at what?" he would be at a loss. Not at anything in particular, just talented. Which was their trouble, Johnny's more than Evelyn's since it meant he could never find a job consonant with his gifts. He was at present the advertising manager of a large Chicago department store, and miserable in it. They were famous on the lower North Side and along the lakefront Gold Coast as a glamorous couple, a term that would never have crossed their lips.

Watching now, Matt Shaw saw Evelyn lean down from her perch on the arm of Johnny's chair and say something. He pushed his teeth up nervously into his gums. He saw them lean together and speak into each other's mouths.

"Wouldn't night before last hold you for a while?"

"No, doll."

"I can always tell when it's going to be a good one," Evelyn murmured with the deliberate shamelessness they had always relished together. "You get hard all over. Your whole body, arms and legs . . ."

He mumbled something not meant to be intelligible, and after a moment drew back and gave her an order.

"You ought to go get their grandfather another cup of punch. He's not having a very good time. And tell him while you're at it who wears the pants in the family where the kids are concerned. He thinks I do."

Watching her walk across the grass, Johnny thought to himself, "She's got the prettiest little tail in Christendom, and she knows it."

This thought having finished reverberating in his mind, he looked around for fresh company. Bushrod had emerged from the house and was striding purposefully toward the playground with a dish in which was a charlotte russe and a spoon. He had the look of a father going to restore order in his household. Johnny rose suddenly and went into the kitchen.

"Moo Moo, where's Harry Mercury? What's happened to him?"

"That's what I'm beginning to wonder," she said, wiping her hands on a towel with a worried air. "I called at the hotel twice but he doesn't answer. It's not like Harry. The last time I called was around one and I left a message for him to call back, but he hasn't. At least that I know of. In all the confusion here . . ."

She had been glancing out the window, and this time saw what she had been on the lookout for. Two young figures were advancing across the lawn in summer evening clothes.

"There's Lee," she said. "Maybe she's heard from him. And that chap she's with, I'm very anxious to have some of you meet him. Come on."

Johnny followed her out the squeaking screen door. He noticed that, as she reached the porch stairs, she drew a deep breath and squared her shoulders, as though she were steeling herself for something.

fifteen

MARVEL stood in the dooryard surveying the scene with his hands in his pants pockets. He had at last removed his white linen coat though now it was growing cool and time to put it on again. "How much will I be able to leave my grandchildren?" he thought, watching them play. Beaumont seemed to be sitting on the swing eating something with a spoon. He remembered the expert advice with which Beau's parents met his forays on refrigerators and pocketbooks — "Give him positions of trust." The screen door twanged open and Alma came down the stairs.

"Why is he getting his dessert early?" Marvel asked.

"He stole somebody's watch." She jerked her head toward more urgent business. "He's here. With Lee. Come on."

Marvel fitted the word "extortionist" firmly into place in his mind, like a bullet into a barrel, as he was towed across the lawn to the oncoming youngsters, calling over his shoulder to Johnny to go back in and set some more champagne in the ice tub.

Lee and Sligh had already been given some. They touched glasses and drank to the happy couple's health. Seeing Lee work her little muckle mouth into the circle of smiles, Ben knew what Alma should have done instead of these head-on heroics: she should have taken the girl quietly aside and told her, for Lee to take from there. The matriarchal principle had led her into permitting the stranger's introduction to the tribe, so there was nothing for it now but to go on with the ceremonial eating and drinking. Or was there? This brat had offended his wife (unless she had been more than normally vague, which was hardly possible), so why not slap him across his handsome chops and send him packing? So they could get a neutral look at him, supposedly. It was at any rate too late to behave as a man might; he must act as a gentleman should.

"Sit down."

It was the elders, the youngsters, and Elsie Trautwig who settled around a small table under a crabapple tree. Seeing the knit group, the returning Johnny wandered elsewhere. After Lee had answered inquiries about Mercury by saying she had heard nothing of him either, there was a silence. Elsie said:

"What do you do, Mr. Sligh?"

"If you'd asked me that yesterday I could have told you — 'I'm in genealogy.' But as of today I quit. The prospects aren't good enough for a man who wants to marry."

"You can always supplement your income," Marvel said dryly.

Things were slipping rapidly out of focus, or rather from that of reality into theatrics. Alma spluttered her champagne as characters do on the stage following provocative lines; Sligh lit a cigarette for Lee with measured nonchalance. The setting sun bathed them in a light as unliteral as that which pours across a proscenium. And there was another character in the wings, fidgeting to go on.

By moving his eye slightly to the left, Marvel saw Malcolm standing just outside their circle, as dressed up in summer whites as the villain, fuming under more than the grievance of not being greeted. He had just dismounted a charger, as it were, and had obviously something to spill. Marvel knew of Malcolm's part in the affair; Marvel had just thrown down the gauntlet to Sligh; why not beckon the rival in from the wings and precipitate the scene they were all quivering on the verge of? Marvel started to rise when Sligh spoke.

"I told Lee about the misunderstanding between Mrs. Marvel and me. We both got quite a bang out of it. I hope it's straightened out in your mind now, Mrs. Marvel?"

"No, it is not."

"There was nothing to it. I . . ." Sligh looked to Lee for support, and for a moment in the overrich light wore the pathetic charm of the victim. Lee had believed him. She had wanted to believe him. Now glancing at Moo Moo she knew she couldn't. His story had been a device to get there first. She leaned back, as from the sunburnt hand at which she now stared, which lay on the table. What liberties had it been given, Marvel wondered as he took in the young breasts behind the pale green dress.

They all watched the hand as it clung a moment to the table edge by its fingers; then the fingers slipped off, like a mountain climber's from an icy escarpment, and the hand dropped. "My mother is very ill," Sligh said. Marvel laughed without expression through his nose. Elsie said, "Will somebody please tell me what this is all about?"

Mrs. Marvel began a passionate account of the economic roots of the Revolution, jabbering disjointedly and in a conspiratorial tone. Washington was a 4-F. Lee sat with her head bowed and her hands in her lap; her cigarette lay smoking on the grass. Sligh nodded and smiled in his way, his jaw thrust slightly forward and to the side, as though he were lining up his incisors. It was then that Marvel rose and beckoned the good guy over, acting on what instinct told him: that the contents of the scene could best be discharged by introducing a note of orotundity. They were not corny enough to motivate drama. They would hack and pick till Doomsday; better to blast.

"May Ah add what information Ah have acquired to what Ah have overheard," Malcolm began when the greetings and presentations were over and he had drunk to the occasion which must now be ruined. A place had been made for him in the tight circle. "It is important to all and crucial to some. Most crucial to one whom Ah have offered mah own favor. That it has been in vain," he continued as Lee popped nervously erect like a puppet, "will suffice as proof that mah investigations — Ah too am interested in pedigree — are neutral and without hope of personal gain. Whether Ah am free of gratuitous spite Ah leave to mah friend Alma to say."

She told them with a nod that he was free of gratuitous spite, as simply as though she were informing them that he had a good liver or took a ten and a half shoe. Malcolm directed many of the rest of his words to Elsie.

"Everything being at stake, for others, Ah have hesitated at nothing. Ah have been some days in Boston looking into the newcomer to ouah town. Ah learned from the firm he represented that he no longer does."

"I told them —"

"He did not represent them when he first called here either, having been dismissed for misuse of information against clients. Chiefly, we may suppose, milking them of undetermined sums. Some of ouah first families! In the interest of honesty Ah won't withhold facts in his favor. He has a mother in a sanatorium for whom he is the sole support. He refused to remove her to a state hospital. We can imagine what the weekly expense of this is."

"You're not just whistling 'Dixie,' " Sligh said.

"But are we to suppose that it justifahs playing fast and loose with ouah finest families? Engaging in blackmail of rich — rich —"

"Snobs? You said it, I didn't."

Malcolm rose and pushed back his chair. His fingers closed around the stem of his champagne glass. Sligh noticed it, and got to his own feet. Thank God, Marvel thought in his riddled heart, for the Graces of Another Day. Here we go.

"You have just spoken in a manner Ah cannot countenance of a lady who is mah friend. Ah therefore demand an apology under pain of requiring satisfaction of another sort."

"You're the Flower of the South."

Malcolm threw the champagne. Sligh ducked, however, in time for it to pass over his right shoulder and catch Matt Shaw full in the face as Matt came up to say he had to leave, hoping thereby to secure the invitation to dinner.

"Please stay," they said as many hands wiped him down. Thus he got what he wanted. He was led away from the scene which now also otherwise rapidly disintegrated. Lee fled toward the house followed by Moo Moo, who was in turn followed, after a moment's hesitation, by Malcolm. Marvel moved off several steps without any clear purpose, or even volition, feeling like a car beginning to roll down a hill with no one at the wheel. Sligh took a step but Elsie held his arm.

"Just a minute, Snickelfritz. I want to talk to you."

Remembering who she was, Sligh played his last card.

After filling in the blanks in her comprehension of events, to the best of his ability, he proceeded to unfold a tale of young love pursued well but not wisely. The only decent thing about him was his love for Lee, he knew, and if he was to leave any proof of his decency, it must be to come clean with her mother. He wished to take full blame for their having let their passions run away with them.

"What! *You* ——!" Elsie sized him up, aghast. She became hysterical. "You're a rotten, lowdown, worthless, unprincipled skunk, and you'll marry my daughter if it's the last thing I see to!"

Marvel stood, an elderly man with his hands in his pockets wondering how much he could believe of what he thought he was seeing and hearing. Nearby, Bushrod dragged himself in a sitting position across the grass to a pretty girl, like a dog with the worms. "I was interested in what you were just saying about the Renaissance. It opened up to man the world but shut him out of heaven." At a somewhat greater distance Matt Shaw was tapping one end of a seesaw on the ground while he listened with his ear at the other; perhaps he was inventing the stethoscope all over again.

At that moment there was an explosion in the house, like a rifle shot, followed by a woman's scream. Running into the house Marvel found Ruby at the sink with a bleeding hand. She had tried to uncork one of the iced bottles of champagne without the time-honored napkin and it had burst. The bleeding was not severe, and presently stopped under the running tap. But there were undoubtedly small bits of glass lodged in her palm, and it was agreed that a doctor should be called. Then Bushrod had a better idea. The hospital was nearby, scarcely three blocks if you slipped out backlots to Adams Street, quicker even than by car. He would take her over himself.

By now Ruby was laughing, admitting she knew now that napkin wasn't for show. "It's to keep a warm hand from contact with a cold carbonated surface," Bushrod explained, hurrying her out the back door. Ruby's sister, May, would have to manage dinner alone, at least till they returned.

"On with the dance!" someone said.

There were twenty-two for dinner, about evenly divided between family and friends. Jack and Mary Hilton, the Marvels' bridge companions, were there by invitation. Jack was a great mixer. He traded stories with Matt Shaw in the tradition to which they were both partial. They went back to the days of "Let's not and say we did," "Don't swear it sounds like hell," and "Jack's going to take unto himself a wife but he hasn't decided yet whose." They teamed up against Johnny and Evelyn in an argument about shaggy dog stories, and another about current comic strips. They could not abide things like Pogo, harking back as they did to those in which characters fell backwards out of the last frame saying "What the—!" They wanted to let the kids decide, but the kids wanted to rig up the stereophonic portable Jack had brought along, and Jack did, and soon there was dancing on the terrace at that. The Glimmergardens led off, swaying dreamily under the Japanese lanterns growing steadily brighter in the deepening dusk. Roy did a tumbling act on the grass, Jenny a recitation, turning her back on the audience as self-consciousness overcame her, giggling the climax into her two hands.

The Sligh-Malcolm scene had been kept from general knowledge. Lee was in tearful hiding somewhere, no one knew exactly where. Sligh hurried at last away from Mrs. Trautwig, who was becoming too shrill in her approval of the match. His movements became a decision to flee the premises altogether. On the way to his convertible, parked away down the street in the long line of cars, he saw someone standing uncertainly on the front lawn, taking in the scene behind. As he drove off, he placed him vaguely as a chap he had seen at the theater.

When Prufrock heard a low sound of sobbing on the front porch and, going up, found it was Lee, he wondered why he suddenly felt a load off his mind.

"What's the matter?"

"Nothing."

Pondering as he often had the truth of the adage that it never rains but it pours, Prufrock wondered if it weren't a mercy rather than a cruelty of fate to deal us one blow while we are still numb from another, if both had to be. Telling Lee what Harry had sworn him to keep secret till tomorrow, so as "not to spoil anybody's fun," would now not be breaking a promise since she obviously wasn't having any fun anyway. That was the load off his mind, or part of it. The other part was having someone now to share the problem of deciding whether in turn to tell the Marvels, or anybody else, and when.

"Your father's in the hospital," he said. "He had an emergency appendectomy."

"When?"

"This afternoon."

"Is it serious?"

"It was ruptured. Yes, I suppose it could be serious. He didn't want to spoil the party. He said it would keep till tomorrow. I've been with him all day, so if anything had . . ."

"Take me there."

"Sure, Lee, but look. Don't tell him I told you. He was his old self again when I just left him, and that's no fun. Wait. Should we . . .?"

"Moo Moo will understand."

Bill threw one more glance back into the yard as they hurried along the sidewalk. A couple standing just out of the light from the Japanese lanterns turned and saw them. Closer to the terrace, three men were singing "My Blue Heaven" with their arms slung around each other's necks. Matt Shaw was doing imitations. He recreated an entire barnyard, reaching his climax as a hen in the throes of ovulation. "Puck, puck," he began, building slowly. "Puck puck *pugaw!*" he finished suddenly, and reaching around behind himself produced in the palm of his hand an egg which they all examined with interest. "It's funnier when he squats down," Jack Hilton said loyally.

That hardly satisfied Matt, who began discoursing on changing styles in humor. He told a story of early vintage and said, "That was funny!" His breathing had become more stertorous and an ominous flush overspread his face. He sat down at the table he had just thumped.

"We'd better call the fire department," Jack said. "I don't like it."

"Or take him there maybe," Marvel said. "It's just as quick, and they'll have the equipment ready. I'll phone on ahead."

Matt was led away between Hilton and another crony to one of their cars, while Marvel ran into the house to call the fire department to have the inhalator ready. "It's Matt Shaw," he told the man at the other end, who said, "Oh, God, not again." Neighbors witnessing Matt's supported departure mistook him for a casualty of another sort, and smiled from their porches, glad to see the popular Marvels having such a jolly party.

"Mother, we shouldn't hold dinner any longer," Evelyn called from the kitchen where she was helping, when at last night had fallen. "I don't think we need wait for Bushrod."

"She's right," said Marvel, walking down the porch steps to join Alma. He was anxious to get his surprise off before there were any other distractions. "So let's serve. But first there's a little something, my dear . . ."

He winked at the vigilant Cotton, who signaled back. The Japanese lanterns were extinguished. So were the kitchen lights. "Gather round everyone! Here!" Sensing a surprise, Alma let herself be led to the porch, on a post of which the new switch had been temporarily hung. The crowd were finally quiet, expectant. "Suppose you just flip that."

She raised her hand with a nervous laugh, and snapped

the switch. A shout went up. "Oh!" she gasped ecstatically. "It's beautiful!"

The yard was a fantasy of blazing green. The light billowed and bloomed against dark masses of shrubs, receded into shadow, gathered and flung itself in another wave across the open lawn to the rock garden, turning the flowers to jewels and the glinting stones to flowers, on over the tiny brook and its ivy-hung bridge to the rosebushes, dusting their pink foam with a tender, powdery glow, sweeping on to the final limit of the grounds, the semicircle of silver spruce like a slice of the moon itself, in whose embrasure it picked out Bushrod and Ruby returning from the hospital, the latter with one hand in a white bandage, standing in a momentary embrace, kissing.

part three:

A FRESH FIRE

sixteen

A CRISIS between the Bushrod Marvels was to be expected. They went up to their room about ten o'clock, for the scene that under the circumstances was now inevitable. Clara went first, slipping in through the kitchen door after coffee, which Ruby's sister looked to alone, Ruby having vanished. Bushrod followed her a few minutes later. He found her sitting on the bed. Her hands were folded in her lap and her feet and knees were together as she stared at the floor.

"The colored maid," she said.

Bushrod had just closed the door behind him, and had begun to cross the room to the window. But now he turned, aghast. He stood over her with an expression of shocked amazement.

"Prejudice!" he said. "To think I should find it in my own family. My own wife."

This brought her to her senses. She saw what she had done.

"I'm sorry. I – I didn't realize what I was saying."

"I should hope not, Clara." He too sat down on the bed, with his face in his hands. "My God. What a blow this is. I thought you shared my ideals."

She raised her hand, but he turned away.

"The thing I've been fighting all my life. All my *life*. And this is where I find it. What a blow."

She dropped her uplifted hand in shame. Her whole world came tumbling down around her ears, the whole painstakingly erected edifice collapsing like a house of cards. What good were all the years of education, the current-affairs quizzes so faithfully taken week in week out, in an effort to make a good wife for Bushrod — what good were they now?

"How can you forgive me?"

"It's hard."

He rose and walked to the window, where he stood in the dim light of the dresser lamp, looking down with a brooding bitterness.

"Everything I've stood for, betrayed in a single word. It just goes to show you. You can live with a person for years and not know what they're like — really. Inside." He put a fist to his breast to suggest what lay within himself — gall and wormwood. "I have seen tonight nothing less than the outrage of my principles."

"Oh, Bushrod." She started toward him with a little cry. He felt her hand on his shoulder but did not turn; he was not to be so easily bought off, considering that hand was stained with the betrayal of all he held dear.

"I mean a man tries to strike a blow for equality —" He finished with a shrug, unable to put into words the degree of his disappointment.

"Give me another chance," she said. "One slip shouldn't mean the end. I've tried, God knows I've tried to be a worthy wife to you. Let what happened — a word let slip I'd give anything to recall — let it show you how hard I've had to. The struggle . . ."

"What if it ever got out? I'd die. We could never go back home again."

"I'll never tell. I won't say anything if you don't."

There was a toss of his head as he straightened his back, behind which his hands were tightly clasped. "I mean if the whole meaning of a man's life has escaped his own wife, then they've been living a lie. What's the use going on?"

She sank onto the bed again. This time she stared at the floor more abysmally, one hand in her lap, palm up, the other hanging at her side. "Need the CLL hear about it?"

"Not from me! All right," he said, large-mindedly, turning around. "We'll consider the incident closed. I won't say anything about tonight if you don't. And I'll try not to hold it against you."

"Thank you, Bushrod," she exclaimed gratefully, and followed him to the door.

"Now let's go back. More guests are leaving. Be careful not to let on anything's wrong. Act natural."

"Of course," she said, and descended the stairs behind him with the air of a woman trying to summon all the courage it would need to make a fresh start.

The elder Marvels too went to their room as soon as they decently could after the party broke up, which was around midnight. When Ben entered he found Alma pacing in her stocking feet, on the verge of hysteria.

"That's the way it always is! Treat them as equals, and first thing you know that's how they're treating you. I've always said it!"

"Shh! Is that how you see it? How about blaming your son?"

"*My* son. That's how you always put it when it's something bad. They're your children when they're good."

"It's an expression. You know all couples do it. It's a joke."

"Not to me!"

"No, of course not. It isn't a joke. I simply meant this business about —"

"I never want to speak to him again."

"You'll have to, at least to say good-by."

"I'll leave them all notes. All of them! For you to distribute at breakfast. Have you spoken to him?"

"I should say not!"

"I mean *spoken* to him, as a father."

"My dear, he's a grown man, with children of his own. He's not six years old. Or supposedly not. My not speaking to him is speaking enough."

"It's the way you handled him when he was six too. You never spoke to him enough. You never whacked him enough. You should whack him now."

"I'm afraid that would not be very mature on anybody's part."

"Oh, mature! Is that all anyone is ever to hear these days? Why can't they see children as bad any more, instead of maladjusted or insecure or whatever, and give them a good whaling instead of more confidence. All this psychological stuff, tension spans and one thing and another — what they need is discipline! Good old-fashioned discipline!"

She banged a hand on the dresser while Marvel spread both his. "Please be quiet!" he whispered. "And do stop raving about how they raise their own children. We didn't raise ours that way, we raised them the other way, and look at them now. We beat them."

"Only when you were angry."

"I cannot lay a finger on someone when I am not. Is that bad?"

"That's the way you handled Bushrod, spanked him when his behavior annoyed or infuriated you, not when it was wrong."

"That is absolutely not true. The two factors often coincided."

"And the broken homes they give their own as a background, to make it worse. What can you expect for the next generation?"

"They're here to celebrate the solid one we gave them. How much good has that been? . . . Oh, God. Maybe they're right in hanging everything on the family. Maybe that is the villain. Maybe it ought to go. Go as such, good, bad or indifferent. Go as an institution."

"I hope for your sake you're drunk."

"Stop to think about it a moment. The implications of what we've just said. It is rather snug quarters you know." Either he was seeking a little comic relief or his own thinking had become tinged with hysteria, he could hardly have told which himself, but he said: "Haven't you often thought about it yourself? To sleep year after year with the same husband or wife, what could be more incestuous than that?"

He had an impulse to climb fully clothed under the counterpane and pull it over his head, but instead of lying on his back with the rough cool feel of chenille on his face he had to hear, and what was worse, see, her say, both fists coming down on the dresser once for each word: *"Stop. Tormenting. Me."*

"All right."

She stood a minute moderating her breathing, as it were, in the same way in which she often tried to moderate discussions, as she had that at the family dinner table last evening, and even disputes such as this. Clearing her throat she resumed, "Were you ever a friend to him?" returning to that. "Did you ever take him fishing—?"

He raised his eyes to heaven, at the same time shoving the door more surely shut with his heel, not speaking again till he had heard the softly chuckling latch. "Oh, my dear God, are we going through all that again? Fishing bores me stiff, and the one time I took him it bored him stiff too. I played ball with him, went on wiener—oh this argument is preposterous."

"All I'm saying is, something might have been done so he wouldn't have developed his hostility to you. It's hostility to the father directed at society that's supposed to make a radical. Well, isn't it?"

"I see you use their jargon when it suits your purpose. And I wouldn't talk about hostility if I were you. I might introduce the subject of Elsie."

Mrs. Marvel's cheeks blazed as with bared teeth she raised her fists. "*If* you throw that up to me one more time I'll never speak to you again as long as I live."

"I am *not* throwing anything *up* to anybody," he said, flapping his hands as though he were shaking water from them. "I'm only defending myself against a charge by showing you the injustice of it when it's laid at your own door. I do not make accusations as such."

"Oh, no? Then why did you throw it up to me?"

He stood in the middle of the room weirdly recalling a lumberjack trying to retain his balance on a log in a river. At the same time instead of rolling his eyes he wearily closed them, rocking his head gently from side to side. "I did not — throw — it — up to you. If I throw anything up it'll be my dinner, in about two minutes."

"Go right ahead and good riddance. That's all the thanks I get for cooking it, going to all that trouble so you could have your old anniversary. This is all you get out of it — out of anything." For a moment she had a triumphant sense of being wronged, like Elsie, as if displaying something she had inherited from her daughter in reverse. "Out of forty years. One puts his arm around everything in skirts, the other can't stand to have a man touch her. I refuse to be held responsible for either — Elsie either. It's from the father girls are supposed to get their preliminary image of the male, isn't it?"

"Again, I thought you were against all that lingo, but all right. Let's do it that way once — just for curiosity trade the charges around for a change and see what happens. You blame me for Elsie and I'll throw Bushrod up to you. 'Bushrod'! What a name to saddle anybody with to begin with. It's enough to warp a person for life. And 'Cotton.' Maybe all their troubles began at the baptismal font. Maybe that Colonial heritage obsession of yours has done more damage than we know."

Her temper now leapt out at him like a beast from a cage. "If you say anything like that to me again I will leave you. Now I mean it! *I will walk out of this house and never come back again.*"

"If it hadn't been for that we wouldn't have the Mr.

Sligh thorn in our side either," he continued unabatingly. "Unto the third and fourth generation. Where is Lee?"

She stood bursting at the foot of the bed. "Is it my *fault* that he — Am I to be *blamed* for what he is? She might have met him at a party, or some other louse. When *I* use arguments of that kind you give me that post hoc ergo propter stuff. And she was also seeing that fancy pants. Did I introduce her to *him*?"

"No, but she mightn't have taken cover with so many others if you hadn't thrown that ass Malcolm at her."

"That does it."

She squeezed back into her slippers, using her finger for a shoehorn.

"I'm leaving."

Marvel had dropped on the bed with his own shoes off and his suspenders down. She now stood over him shaking her finger in his closed eyes.

"I will not have you talk that way about him. You can say what you want about the children, but I will not have you criticizing my friends."

"Malcolm is all right," he said lethargically, rolling his head away on the pillow.

She paced again among the braided rugs. It was the rag rugs he thought of as he stared at a soiled spot in the ceiling, the notion dangling before his mind like a piece of worthless symbolism. How many discarded stockings and hanks of outgrown little girls' dresses were not woven into their bright designs. The refuse of Time, Marvel thought, feeling like a discarded emotional rag himself, and weary beyond belief.

"If you were so worried about the children why did you

let me raise them?" she said, faintly rekindling his interest in life. He sat up on his elbows again, like the man in the Seurat.

"A minute ago you said I did, and didn't do a good job. Will you kindly reconcile those two statements?"

"You reconcile them. I'm busy."

She was at her desk, her pen flying over a sheet of note-paper as it had that night when all this had begun, with the Guest List.

"What are you doing?"

"Waiting for a streetcar."

"Do I get one?" For she had begun a second; evidently they were to be crisp.

"They're awful, if I do say so myself. This is the ghastliest night of my life."

Listening to her write, he remembered there had once stood on that antique desk a potato bristling with pens. He tried to open once again the valves of tenderness. "Of mine too," he said, as though they still had that in common.

"Ben, I feel as though nothing can be the same between us again, after some of the cutting things you said. As though I don't ever want to speak to you again as long as I live."

"Then perhaps we shall have some peace," he said, and hated himself. "Oh, Alma," he said, falling back.

Marvel felt something from the young people's lives like a stain spreading into theirs, like a poisonous mist curling slowly up the stairs and under the door, to infect them in the very bedroom that he had always thought of as a haven, and that had once been a bower.

"But you can give me some idea what you're doing? Are

you really so fed up you're going to leave them notes? And shall I get one? Will there be a divorce?" he added, to shock her back into her senses. "I'm sorry, you know."

She tore up everything she had written and threw and swept the shreds into the wastebasket.

"What did happen to Lee?" she said, in a suddenly different tone. "And why didn't Harry show up? It's all very odd."

"Lee was too upset to stay and Harry didn't want to see Elsie again. It's understandable."

"No. He would want to see Chester. And us. No, it's not like Harry. Now I feel very much as though I've got to see him. I have a premonition something happened."

At this Marvel could only rise, smiling, and lay a hand on her shoulder. "I'd like to see him too. What do you suppose we ought to do?"

"Is it too late to telephone the Inn again?"

"My dear, it's never too late to telephone a hotel. Call them by all means."

"You go see if everything's O.K. then. The children and all."

Marvel put his shoes on again and went out, snapping his galluses over his shoulders. He looked first into the smallest of the rooms at the other end that had always been known, collectively, as the nursery. Jenny and Roy were asleep in the beds. Roy's disordered blankets had a chaos of treasures including a plumber's plunger, with which Marvel had let him play all day since it was new. He covered them both up, kissing their cheeks and smoothing the hair back from their damp brows. In the light from the hall he could make out a dishevelment of toys and clothes. In a corner, one of them on its side, was a pair of unmatched sneakers. Neatly stacked on a table were Jenny's letters from her chum. Going into the next, slightly larger, room, he saw Beaumont and Chester looking almost equally fat on their stomachs. He smiled down at Beau, a smile of conscious benediction, as though by an effort of sheer yearning he might distill into the boy some current of the love he could not consciously and by daylight extend. Covering Chester, he remembered the ode. They must ask him to deliver it tomorrow without fail. He went downstairs to make sure it was still in the kitchen cabinet.

In the parlor he saw someone was stretched out on the couch. It was Evelyn, smoking a cigarette. She reached out a hand to him.

"Hello, Daddy. Never a dull moment, eh?"

"No, never a dull moment." He glanced at the ceiling, reading her thoughts; he dropped her hand and ruffled her hair, the yellow locks he had always loved to fondle. He saw that with her released fingertips she was brushing at her cheek.

"What's the matter?"

"Nothing. You can't be happy for people without being unhappy for them too, can you? It's a wonderful party. Pour me a little more champagne. I took a bottle in here with me with some in it. Some sentence. Have a nightcap with me. Over there on the table. Must be glasses too."

As he poured them drinks in jelly glasses he could hear Ruby's sister cleaning up quietly in the kitchen. Evelyn said rapidly to his turned back:

"I want to tell you this. You're the best parents anybody could have. I've always loved you, Daddy. And don't ever worry about Johnny and me. We're fine. He's got a lot of you in him. This intellectual thing for one, detached but at the same time deeply involved. I suppose it's what you call sensitivity. We fight but we're fine together. And he's such a nice sex fiend. An *appreciator*. Remember that joke we used to have about a coin bank? I told it to him and now he calls me that — his little coin bank. Kind of awful telling it that way. Where were we? We got off the track. No we didn't. The thing is that life can have such wonderful purity if you don't let it get mucked up. I think you've taught me that. Well, there weren't supposed to be any speeches."

"I'm glad to have been such an edifying influence," Marvel said, turning around when he felt he could safely carry the drinks without spilling his tears into them. "Well, here's to us. I mean to all of us."

"Oh, sure. To all of us."

Evelyn sat up to drink. After setting her glass on a table, she curled her legs up under her on the couch.

"Has everyone else gone to bed?"

Before he could answer, Mrs. Marvel's footsteps were heard coming down the stairs. She entered hurriedly.

"Harry's at the hospital," she said. "Emergency appendectomy and — He's not allowed to have any visitors. So in that case . . ." She stared at the floor in thought a moment. "In that case maybe we'd better go on over."

seventeen

WHEN THE THREE of them walked into the hospital — having decided between them that getting Elsie out of bed to tell her would serve no immediate purpose — they found two others in the lobby. Lee was sitting on the edge of a chair while Neil Sligh stood comforting her. After driving around for hours, following his departure from the party, he had telephoned back to ask for Lee. On being told she too had left, he inquired at the Hickory Inn, and having learned themselves by this time what was going on they suggested where Miss Mercury might be found.

Neil was now being a tower of strength. He was showing his stuff. He stood with a hand on her shoulder, which from time to time he patted. "Easy baby, easy. He'll pull through." At these words she burst into tears, needing the ministrations that had brought them on.

"Have you got a handkerchief?"

He drew one from his breast pocket and flapped it open. By this time the Marvels and Evelyn had left the desk where they were able to learn no more than they already knew, and begun to come over. Sligh had to be introduced to Evelyn, who had not had a chance to meet him at the party.

"I'll stay with her," Neil said, looking down at Lee. "I'm used to hospitals. It's the story of my life."

"Have you seen your father?" Marvel asked the girl.

"About half an hour ago. He was asleep then. They've pumped him full of antibiotics. The reason he didn't want you to know about it till tomorrow was he didn't want to spoil the party."

Marvel sent a speculative look down a dim corridor, past the elevator to a stairway.

"I'm going to slip up and see the floor nurse. What's his number?"

"Three fourteen." Lee had finished with the handkerchief, which Neil declined with a shake of his head – she'd better keep it. To Marvel he said, "Yes, you might slip upstairs, sir. The night nurse will be on now, and they sometimes tell you more."

Marvel found the floor nurse bent over a desk making entries in a book by the light of a gooseneck lamp. He introduced himself as the patient's father-in-law.

"We're treating him with penicillin, Chloromycetin, everything," she said, straightening her uniform at the sides. She was a thin and rather formidable woman in late middle age. "He has a high fever and it may be touch and go, even though we have these antibiotics. I've been nursing long enough to have a nose for this sort of thing, and I've found it a good sign when patients are assertive, the way he is. The will to live. He was delirious a while ago and kept calling for Chaucer. Is he literary?"

"In a way. Who is his doctor? Perhaps we could get some information from him."

"Dr. Nethersole. He keeps saying all writers are alike. When you've been nursing as long as I have you get to gauge a patient's spirit. That's as important as taking their temperature or their pulse. The will to live is the thing."

"What is his temperature?"

"I'm not allowed to give out that information."

Marvel went back wishing people would stop using terms like pulling through and the will to live. Seeing them all waiting for him in the lobby he squared his shoulders as he strode up the corridor.

"He's a good deal better. And I think we should all go home and get some sleep. We won't be any use to anybody going around half dead ourselves. One thing, should we call the doctor first?"

"Who did the operation?" Mrs. Marvel asked.

"Dr. Nethersole."

"Blllk," she began automatically, but checked herself and for Lee's sake said, "He's the best we have in town." This was a verdict she had often extended to other women, but as a measure of their pickings, not any merits of Dr. Nethersole's. "Don't call him at this time of night. I know all of them. Our doctors mustn't be disturbed." To Lee she said, "One more thing. Does he have a nurse?"

"Not yet. We have our name in and they're trying to locate one for tonight."

"Then I'll stay."

"They won't let you. They wouldn't let me. From that he can't be in any immediate danger. They let you stay if there is."

"Of course," said Ben. "Now let's all do the sensible thing and try to get some sleep. Lee, can we—?" Seeing him look around, Alma said, "He's gone," and from her tone he knew that she had sent him packing, diplomatically or otherwise. He learned later that she had simply assured Sligh that Lee's mother was on her way and would be along any minute. Mr. Convertible had scuttled.

The upshot was that, the Marvels not having their car, having slipped across lots to Adams Street the way Bushrod had with Ruby, a taxi was summoned for Lee. They phoned for one at the desk. They parted outside, the Marvels and Evelyn returning home through the back as they had come, leaving Lee to wait for her cab on a bench in front of the hospital.

As she sat there, she heard a stir in the darkness behind her. She rose and walked to the lawn, where she traced the sound to another stone bench, behind a shrub. Prufrock was sitting there with his head in his hands.

"I thought you went home ages ago."

He shook his head, turning a little away from her. *He* was certainly not behaving like a tower of strength.

"What good does it do anybody to wear yourself out hanging around here?" A white figure moving behind a curtain made her look up. She had an image of faithful dogs waiting under their masters' windows.

"You're really very fond of my father, aren't you? You love Harry."

"Have you got a handkerchief?"

She gave him Neil Sligh's.

eighteen

THE SUN BLAZED as it had for many days, but the morning was not hot and a breeze shook the smells of rose and heliotrope from thrashing bushes and blew the curtains at the open windows, behind which were heard the revived commotion of children and the murmurs of awakening adults. Mrs. Marvel stood at the stove frying ham and eggs. Marvel came up from behind and undid the bow of her apron as proof of his affection.

"Roy sit down. Jenny sit up."

"I don't see any butter on this bread."

"Turn it over."

"Isn't six times four twenty-one?"

"Easily. Eat." Moo Moo went gently as she could on Roy, whom one understood to be suffering from a basic insecurity dating from a role in an allegory in which he hadn't been quite sure what he symbolized. Were inner things like that worse than external plights like Beau's who had to hit a triple to get on first, he was so slow?

"Ask me how far away the moon is."

"How far is it?"

"Twenty-three thousand miles."

"Liar."

"The sun is ninety-three million."

"Liar, liar, pants on fire."

Bushrod entered.

"Play with, not at, one another."

Marvel, who had been watching Chester slump over the kitchen table with his chin in his hand, said: "Wouldst favor us now with a rendition of yon prothalamium, Chester?"

Chester apathetically spun his knife on the table, making a face. "I have to make some changes. It's not right the way it is."

"Oh, come now, we're dying to hear it."

"What's prothalamium?"

"Skin."

"And now would be a good time." Marvel glanced at the cabinet shelf to confirm his impression that the scroll had been removed. "I'll mail it back to you when I've revised it." Chester dropped his knife and sat up straight with an air of finality.

"Guess what the man next door to us died of."

"Oh, eat!"

"What?"

"Guess."

"I don't feel like guessing. I don't feel like eating either."

"Why must you hum that song all day?"

"Because I don't know the words."

"Guess how much you'd weigh on Mars."

"She thinks she's so great in school. She didn't understand a thing in the planetarium. I don't see what the sense was of taking you."

"I did too understand it."

"You had an accident when they showed the end of the world."

"Well, that shows I understood it. I understand it in school too."

"Not in Sunday school. We had to learn the Twenty-third Psalm, and she said 'Thy rod and thy reel they comfort me.' "

"Eat your ham and eggs, Chester."

"I don't feel like eating. Give them to Mr. Glimmergarden. Uncle John I mean."

But Johnny had left the back porch where he'd been standing in the sun buttoning an elusive cuff, and sauntered off into the yard. He debated throwing gravel at his bedroom window to see if he could fetch Evelyn to it, but was diverted by a murmur of voices from an unexpected direction. Lee and the dark young man were sitting on the grass. He turned their way, but sensing from a vibration their reluctance to being interrupted struck off obliquely in another, as though in response to a military command. He made for the apple trees, underneath whose rustling boughs he resumed again his endless, patient dialogues with Ibsen.

"Everything in our time is phallic, Henrik," he said, "except the male. He's in the kitchen washing dishes while the wife is off listening to some lecturer explain the sexual symbolisms in Dylan Thomas. If you ask me, Henrik . . ."

"You can tell me frankly, Bill. If you are."

"It would be better if I were."

"What do you mean?"

"Because then you're halfway home. It and the normal have a lot in common. After all, sex is sex."

Lee brushed the tops of the grass with her palm while he rolled over on his side and chewed another spear of it. He had been chewing so much grass in the last ten minutes that he felt like Nebuchadnezzar. He spat this one out.

"The thing is, seeming to be incapable of any emotion — any emotional relationship whatever. That's the bad thing. That's the trouble. No, I'm a virgin."

"But what *as?*"

This made him lie on his stomach with his head on his arms, sobbing with laughter. She sat staring at him.

"An unstable Indian is not a pretty sight."

"That's like that joke of your father's, about what the coffee the waiter is bringing him is instead of — milk or tea. What difference does it make? What I'm trying to say is when a man — or a woman — is gummed up in his emotions — call it the inability to love. Curse of our time. We're breeding too ingrown an individual."

"You like me, don't you?"

"None better," he said, rolling over on his back.

"And when we were experimenting there on the beach — what a word — you could have, um, managed."

"Oh, God, what's that got to do with it? Of course. I understand a man's role in the home, and also in the hay, I'm talking about the whole thing."

"You'd think it would be better for a person closer to the, um, primitive . . ."

"Me not primitive. Me Prufrock — you Jane. No, you not Jane. You little Salinger girl. Tortured and O.K. But Eliot had all this taped forty years ago in that damned poem. The exquisitely self-conscious, hypersensitive, super-distilled but gummed-up first person singular. Curse of our time. The two I's —" he held two forefingers erect then locked them into a puzzle — "that can't make a We. And it's going to get worse before it gets much worse. The wave of the future. That's all I know. All I know is, tomorrow will be tough."

"If *Prufrock* can reach you way out there in Saginaw, Michigan, there isn't much hope for the human race."

"Me not holding out hope. Me holding out my hand." He drew closer, whispering further words of exegesis into the pink shell of her ear, rather than any lines from the poem in question. Thus he wooed, in an age of Criticism, under the apple trees.

Lee jerked her head toward the house, in which the sound of adult voices grew. She chewed a blade of grass thoughtfully herself. "If that's the percentage in being normal, well, the odds can't be much worse for us. With one out of four ending in divorce, and half the rest muddling along on God knows what . . ."

Stroking his hand, then his forearm, she felt a tenderness spreading through her loins. She remembered that women learned sex through love, while men were supposed to learn love through sex. Or so legend had it. Perhaps it could be the same for both . . .

He withdrew his hand from hers and laid it on her knee. She was in shorts. He caressed her there, moving his fingers upward delicately along the soft bulge of her thigh. "You're an unlighted candle," he said. "Or are you? How should I know?"

"That's the impression he tried to leave Mother, I heard

— his last trump card. That they'd *have* to take him to make an honest woman of me. God."

"I wish I could be a rat," Bill said wistfully.

Bushrod came out on the porch, looking around. They rose and brushed themselves off.

"Of course I came by my own honestly. I've told you about my mother's trouble?"

"Nothing to do but grin and bare it."

"Are you sure you won't come in for some coffee?"

"No, thanks."

"I thought that was the idea, to meet them all. Oh well, what's the difference. Thanks for coming by anyway. Moo Moo insisted I have breakfast here and I'd better go eat it if I'm to get to the theater by ten. Are you going to talk to Daddy?"

"Just about business. The other can wait till he's stronger. What about your mother?"

Lee smiled and shrugged. "I'll write her about it when they've gone. You're going to drop by the barn? I'll try to get a good hour for dinner."

"And I'll take you to that chop house. The waiter carries the silver in his pockets. You mustn't miss it."

When Mrs. Marvel hung up after phoning the hospital to inquire about Harry she was smiling. "His condition is serious," she said. "Good. Because yesterday he was listed as critical. Now then!"

Looking round the kitchen she saw that only Clara had heard her announcement, and Clara had other matters on her mind. She had obviously been waiting for a chance to tell her something.

"Look, I think I may divorce Bushrod," she said.

"I can't say I blame you," Mrs. Marvel said, going to the sink.

"Because I can't ever come up to his standards. I know that now. It's no use. It would be better to go our separate ways before it gets any worse, or I make some other *gaffe*. Fairer to him while he can still find someone more equal to it. You can't imagine what it's like being married to a perfectionist."

"When will you all be leaving?"

"When the twins have had the chance to visit with you. Tomorrow or the day after. He's gone to get them now from the train. They've been with their other grandparents on the Cape, as you know, and we're to send them back as soon as you're finished with them."

Bushrod strode importantly across the lawn.

"The twins have disappeared."

They gathered round him on the front porch. Judy and Nick had been put on the train at Boston by Bushrod's first wife, according to plan, for him to meet in Hickory, just as she had put them on the train in Baltimore for him to meet in Washington, for innumerable custodial weekends with their father. This time they had up and vanished somewhere between delivery and pickup, either because of some confusion or misunderstanding about where to get off or because they were fed up and running away (from two homes instead of the traditional one).

"How about that for a railroad?" Bushrod said.

They all went into the house for a conference.

The train made only two stops, so they telephoned the stations there. The station masters said they had seen no two children answering that description wandering around, either at a loss or in any other condition. No, there were no Travelers Aid units there. They then telephoned the state police to report the children missing.

Wringing the neck of a fresh bottle of booze, Marvel said through the crackling seal, "I think we ought to do something too. Drive back along the train route and look around in those stops. I can't just sit here waiting. So let's drink these and get going."

In a few minutes he, Bushrod and Johnny were on their way in one of the cars. "Talk about the railroads going to hell," Bushrod said. "Now who doubts the government should take them over? Let a thing like that happen."

Bill was watching Mercury eat his dinner, no new experience. This one he had brought in himself. The hospital dietitians were very sad. They sent out from the kitchen meat loaf, liver, boiled cabbage and so on, and had sent back, from one of the rooms, duck Bigarade, filet mignon with sauce Béarnaise, lobster thermidor and even pheasant under glass. They took it personally, as a form of comment, of satire. This evening Mercury sat up and toyed with a little chicken in red wine.

"I had a chance to look at some of the new stuff," he said, patting a sheaf of papers on the bedspread, the moose eyes bleeding reproach. "You've got me walking funny through Oregon because the Northwest is famous for lumbering. That some more of the intellectual wit I hired you for? And where's Chaucer?"

"At the hotel batting out a revise of the Western. You're not going to send that *coq au vin* to the kitchen? And how about the strawberries Romanoff?"

"I'll eat a few of them."

Bill watched him, the long-suffering and eternal human Sad Sack in his caricature of a nightshirt; the heavy-hooded eyes looking more than ever like those of a Hashemite king weary alike of the cares of state and nights of love.

"You going with Lee?"

"I thought I'd like to marry her."

The spoon dropped in the dish. Chewing, looking out the window, wiping his mouth and scratching his head all at the same time, Mercury said, "I wouldn't."

"Why not? What's the matter with her?"

"Aren't you a fag?" Harry asked, the eyelids coming down like little veils.

"That depends —"

"Don't split hairs with me."

"I'm pure as the driven snow. Whether the same can be said for your daughter, sir, I wouldn't know."

"Are you giving me that it's-all-a-matter-of-terminology stuff? That we all got a dash of that in us? There is a period when it's even normal — adolescence." Mercury dabbed his mouth with the counterpane, thinking it to be his napkin. "There is a comradeship of boys who are out of it before they know the significance of what they have been through. An attachment of the same sex is a midway point — we're now in psychology — in the transition from the self to another person of the opposite sex. In men's clubs, and women's, it persists in a sublimated form."

"Why, sir, this is all very instructive. I didn't realize . . ."

"How will you support her?"

Bill coughed into his fist, bending over a little in his chair. When he had straightened up he said, "Lee will want to finish college, so the problem won't come up for a few years yet. But you're right — I shall have to have more money, sir."

"Never mind that sir stuff. It's a damned impertinence. You don't have to put me in my place yet."

A cart rattled along the hall, collecting trays. Mercury combed his mind for other objections.

"Aren't you part Indian?"

"Yes, but I'm not snobbish about it. Just because my ancestors were here waiting for your first families when they arrived on the *May* —"

"Look, the other night at the Sizzling Platter you told me something about your old man that I didn't quite get all. In our condition it was all vague to me. I asked you if your old man was Cherokee and you said yes but it was all right, because something else. What was that? A qualifying factor, I dimly remember. Exonerating, like."

"I said it was all right, I'm illegitimate. That my mother had more self-respect than to marry a man like that. A man who had seduced her and all. They just lived together."

"I see said the blind man." Mercury pondered the situation further, mulling additional objections to the union. Presently he said:

"What will you do if you have children?"

"Send them to a dog obedience school. God knows parents can't raise them any more. People are no better at that any more than they are at marital relations. But the thing I wanted to say is, think it over. You don't have to give me your answer now."

The twins had ridden all the way to Hickory on the train, but seeing their father, Bushrod, on hand to meet them, they had slipped through the crowd and hurried into a taxi, banging their luggage against the cab and against one another.

"Take us to the summer theater," they said, sitting well down in the back seat.

"Have you got three dollars?" the driver asked them first. They showed him their money and he made off, shrugging. They sat close together, and after a moment began a grave conversation or rather resumed one they had been conducting on the train.

"He didn't have you in mind when he conceived you," Nick said.

"Are you sure?" Judy wasn't doubting it, she just wanted it confirmed. She couldn't hear it often enough, not so much because of dislike for her parents as because of a revelation it consisted in to her — a kind of apocalypse. Mary Cofelice had told her the same thing, and it opened vistas; sudden lyric vistas, a vision of one's own individuality. Her cheeks flamed, she could hardly breathe: your parents hadn't asked for you: you were yourself: free. The world was full of mystery and liberty and wonder.

"Are you sure you want to go into the theater?" Nick said.

"Positive."

"She may not be able to help you."

"She'll be there. She can tell me something. You have to find yourself — live your own life."

"I'm sure you have to be more than twelve though. And you look young, not old, for your age."

"We'll see."

The road ended in a dappled shade of pine trees burningly strange. They gave the cab driver his three dollars and a nickel tip, which he generously declined. He backed out of her dream at high speed, shaking his head. She had one of those twinges of pity children on fire feel for adults locked in the commonplace.

Two boys floated by on the soles of their feet, rather as kites to which someone held the invisible string.

"I thought of doing the whole thing in polka dots."

"Sometimes you frighten me."

The twins stood in the path looking after them, their valises in their hands.

"What are they?"

"I don't know."

Nick decided they might as well make their inquiries of them as anyone else, so he overtook them. "We're looking for Lee Mercury. Is she in?"

"Who are you?"

"We're her cousins," said Nick. "This is my sister. She wants to get into the theater."

"Well, it's open. Go right in. No, wait – she's in the box office this week. Around there to the front door."

Lee had never met them but was glad to now. She assured them that she would tell them all about the theater – later; she was tied up in the box office now. Why didn't they go to the Marvels' for the time being? And how had they got here? Something rapt and evasive in their manner prompted her to pick up the box office phone and call the house.

That was how the reunion was completed. The telephone calls to the state police were repeated and the hunt thrown into reverse: cars now to be on the lookout for three men on the lookout for two children. The children stayed at the theater until they could be called for, which was not very soon since all family resources were for the moment focused on the chase and Moo Moo was home alone. By that time Bill had arrived to call for Lee, who was tied up in the box office for a bit yet, during which interval it fell to Bill to amuse the twins. The menfolk cruising the Massachusetts coastline were finally located about six o'clock. When all the pieces had been reassembled in Hickory, the entire crowd went out, exhausted, their hysteria spent in relief, to dinner at the fish house in the Inn.

It was Bill's first family dinner, at least on anything like such a scale. The Institution swallowed him like a Venus flytrap. His *geist* was on the way out.

Lee was wedged in between the twins at table, who had now to hear all about the theater. She didn't know that she could stay through coffee with them, since she had to get back into the box office for the performance. That was another revelation to Judy. One bolted one's dinner: one flew: one was free. Even Mary Cofelice wouldn't know that. It was something she could tell Mary Cofelice. In her dithers she choked on a fishbone.

"Eat this," Bill said handing wads of bread across the table to her. "It'll force it down. Another . . ."

It did no good. Lee took her to the ladies' room from which she emerged five minutes later gasping and coughing as bad as ever. "We'll have to take her . . ." Mrs. Marvel whispered something to Ben. She was not too put out by the suggestion she had to make. She shared the superstition about misfortunes coming in threes, and a third member of their number going to the hospital (albeit only for a moment in the emergency room) in almost as few days would close the ring on their present cycle of calamities.

Bushrod took Judy by the hand and led her out of the

restaurant. The person in the sou'wester held the door open for them. Judy insisted Lee come along, and Bill trailed Lee. The child sat between the two on the back seat while Bushrod, and then at the last moment Marvel, hopped into the front. Bushrod drove, it being his car.

"This is a great place, Judy," Bill said as they approached it, to keep her spirits up. "And they have a world-famous bone specialist there. He'll get it out in no time."

Lee looked at him in surprise, and Marvel turned around too. But they saw that the girl was smiling up at him, getting the joke all right. Bill had the child's hand in his. Lee reached her own arm around Judy till her hand rested on Bill's shoulder, and Bill raised his free hand to hers as they sped on through the summer dark.

Mrs. Marvel made a point of finding a minute alone with Lee the next day. The subject of Bill was brought up, and Lee said directly how much she liked his company, how amusing he was, and also how bright. "I think I may even consider myself as going steady with him."

Moo Moo was sympathetic, either because she actually approved or had learned from long experience what opposition got you. She admitted he seemed nice — he had certainly been so at dinner, well-spoken, able to talk on subjects, and fun for the children.

"But there's one thing you should think about before coming to even any temporary decision, and that's meeting some of his people. That's important. Because you see, Lee," she said, reasonably, "after all," laying a hand patiently on the girl's, "after all, my dear, what do we know about his family?"

EPILOGUE

WILL the healing streams of simple humanity flow unhindered, till a child is born of this union, then another, and it shall bear at last its normal share of the long human burden? Or will wiser heads prevail, scattering its members before howls of protest from all sides of the family? In that case Bill Prufrock is relieved of his job and drifts farther into the theater, where he again runs into Cotton who is carrying an imperfect script under his arm. A collaboration is arranged which in due course betakes itself to some Manhattan apartment, where the friendship deepens . . . "If you ask me it's time they gave the country back to the Indians," one choleric tenant observes to his wife on hearing of the new neighbors . . . Lee returns in tears to school, where Betty Markham, she of the sisterly instincts, befriends her, takes her into her room, into her arms, and by morning — But these are alternatives fortunately not ours to ponder, since our story ends — or rather one is given his choice of endings — at this point in the endless ramifications of human chance and fate. Except for a brief bit of unfinished business Mrs. Marvel has promised herself with you know who.

Sailing by car down the new turnpikes that fall, she and Ben went on a week's holiday in New York City, just the two of them. In the gay round of shows and dinners and luncheons, she slipped away one afternoon on a pretext of shopping, to keep an appointment secretly made with the marriage counselor.

Patchkiss was a man of middle age dressed in tweeds of muted green, with the whitest linen and the leanest wrists imaginable. They were like rapier steel in the spotless cuffs, pliant and strong. He sat behind a desk the shape and color of a wiener, among many leather and chrome appurtenances including a quiver of sharp pencils. He did not bat an eye when she told him she was Elsie Trautwig's mother — Case Nineteen. He believed it. It was his business not to be amazed.

"Do you really think you can hang all these troubles on the Family?" she blurted in the burst of courage that freed her from her hemming and hawing. "The parents —" She wriggled forward on her plastic chair, gesturing in the blinding sunlight in which she had been installed while Patchkiss sat in a pleasant shadow. She told him what she had told Elsie she would to his face: "Because if they want to blame us, we can blame our parents, and they theirs, and so on, and nobody will ever take any responsibility for anything!"

"You seem very heated in your defense of yourself." Patchkiss smiled, with his little finger sweeping cigarette ash from the sheet of white paper on which surely enough he had begun to make notes in his neat hand. "Why?"

She should have known better than to fall into that trap, having lived long enough in the multi-level world their children had passed on to them. She sat back a little as Patchkiss went on like a suave prosecutor:

"Nobody has accused you of anything, so whom are you trying to convince — yourself? Nobody really *blames* you for raising your children according to your lights. I'm afraid you're the one who's protesting it. Guilt is a universal sensation. What are you feeling guilt about?"

"What?"

"Perhaps I should say what are you upset about? That you should feel the need to come to me. That's what people do come to my office for, I'm afraid. They feel they need help. There's no more disgrace to that than there is in guilt — every marriage has troubles. The folly is in letting them fester till it's too late. The fact that you are sitting there indicates the need to air something." His voice became very gentle and encouraging. "Now what is wrong?"

Frantically she thought of the blaze of dispute in which the celebration had ended, the bedroom discord such as those four walls had never heard. She thought of Ben alone in their hotel room turning the pages of a newspaper while he smoked, and the need to protect him seized her. To protect their home from the lance thrust of that sharp pencil poised even now over the sheet of notepaper. She quickly extemporized a woe.

"Well, I have this —" A word from the lexicon flung itself out like a life preserver. "This compulsion."

He raised his eyebrows in new appreciation. "Oh? What compulsion?"

She swallowed and sat up, tidying her blouse.

"Well, every time I hear a song played, I make a white ball bounce from one word to the next."

"You make a white ball bounce from one word to the next?" he said softly.

"Yes. Like a Ping-pong ball. You know what I mean."

He lowered his eyes as he said, "I'm afraid not."

"The white ball that bounced from word to word of the verses that were flashed on the screen in the silent movies in the old days, while the audience sang. To lead the singing while the organ or piano played. Surely you remember that?"

He rose to lower the window blind, retreating to finer shade when this was done. He shook his head, pleading ignorance.

"You mean to sit there and tell me you're not old enough to —?"

"I'm afraid I really don't know what you mean," Patchkiss said. "Of course I do know now that you've explained it to me, but I'm afraid —"

"Don't be so afraid of everything!" she exclaimed, surprising herself. Seeing him wince she added with an amiable laugh, "Everything you say, you begin 'I'm afraid.'" From a ray of light invading his lair she caught a wattled line above the gay bow tie, a speckled hand writing again. He must be over fifty, she thought. He's lying. He knows what I'm talking about. She continued, reveling in her newfound affliction:

"I used to do it voluntarily but now I can't help it. *I have to do it.* Make the ball bounce. It's spread from songs I hear people sing to poems I might hear recited to anything at all."

"You see this white ball bounce on every word?"

"Every *syllable*. The way it used to."

"All poetry?"

"Everything anybody says. I'm doing it right now with you. Don't you notice my eyes? On 'All poetry' there were four. Bounce, bounce, bounce, bounce."

"Yes but wait," he said, passing a hand across his forehead. "Before we go any further let me visualize it myself. Let me get the picture clearly in my own mind. You mean to say that everything you hear spoken," he went on, turning away from her a moment, "is transposed into an image of written words in your mind's eye, from syllable to syllable of which then a ball bounces, also in your mind's eye?"

"Yes!" she cried, copyrighting her madness. "That's me."

"Would you mind giving me a demonstration?" he asked, swinging back in his chair to face her again.

"Certainly. Say something. Anything. The first thing that comes into your head."

Patchkiss thought warily a moment. Then he began, "Fourscore and seven years ago —" He caught himself, too late, and continued, "— our fathers brought forth upon this continent . . ." As he spoke he watched the woman, now quite erect in her chair, roll her eyes steadily from her left to right in a series of vast loops from ceiling to floor. ". . . conceived in liberty and dedicated to the proposition that all —"

"Wait! Not so fast please. That's part of the nervous state I get into — that I can't keep *up* with people. Go ahead now, slower."

"I get the idea," said the flinching counselor, who turned aside again and continued without the view of her, "Of course I am not a therapist, you see, so problems of a personal psychiatric nature —"

"It's driving my husband crazy."

"Ah!" he said reaching for his pencil again. It flew across the virgin white. "A device to gain the attention of a husband who ignores you perhaps? Spends the long evenings with his nose in a newspaper —?"

"Or book! And the magazines that come to the house. He subscribes to everything!" she cried, feeling the inebriation of complaint. "He'll hardly play bridge any more with some people we've spent every Thursday night of the past ten years doing that with. He won't — he has this habit of —"

"Wait." Patchkiss raised a hand. "I'm afraid we can't take in everything today, and before we proceed any further I must outline for you my policies and procedures as I do for everyone. Now, I am a counselor of the kind we call non-directive. That is to say we do not *advise* clients to do this or that. We help them gain enough enlightenment into their problems so they can intelligently, with a knowledge of all the factors we have unearthed and examined, make their own decisions. It will be up to you to decide what you want to do, and when and how. Whether you want to work things out, try again. Or if you decide that divorce is best . . ."

"Fine," she said.

"You have life ahead of you, Mrs. Marvel," he said encouragingly. "Don't think that just because you can recall the time when balls bounced on silent screens — the obvious fear behind your obsession — you are too advanced in years to have many happy ones yet. Geriatrics —"

"Oh, I know!"

"The possibilities that life opens to each decade . . ." He cleared his throat into his fist and looked at what he had written. "Now the question whether your husband is to come and see me. Sometimes it helps. Sometimes it enables one to see all around a problem —"

"I'll try to get him to come. At least I'll talk it over with him."

"Splendid."

Arranging for the next appointment she gave a fictitious New York address and phone, or hoped they were fictitious and that no innocent apartment dweller would be called about a skipped visit or dunned for professional services.

He saw her to the door. When she had gone he admitted from the anteroom his secretary, a beautiful young girl who took the vacated chair and jotted in shorthand some notes dictated on the patient just gone. Patchkiss tilted farther back in the shadows with his fingertips together, leaving the girl to cross in bright sunlight the silk legs at the sight of which a familiar bolt of hunger struck him. He resumed in return the five-weeks campaign to dazzle her with his gift of précis.

"Now will you read back what I've dictated please, Millicent?" he said after five minutes. The young warbler's voice came on:

"This seems to be a case of delayed resentment suddenly erupting after one of those threshold years have seized the patient with the fear of passing time . . ."

Something happened to Patchkiss here. His eyes left the crossed knee on which the dictation pad was settled and described a wild arc around the room. He sat up, wetting his lips nervously. His gaze repeated the gyration, then again, till his eyes were rolling in a series of scallops rhythmically synchronized with the flow of words from the divine young lips and throat, syllable by syllable. Had she glanced up she would have thought him making the most amazing goo-goo eyes at her; but she did not glance up.

"Would you go not so fast a moment, please, Millicent?" he said, wetting his mouth again and raking his hair in something like terror. "*Not . . . so . . . fast!*"

The Marvels had a pleasant drive back to Massachusetts. They took the turnpikes up as they had down. After chatting of the fun they'd had and comparing notes on the four plays they'd seen and the four expensive dinners they'd eaten in four separate restaurants, they lapsed suddenly into silence. It was a companionable quiet, born of long years of respect for one another's reveries. But the revery this time was a common one. Each knew the other was reviewing the eventful summer this lark was bringing to a close. The Anniversary; the children and the guests; the troubles and rewards; what had come out of it, what had led up to it. Here their thoughts parted company, for Marvel had his own clear memories of the day preparations had begun. He may have been musing on the sorrows of automation when another arose. The trouble was the assumption of established reflexes at moments when they are not called for, as in so many matters of the non-mechanical world too, he was thinking . . . This time he was at fault but not the victim, in contrast to that at the supermarket of which he was the butt though not to blame.

The many miles on the turnpikes had now so accustomed him to flinging money into the exact-change hoppers that the act had become as automatic as responding to traffic lights and other aspects of driving a car. So that when now, partway on the journey home, in the new Renault of course, he edged into a lane that was not going through an exact-change passage at all but a manned gate, he absently behaved as he had anyway. The uniformed attendant received a spray of small coins in his face.

Not even Mrs. Marvel heard the imprecations fading in their rear, so deep was their abstraction. She heaved a sigh, thinking of all they'd been through, of all of the Twentieth Century that had been brought to their old door. What was happening in and to the world, including supposedly rock-ribbed New England Massachusetts?

"What are we coming to?" she wondered aloud.

"Connecticut," said Ben Marvel, who had been watching the signs.